Mind Portal

MW00985421

Alan H.B. Wu, Ph.D.

Ilee

Pay, CA

Feb 2015

Mind Portal is a work of science fiction based on real individuals in history. The dialogues portrayed by these characters are fictitious.

ISBN-13: 978-0-9863634-8-1
eBook ISBN: 978-0-9863643-7-4

Dedication

This book is dedicated to my wife who continues to challenge me to achieve.

Acknowledgement

Some of the ideas for these stories in this book were derived from the University of Maryland's Historic Clinicopathologic Correlation Conference held each year in Baltimore. Since 1995, this Conference invites noted doctors and medical historians to discuss the deaths of prominent individuals. Based on archives, these individuals offer alternative disease diagnoses and cause of deaths than what was known or reported at the time of that individual's death.

I thank Pat Beatty for her review and editing of this work.

Table of Contents

Prologue...vi

Mind Portal: How it Began....................................1

Biocide..12

He Has Not Left The Building............................22

iBrain...32

TBI...44

Sweat Shop..56

A Wall of Stone.............68

Ashwood............................80

Point-of-Care...92

Bladder Control...104

Dishwashing Liquid...................112

George's Last Legacy...122

You Vee to the Rescue...132

Purple Reign...144

Cursed..154

Libertadore del Liberador!...................................168

Behind Every Man...182

Purged..194

Atomic Barré...204

The Butcher...214

The Collaborator...226

Skyweb...236

Amit's Altered World...248

Prologue

The concept of time travel for the purposes of reviewing history and perhaps even changing critical events in the past has been explored in books, television shows, and cinema since the very beginning of the science fiction genre itself. For example, H.G. Wells penned the *Time Machine* back in 1895.

In the late 1950s and early 1960s, Rod Serling often used time travel in his television series, The *Twilight Zone*. In one episode entitled, "Walking Distance", an overworked advertising executive takes a train which delivers him back in time to the town where he grew up. As an adult, he sees himself as he was when he was a child. He tries to communicate with the boy, but the boy runs away and suffers an accident that injuries his leg. He has a discussion with his father who is aware that he is talking to his son from the future. The father has the wisdom to know that his adult son needs to return to his time and place, and he is not allowed to relive his childhood again. But now, he has a limp that he didn't have before he went back in time.

The 1960's television series *Star Trek* also explored the time continuum on multiple occasions. One of the more popular episodes was when Doctor McCoy was accidently transported back in time to America during the mid-1930s. While there, he prevents the death of Edith Keeler, a pacifist whose protests lead the U.S. government to delay their entry into the Second World War, enabling Nazi Germany to develop nuclear weapons and altering the outcome of the war. Captain Kirk and Spock realize that Dr. McCoy has changed the past to the extent that their current reality no longer exists as a result of the doctor's action. So Captain Kirk and Spock enters the same time portal a week before McCoy's entry not knowing if and how Edith is involved with the time rift. Spock finds out that history is changed with Edith's survival and Kirk must stop Dr. McCoy from saving her life.

The 2016 television show *Timeless* is yet another series where characters physically go back into time via a "time machine," interact with important historic figures or events, and change the current reality upon return to their present time. Most of the changes are to the personalities involved in the show and specific details of history, but no major alteration in the civilization of man.

This book is a slight departure from these stories in that nobody goes back in time to change history. Instead, Amit Savjani, a clinical laboratory scientist, has the unique ability to implant ideas and knowledge into key individuals in history. Now armed with this information, these notables change what they did in history, resulting in significant consequences to the course of human events.

Beyond entertainment value, the ultimate objective of these stories is to show the importance of clinical laboratory tests in health and disease. I am a clinical laboratory director and have 35 years of experience in directing testing for patients and the development of new tests. The laboratory science portrayed in these stories is accurate and has not been fictionalized. The medical history of the individuals involved, and their role in world history are also accurate up until the time that the central character intervenes. The events that follow the survival of the central person in each story are fictional. However, the rift that is caused by that character's survival is based on the view of historians as to what could have transpired had these key people survived.

Six of these stories have been previously published in my earlier books. I did not explain how an individual in history could acquire the medical and laboratory knowledge of the 21st century. They also did not fit with the overall themes of the other stories in those books. Therefore, I have taken them out of my previous books, and added the involvement of Amit Savjani's unique mental capabilities as a common theme for all of these stories.

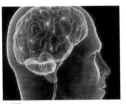

Mind Portal: How it Began

****

They came from Mumbai and settled in Sunnyvale California. The father was a brilliant software engineer and he worked for one of the pioneering companies in a region that became the Silicon Valley. After a few years, he and his wife had a son. They named him Amit Savjani, which in Indian, means "limitless." He would be their only child. Amit was a small boy for his age. In the early 1960s there weren't that many Indian families living on the San Francisco Peninsula. He was shy, and somewhat of an outcast. He had few friends. Many of the other kids in his school lived on farms and orchards that were abundant in the area then. These kids had nothing in common with Amit who had darker skin.

From his early teenage years, Amit knew that God had given him a unique gift. He could look at someone and not only know what they were thinking but also he could plant thoughts into their mind. He first discovered this ability on the school's courtyard when the school bully, Samuel, was trying to take Amit's lunch money. Samuel had numerous fights with other boys in school. The much larger kid saw Amit from across the courtyard and went over to him with an angry and determined look on his face. Samuel was sporting a thin beard while Amit had not yet begun to shave.

Amit knew he could not avoid Samuel so he braced himself for a face-to-face confrontation. Their eyes locked on each other despite the height difference. There were no words spoken. They just stared at each other for a solid two minutes. All the other kids stopped their conversation and what they were doing to watch this confrontation. There was total silence on the courtyard. Some of the girls were fearful that Amit was going to get hurt but they stood motionless and powerless to say or do anything. Nobody left to get help.

With deep concentration, Amit began sending out his thoughts from his mind to Samuel's. He didn't know why he would try this. Amit was just hoping for a better outcome. *You don't want to do this. This is not right. You are a good person. We could be friends. You don't want to do this.* At first, there was nothing. But after another minute passed, Amit could see that it was working. Samuel was getting the non-verbal message. He backed off a step and dropped his head. His facial expression went from aggressive and angry to calm and friendly. His conscience was talking to him. *I don't need to do this. This is not right. I am a good person. We could be friends. I won't do this.* Samuel extended his arm and he and Amit shook hands. Samuel then put his arm around the smaller boy's shoulder.

"Maybe you can help me with my homework," he said to Amit. "I have trouble with just about everything."

"Sure, anytime," Amit remarked with a renewed sense of confidence. Samuel backed away. He thought, *why did I say that to that kid? I was going to pound him into the ground. I don't give a crap about school. What has gotten into me?* He shrugged off these thoughts and left the school yard. He went to his car in the school's parking lot for a beer and a smoke.

The kids who were watching this could not believe this transformation. Some of the other boys who were playing basketball and stopped to watch were noticeably disappointed. "Damn, I was looking forward to a good fight," one of them said.

"Naw, it wouldn't have lasted long," another said. "Look at that puny Indian kid. He would have folded into a heap."

"I suppose you're right," the first kid remarked. "But we haven't had a good fight in a long time. What else is there to do here besides gawk at the girls?" The boys went back to their game.

On the other side of the courtyard, a group of girls were also commenting. "Who is that Indian boy? There was something about his look that defused the situation."

One of the more attractive girls commented. "I don't know who this boy is but I am going to get to know him. He has something special. Unlike that loser Samuel, this kid is going places." A few minutes later, the class bell rang and recess was over. The students slowly headed back to resume their classes. There was a continuous murmur of what they had witnessed.

Amit wasn't sure what had just happened. He didn't plan on staring down Samuel and he had no reason to believe it would work. But at the critical moment of his confrontation, he had no fear. He knew that he could transmit his thoughts to the bigger, older boy. He went home that night with a confidence that he never had before. He did not tell his mother or father about what happened that day or what he was able to do. He needed to know if he could do it again and learn the limits of his mind.

*

Amit graduated from high school and was admitted to

3

college. He majored in biochemistry excelling in his classes. He also minored in world history. It was an unusual mix. Amit realized that his future vocation was likely science but he felt a connection with individuals who made major accomplishments during their lifetimes.

In his sophomore year, Amit was enrolled in an organic chemistry class. During the laboratory portion of the course, he was paired with Angie as a lab mate. Together they worked on the chemistry experiments assigned by the professor. Angie was very attractive and smart. Amit thought that she would never be interested in him romantically. Over the next few weeks, they became friends and they would often meet to have coffee. One day, Amit asked Angie about her weekend plans, hoping that she was free so he could ask her out.

"I got fixed up with a guy named Carl." Angie lived in a sorority that was friendly with one of the fraternities on campus. *I wish that was me,* Amit thought.

"We're going out hiking by the dish." There is a park with a radio telescope near the campus where students go to exercise and relax. Amit looked into Angie's eyes and after a brief moment, he saw a vision that noticeably startled him. Angie saw that Amit's expression had dramatically changed.

"What?" Angie asked. "Why are you looking at me like that?"

"I'm sorry, I didn't mean to stare. It's just that, that... Oh, it's nothing. I hope you have a good time," Amit said.

Angie sensed that Amit was attracted to her. But she didn't want to encourage him so she said nothing further. *I've never seen him like this. He's acting weird,* she thought. After a few minutes,

4

she said she had to go to class, and she departed without looking back.

Amit remained in the coffee shop and was in great distress. He had seen in Angie's eyes that she was going to be raped by her date in the park that weekend. But he wasn't sure if it was real, so he hadn't said anything to her. He didn't know what to do. *Should I warn her? Should I call the campus police? What real evidence do I have? He'll deny his intentions and I will look foolish. Should I follow her on her date? If she saw me following her, she would really think I am a weirdo.* In the end, Amit sat in his dorm room on that early Saturday evening and did nothing hoping that his vision was wrong. But somehow, he knew he was right.

Unfortunately, Angie during their date was assaulted by Carl when they were in a secluded part of the park. "Stop! What do you think you're doing" she pleaded with him as he groped her.

"I know you want this bitch. Shut up and enjoy it," Carl said.

She saw rage in Carl's eyes. Fearful that she would be harmed, Angie did not resist any further. After it was over, Angie left the park alone and ran to her dorm room. The following day, she called her parents who came and took her home. They called the police and charges were filed against Carl. Angie was so upset that she dropped out of school. Carl was convicted of rape and was given a prison sentence. Angie did not return to the school. Amit never saw Angie again.

When Amit heard the news, he was crushed that he had done nothing to prevent the attack on Angie. Over and over for the next few weeks, he agonized about the options he could have taken to prevent this attack. He let down his classmate and felt

5

cowardly and depressed. He questioned his maker. *Why was I given this ability? What am I supposed to do with this? What good is it? I don't want this!* While his grades suffered temporarily, nobody knew the torment he was facing. He wanted to call Angie at her home to tell her what he had sensed in that coffee shop but decided against it. She would not believe him and it would serve no purpose.

For the remainder of the semester, Amit got no more visions and he immersed himself into his classes. The chemistry professor assigned another individual to be his lab partner during the course, but it wasn't the same as being with Angie. This made him realize that he loved Angie and regretted that he had never told her of his feelings. Two years later, Amit received his undergraduate degree and enrolled in graduate school majoring in clinical laboratory science. He was hoping to become a professor at a major university medical center.

During his third year of grad school, another event occurred that would change his view of reality. He read in the newspaper that Carl had served his time in prison for his attack on Angie and was released on parole. While in prison, Carl had been trained as an auto mechanic and when he was released, the prison arranged a job for him at a local garage. Somehow, Amit knew the garage where Carl was employed. A few months later, Amit brought his old car into that garage. Carl had never met Amit and didn't know about his connection with Angie. Amit asked for an oil change, tune up and tire rotation, but his real objective was to study Carl. While in the waiting room, Amit focused his attention on the mechanic. Amit's eyes followed Carl's every move. After a while, Amit sensed that Carl had rehabilitated and that he was sorry for his rape of Angie. Amit was able to get Carl to think back about his attack on Angie. *That is not who I am now.* Carl thought. *If I could start college again, my attitude and behavior would be very different.* Amit sat back in the waiting room and wished that he too could go back and start college again. He missed Angie and wished she was in his life in some manner or another. Lost in these thoughts, he was startled when Carl came back to the waiting room to speak with him.

"I noticed when changing your tires that your brake pads are worn to a dangerous level," Carl said. "You should get them fixed."

"Can you do that now?" Amit asked.

"It is 5 o'clock and we're closing soon. But if you bring the car back tomorrow, I will do it first thing in the morning," Carl said.

"Ok, I'll be back." *This will give me a chance to study Carl some more,* Amit thought. Throughout that evening, Amit kept playing the "what if" game again in his mind. *How would things be different if I could have prevented that attack? If I had seen Carl before the date, maybe I could have changed his intention with my thoughts such as I had done with Samuel that bully from junior high school.* Thinking that he had lost his opportunity for true happiness, Amit went to sleep in his apartment.

The next morning, he arose and drove to Carl's garage. When he arrived, Carl was nowhere to be seen and another mechanic came to greet him.

"What can I do for you today, sir?" he asked.

"I have an appointment with Carl to have my brake pads replaced," Amit said.

There was a hesitation. "You must be in the wrong place,

man. I am the owner of this garage and there is no one by the name of Carl here."

"What? He was working on my car yesterday. I sat right there waiting," Amit pointed to a chair in the waiting room. "I was reading THIS magazine," as Amit pointed to an issue of *Newsweek*.

"Look buddy, I was here all day yesterday and you weren't here. I don't have time to play games. I can fix your brakes but you will have to wait until I have time later this afternoon."

Amit was baffled. He left the garage and drove to his office at school. A few minutes lapsed when he received a call. A woman was on the line. "Honey, do you want me to come over tonight? I can fix you a special meal."

"Who is this?" Amit asked.

"Very funny. Who do you think this is? Do you have another girl over there?"

Then Amit recognized the girl's voice. It was Angie. But how can that be? I haven't talked to her since she left school? "Ah, ah..., sure, ah..., okay, that would be great. Do you know where I live?" Amit said.

"I said, quit playing games Amit. I had a big day at the hospital." Angie was a registered nurse at a hospital near the school. "If you don't want me to come...."

"No, no, that would be great. I'll see you tonight," Amit said.

That evening after school, Amit rushed home. Was he dreaming or was Angie truly in his life? He went into his apartment and immediately noticed some changes inside. The room had different furniture and there were flowers on the table. There was a noticeable pleasant aroma in the apartment. He went to the bathroom and saw that someone else had left their toothbrush. In the shower, there were aromatic shampoos and conditioners. *These things are not mine. What is going on here?*

A half hour later, there was a jingling sound at the front door lock. Angie came into the apartment. She had her own key. She gave Amit a big kiss and asked him about his day. Amit fell into his chair astonished to see her. Her hair was longer and styled differently and she was a little older than he remembered. But she was more beautiful than ever. He could not figure out why or how she was there. Angie acted like they had been together for years. As promised, she cooked him dinner. Afterwards, they sat in the living room and Angie told him about her day. Amit wasn't hearing anything she said. He just stared at her in disbelief that she was in his apartment. Amit had not been with any women. When it was time for bed, they made love like it was their very first time. For Amit, perhaps it was.

Later that night, while she was lying next to him asleep, Amit tried to make sense of the change in events during the last 36 hours. After staying awake for most of the night, he concluded that his will had changed the course of history. By planting ideas into the minds of people he encountered, he could change their actions. More importantly, he could project his wishes onto people before they undertook some event, whether it was in the past or present time, thereby preventing the actions that were to come. Or at least the actions that he thought were to come. Through his mind implantation, *did I prevent Carl from raping Angie? Or was this current reality with Angie real and the rape imaginary? Was his previous memory a dream?* But his memories are so vivid. Amit's was getting dizzy thinking about these various explanations. In the end, he was happy that he now had a life with the woman of his dreams and he did not tempt fate by trying to use his gift again. If he is able to change the future, he didn't want to risk losing his current reality.

Angie and Amit married later that year. Amit completed his doctoral degree and went on to complete a postdoctoral fellowship in clinical chemistry. Soon thereafter, he accepted a position as Assistant Professor of Pathology and Laboratory Medicine at the state's major medical school, and he was appointed as the Assistant Director of the Chemistry Laboratory at the University Hospital. Angie worked at the hospital as a registered nurse.

Amit enjoyed a productive career in clinical laboratory science. He was the director of a lab that had a staff of 50 techs and produced millions of test results for patients seen at his hospital. He was also well funded to conduct research and publish his findings in peer-reviewed journals. His students loved his passion for the field and he trained many individuals who themselves went on to become laboratory directors. Perhaps his only disappointment was that he and Angie did not have any children. Angie died of an autoimmune disease when she was in her early 60s. Amit was distraught at the loss of her friend and lover. He was again alone in the world.

*

Many decades after his encounter with Carl in the auto shop, Amit began to think about how his life appeared to have changed that day. *Do I have the ability to change the will of people's intention? Can I implant seeds of doubt? More importantly, can I implant modern-day medical and laboratory knowledge that when acted upon, can change events?* Amit decided to tempt fate. He learned that through a "mind portal" he had access to, he could target a key scientist or doctor in history and that he had the ability to transplant an idea or suggestion without even seeing or meeting that individual. Once the seed has been planted, the individual would believe the idea was an original one. A little assistance from Amit would produce ripple effects that could change the modern world.

Amit was nearing 70 years of age. He had made his mark in the field and felt he now had a bigger calling. He has this talent that he did not dare to use before. But now that he was alone, he thought that his knowledge of laboratory medicine could influence important people in history and change the course of events for the better. He was willing to tempt his own reality for the sake of helping mankind in some manner....

*

Telepathy is a form of non-verbal communication whereby a person can implant an idea or image onto the brain of another. Usually the individual who has received the implant is unaware of the transfer, and believes that he is the originator of that implant. There have been many science fiction movies about an individual who has telepathic powers. In the Star Wars movies, many of the characters including Luke Skywalker and Obi-Wan Kenobi have telepathic powers that they use to alter the behavior of their enemies. The movie, Inception (2010) involves the use of telepathic powers for stealing corporate secrets. The movie, In Your Eyes (2014), is about a paranormal romance.

The concept of using telepathic powers to affect events that have already occurred in history has not been explored in the science fiction genre. An individual with this telepathic ability, coupled with today's knowledge, could produce fascinating changes in the course of human history.

Biocide

****

The year was 1958. By then she was a world renowned New York Times bestselling author. She was asked to speak to groups all over the country. She was alone in her hotel room after one such lecture when she felt a small bump in her left breast. When she was introduced as the keynote speaker, Rachel was gathering her notes as she approached the stage, her accidently bump the left side of her chest against the sharp edge of the podium. That night, she took off her blouse and while looking at herself in the mirror, she didn't see a bruise or any redness on the underside of her breast where she had bumped herself. *It will go away,* she thought and she did not think about it again for another 18 months.

*

Rachel was born on a small farm in Pennsylvania in 1907. She was an avid reader and began writing stories at the age of eight. Two years later, she had her first article published. After high school, she entered the Pennsylvania College for Women majoring in biology. She became interested in zoology and genetics and entered graduate school at Johns Hopkins in 1929, earning a master's degree while studying zoology and genetics. Although she couldn't predict this at the time, both of these fields would be key in her future research. Prior to earning her doctoral degree, Rachel withdrew from graduate school and accepted a job at the U.S. Bureau of Fisheries. There she continued writing non-fiction essays and wrote her first book about life in the sea in 1941. America and the rest of the world were consumed by the Second World War, and the book did not sell well. A few years later, she became interested in a particular pesticide and tried to convince the editor of a popular magazine regarding the importance of this chemical.

"I want to write a piece on dichloro-diphenyl-trichloroethane," she said to John, the senior editor of the *Sunday Evening Digest*.

"Dichloro what?" John asked.

"It is call 'DDT' for short. It is a pesticide that is being used by our troops to control the spread of malaria, typhus, yellow fever and dengue fever," she explained.

"That is great idea. I heard about this, many feel it helped the Allies shorten the war in both Europe and in the Pacific," John said. "But I didn't know you were interested in military history?"

"No, I'm not interested in that role. DDT is being sold as a pesticide for our farms in the U.S. I am concerned about what it is doing to the environment and our health," Rachel said.

"Human health? Is DDT poisonous to our troops?" John asked.

"There is scientific evidence that DDT washes into lakes and streams and is absorbed by fish," Rachel said. As an environmentalist and employed by the Bureau of Fisheries, she knew what she was talking about. "When game birds such as eagles and hawks eat the fish, they are poisoned. I believe that DDT is also harmful to humans but I don't have evidence of that."

"The last thing I want to do is to create a fear that is unfounded. DDT saved millions of lives by avoiding insect-borne illnesses and it helped us win the war. We don't want people to think that this was now a bad idea. Rachel, come back to me when you have some concrete proof regarding the human health effects. Everyone is elated that we're at peace. We don't need any stories that show a negative side as to how it was done. Not right now."

*

In the 1930s, Paul Müller was a chemist working in Basil Switzerland. He was given the assignment of finding a chemical that is toxic to insects but safe for plants and animals. He and his company Geigy were motivated by the fact that Switzerland had a food shortage due to crops damaged by insects and that there was a typhus epidemic in the Soviet Union. When it comes to a drug company, epidemic maladies are opportunities to profit.
Typhus disease is transmitted by infected fleas. Müller scanned the world's literature for potential chemicals and tested 349 of them without success. One chemical was affective in killing bugs but it contained arsenic which is highly poisonous to humans. Müller's work was tedious and unrewarding. Many times he said to his wife that he wanted to switch projects to something else. But he persisted.

Then one morning, he arose from bed and said to her, "Today is the day I find the answer." The 350th tested compound was DDT, a chemical that was synthesized in 1874 by an Austrian pharmacologist, but never tested as a pesticide. In September, 1939, the month that Germany invaded Poland with soldiers to start World War II, Müller invaded a fly cage with DDT. The effect was the same: those invaded were eradicated by the invaders. Geigy produced a dust that was used by the British and U.S. Army during the war to protect their soldiers against insect-borne infections. Müller went on to win the Nobel Prize in Physiology and Medicine in 1948.

*

Rachel kept quiet regarding her concerns of DDT and other insecticides for another 15 years, all the while keeping track of research studies and publications. She went on to write other non-fiction articles and books about the ocean. She was so successful that she was able to leave the Bureau in 1952 and became a full-time author. Then in 1962, she released the book, *Silent Spring*, a description of the harmful effects that pesticides had on the environment. Rachel documented hundreds of incidences where indiscriminate spraying of pesticide to farms and fields resulted in human diseases. She also showed that insecticides were killing off the population of birds. The toxic effect of DDT was the focal point of the book. There, she accused the chemical industry of poisoning the environment for financial gain. The pesticide industry, in return, countered with data on the number of humans that use of DDT saved, by preventing diseases transmitted by mosquitos. Rachel's call to action was not the banning of insecticides, but rather the discriminant use of the chemicals. She opined that through natural selection, that widespread use of pesticides promotes the mutation of short-lived insects that are resistant to DDT:

> "The world has heard much of the triumphant war against disease through the control of insect vectors of infection, but it has heard little of the other side of the story- the

defeats, the short-lived triumphs that now strongly support the alarming view that the inset enemy has been made actually stronger by our efforts. Even worse, we may have destroyed over very means of fighting."

*

Rachel was diagnosed with metastatic breast cancer a few years before finishing her book, *Silent Spring*. She was wrong in thinking that the lump in her breast was caused by a bump from the lectern. She underwent radiation therapy and a mastectomy shortly after her diagnosis of the malignancy, but it was too late. Rachel died two years after the publication of her best seller, at the height of her popularity, at age 56. Six years after her death, President Richard Nixon created the U.S. Environmental Protection Agency (EPA) responsible for wildlife and other environmental concerns. It was independent to the US Dairy Association which was more concerned with the success of the agricultural industry. Hence Nixon's cabinet felt that the USDA might have a conflict of interest with regards to conducting scientific studies and regulating the use of pesticides. Rachel Carson's unbiased work was considered the impetus for the creation of this new Agency.

*

As a toxicologist, Amit Savjani followed the history of environmental toxins with specific reference to its effect on human health and disease. Having worked in California, he was involved with several studies of organophosphate insecticides, the successor to DDT. Amit wondered how the pesticide landscape would be different if Rachel had survived her cancer and continued her work. He went into his mind portal and instructed Rachel to seek a medical examination right after her lecture that day and not wait for the tumor to grow and progress for two more years. She was given radiation therapy and mastectomy before the tumor had metastasized to the liver which led to a permanent period of remission.

In 1967, pharmacologists were trying to identify a contraceptive drug and first synthesized tamoxifen, a drug that blocks human estrogen receptors. While the drug failed to block pregnancy, it was soon studied as anti-cancer drug. Many specific tumors of the breast require the hormones estrogen and progesterone to grow and proliferate. Tamoxifen is effective in treating patients with breast cancer and to prevent its recurrence for those who have been treated. The first clinical trial for tamoxifen in breast cancer began in the UK in 1970.

For many years, Amit's clinical lab performed estrogen and progesterone receptor assays on breast cancer patients as an entry criteria for tamoxifen. They also test for genetic variances in the liver enzymes, collectively known as "cytochrome p450." Tamoxifen is known as a "prodrug" that requires breakdown by this liver enzyme to its pharmacologically active form. Someone who has a defect in producing this enzyme will not produce sufficient quantities of the drug in their bodies and will not benefit from use of tamoxifen. None of these breast cancer predictive tests were available to Rachel at the time of her diagnosis. However, as a Caucasian, she was in a population with the highest incidence of estrogen positive tumors compared to the other ethnicities. Moreover, the p450 null gene variant that reduces the value of tamoxifen is also rare among Caucasians. So despite his inability to test Rachel's blood, Amit was confident that tamoxifen would be an effective drug for her. Because of her celebrity status as a scientist, and with a little help from Amit's Mind Portal, Rachel Carson was enrolled in the first tamoxifen clinical trial. Her treatment was a success, and as a result, Rachel remained cancer free. She died of natural causes in 2003, at the age of 96.

*

The next major environmental issue was the herbicide glyphosate, discovered in 1970 and made commercially available in 1974. Glyphosate inhibits the synthesis of essential amino acids in rapidly growing plants such as weeds by inhibiting a key enzyme. Key to its use was the finding that the "shikimate" pathway is absent in humans, therefore it was thought to be safe. In 1976, Rachel Carson was appointed by President Gerald Ford to head a special EPA advisory panel for the evaluation of the health and environmental effects of glyphosate. With guidelines produced by her advisory panel, the manufacturer of glyphosate had to undergo many more human and veterinarian toxicology studies than were conducted in actual history. In 2014, a statistical analysis that combined the results of several epidemiologic studies concluded that workers exposed to glyphosate were twice as likely to develop B cell lymphoma. Having the benefit of hindsight, Amit directed Rachel through his mind portal and her panel to specifically look at glyphosate's ability to produce lymphomas among animal models.

Rachel and her committee also became involved the role of glyphosate and how it relates to the production of genetically modified crops. In 1994, a company developed a soybean plant that was genetically engineered to be resistant to glyphosate. Two years later, Rachel was invited to speak at a Congressional subcommittee on this topic. She was 89 at the time but she was still widely respected and her mind and logic were as sharp as ever when it came to these issues.

"Knowing that their transgenic soybean crop will not be affected, this really kicks the door open for farmers to use glyphosate to control weeds. But the concentration of glyphosate for those who consume these soybean products will be high," she said in a calm and steady voice. "What we really need to understand now is the medical effects of regularly consuming this herbicide."

The publicity of this hearing led to the funding of subsequent scientific studies many years sooner than in the actual history. One study specifically examined the glyphosate's effect on stomach and intestinal microbial function.

"Glyphosate inhibits the growth of beneficial bacteria in the gut. The presence of normal bacterial flora helps control the population of harmful bacteria. When the good bugs are gone, the bad bugs take over resulting in significant gastrointestinal disease," Rachel stated at a well-attended news conference.

Later research also showed that glyphosate inhibited the human liver cytochrome p450 enzymes that break down toxic compounds. These are the same enzymes that were needed to convert Rachel's tamoxifen to its active form.

"Because of my breast cancer and treatment with tamoxifen, a high consumption of glyphosate will adversely affect the ability of this drug to prevent recurrence. There are other drugs that require activation by the liver for them to work. How many other people in this world are unknowingly vulnerable to the effect of this chemical?"

Rachel was not able to ban the release and current widespread use of glyphosate-containing pesticides. However, the work continued by her committee after her death would lead to a movement banning glyphosate-containing herbicides a decade sooner than what is occurring today. Without Rachel's help, the countries that have eliminated glyphosate include El Salvador, Netherlands, Sri Lanka, Bermuda, Columbia, and eventually France (scheduled for 2022).

*

Newer drugs called "aromatase inhibitors" have been effectively used for women with breast cancer who have reached menopause. Tamoxifen continues to be a widely used drug for breast cancer patients particularly for younger women who have not yet reached this stage of life. Tamoxifen is preferred because for aromatase inhibitors to be effective, these women must be pharmacologically induced into menopause.

DDT acts on insects by opening sodium channels in neurons causing them to fire spontaneously. This leads to spasms and eventual death. Overuse of DDT led to the proliferation of mutations in the sodium channel of some insect species that resulted in resistance to the effect of DDT. Rachel Carson was ahead of her time in thinking that indiscriminate overuse of pesticides would eventually be counterproductive, that is, accelerating the production of resistant insects. A similar situation exists with overuse of wide-spectrum antibiotics to treat human infections. Microorganisms, which have an even shorter half-life, will produce mutated bugs.

Rachel Carson's career was cut short by the delay in diagnosing and treating her breast cancer. There have been many critics of her work, beyond the chemical companies who stand to profit from the sales of pesticides and herbicides. Some have claimed that the ban on DDT has led to the death of millions of people due to malaria. *The removal of DDT was never banned for its anti-malarial use in poor countries. In Sri Lanka, the use of DDT to control malaria-carrying mosquitoes was abandoned because the chemical was no longer effective on these mutated insects. The natural selection theory that Carson predicted in her 1962 book came to fruition some 20 years later.*

The epidemiologic evidence of glyphosate's role in human disease remains controversial. Today it remains as the most commonly used herbicide among farmers in the U.S. Several groups such as the German Federal Institute for Risk Assessment and the European Food Safety Authority have stated that the data on glyphosate toxicity are mixed. The US EPA stated in 1993 that glyphosate is non-carcinogenic. However, they are currently re-evaluating the evidence and may alter their conclusions based on more recent data.

He Has Not Left The Building

****

He arrived at the northwest gate without an appointment. He stepped out of the limo and walked alone towards the guard.

"I'd like to see the President."

"Do you have an appointment, sir?"

"I didn't think I needed one."

"Everyone needs an appointment. Even you." The guard recognized the man, even while wearing sunglasses. The date was December, 1970. One of the most recognized icons of his era, Elvis Presley flew to Washington DC in hopes of seeing President Richard Nixon. He was concerned about the abuse of recreational drugs among the youth and he wanted to be personably involved in the fight against it.

The guard's supervisor saw that the King was at the gates and quickly came over. "What is the nature of your visit?" the senior guard asked Elvis.

"I want a badge. I want to be an undercover agent at large. I want to fight the spread of illegal drugs in America. They're killing our youth. I wrote this letter. Can you see that this gets to Mr. Nixon?" Elvis said.

"I will pass this letter on. How can we contact you?" the guard asked.

"I'll be at my hotel waiting for your call." Elvis gave him the hotel's telephone number and retreated to his limo.

In his office at the White House, Egil Krogh was given the letter hand written by Elvis Presley. It detailed how Elvis wanted to help his country by being an undercover agent. As a veteran of many movies, he was a master of disguise. He was trained in the martial arts and carried his own firearms. As a man of economic means, he could make drug purchases and incriminate drug dealers. He had been given an honorary police badge from the Memphis PD. He wanted an official Federal badge that gave him the jurisdiction to fight crime. Egil thought that Elvis' fame could help the President's popularity with Southern voters, particularly young women. He went into the Oval Office and asked the President if he could schedule a brief meeting with Elvis shortly after lunch when there was some free time. Egil showed the President the security video of Elvis' encounter with the White House guards. At first Nixon refused to meet with Elvis, stating that it would cut into his afternoon nap. Eventually he agreed and a date was arranged for the next afternoon.

Elvis and his colleagues came to the Oval Office and met with the Commander-in-Chief. Elvis gave the President an antique Colt 45 pistol as a memento of their visit. In return, Nixon gave Elvis an official badge and he became a "Federal Agent-At Large" within the Bureau of Narcotics and Dangerous Drugs. Elvis told the president that he knew martial arts from his time in the U.S. army and knew how to defend himself. The two posed for pictures. Overall, their meeting was casual and friendly rather than a high level discussion. Today, of all the photos contained within the U.S. National Archives, the one with Richard Nixon and Elvis Presley is the one most frequently requested by the general public. Presley vowed to help the nation's battle against drugs. But they both knew that this would not happen because of Elvis' celebrity status.

*

It was somewhat ironic and very tragic that over the next few years, Elvis' health would decline through recreational and prescription drug abuse. He could not see that he was part of the problem and not the solution. His increasing use of drugs altered his demeanor. Elvis began to become highly erratic and uncontrollable with his entourage. As a result, he had to cancel several dates on his world concert tour. His wife, Priscilla Presley, left him shortly after his visit to the White House. She and others close to him knew that his life was spiraling to down ruin, and they were powerless to stop it. On August 16, 1977, Elvis died at his Graceland home in Memphis at the age of 42. The pathologist at the Shelby County Coroner's office ruled that Elvis died of a heart attack. At the request of Elvis' father, Vernon Presley, the final autopsy report would not be released to the public until the year 2027, exactly 50 years after Elvis' death. Many in the media suspected that Elvis died of a drug overdose. He had been taking many analgesic drugs and sedatives at the time of his death.

*

As a child, Amit was a fan of Elvis Presley's music. He saw most of Elvis' 31 featured films and loved them at the time. But when he saw them again in later years, he could not understand how he could have like them before. Amit was in graduate school when Elvis died. He didn't think much of his death until a 2016 report was published by Dr. Forest Tennant, a pain management specialist. In 1981, the doctor was contacted by James Neal, the attorney defending Elvis' personal physician, Dr. George Nichopoulos, on trial for the singer's death. Dr. Tennant waited 35 years until medical science had progressed in order to make better sense of Elvis' medical condition. In the most recent report, Amit learned that Elvis suffered from many medical problems besides his drug addiction. These problems included and a series of traumatic brain injuries and an autoimmune inflammatory disorder. In 1967, while filming the movie *Clambake*, Elvis slipped in the bathroom of a hotel in Hollywood, hit his head on the bathtub. He was unconscious for an undetermined amount of time, and had a large bump. Although this was not the first time Elvis experienced injury to his head, on this occasion, it may have been the most serious. Dr. Tennant hypothesized that head injuries to Elvis' pituitary gland caused a combination of low hormone output and the production of autoantibodies that were then in turn destructive to his brain and other tissues. Lab tests conducted on Elvis also revealed very low levels of natural antibodies. As a result, he was prone to many infections throughout his adult life.

Amit decided to alter the course of Elvis' health by entering his mind portal in an attempt to prevent him from falling in the bathroom 10 years before his death. Much to his surprise, he was not able to reach the late Elvis Presley despite numerous attempts. Amit was dumbfounded as to the reason for this failure as it had never happened to Amit before. After several weeks of thinking about this problem, Amit came up with a hypothesis for this failure. Even in 1967, Elvis had chronic pain and was regularly

25

using pain killers and sedatives. Perhaps this altered his brain function to the point that Amit's normal route of entry was blocked. To test this theory, he visited some patients at his hospital's pain clinic who were treated with the same drugs that Elvis was using. Amit planted a simple suggestion to several of these patients through his mind portal.

Ask the dietician for a cup of New England clam chowder today. Amit had checked the menu and knew that the kitchen was not offering this soup on this day. For a "control group," he implanted the same idea into two of his lab techs. He confirmed that they were drug free by seeking their permission to test their urine for the presence of these drugs. Within the hour, he knew that his theory was correct. None of the patients on opiates asked for the chowder, while the technicians, who Amit confirmed, were not taking any pain killers, asked for the soup at the cafeteria. Amit was not able to alter Elvis' behavior during the late 1960s. Amit didn't have any details as to which hotel he fell or who he was with at the time. Since he could not prevent the accident that caused Elvis to suffer brain injury, he set his attention on the behavior and knowledge of Elvis' physician, Dr. Nichopoulos.

Knowing that Elvis had damage to his pituitary following his head injury, and therefore he could not produce enough hormones, he instructed Dr. Nichopoulos to replace Elvis' missing amounts through direct injections. Since Amit knew that Elvis was also deficient in antibodies, he directed the Doctor to regularly inject human IgG antibodies into his famous patient to boost his immune system. Perhaps the biggest effect was how the doctor convinced Elvis to stop smoking. The doctor ordered the appropriate laboratory tests to ensure that the concentrations were within the correct limits. Each of these therapeutic measures resulted in a dramatic improvement in Elvis' health relative to what was documented in history. His energy and pain threshold increased, resulting in a decrease in the dependency of pain medications. This enabled him to expand his world tour to his adoring audiences. With renewed energy and activity, Elvis did not gain the weight that he exhibited at the time of his death. Instead of passing at the young age of 42, Elvis Presley is alive today and in his 80s.

Eventually, his popularity declined, as occurs for most aging singers. His movie career also began to wane. Because he didn't die young, the country did not have the same mystique of his life and legacy. Therefore, there is not the phenomenon of Elvis impersonators that exists today. There are no "Mecca-like" pilgrimages by fans to Graceland. During his later years Elvis directed his attention towards making good on his promise to Richard Nixon. However, nobody expected Elvis to actually become an undercover agent. His entourage knew that he could never disguise himself to be unrecognized to dealers or anyone else working in the drug cartel. They also felt it was much too dangerous for him to confront these pushers as a potential customer. Instead, Elvis used his status and economic means to contact other celebrities who were suffering from drug addiction. Nobody would turn down a meeting with the King of Rock and Roll.

In 1981, Elvis introduced himself to John Belushi, who was suffering from cocaine and heroin abuse. John was a big fan of rock and roll and loved Elvis. Born in Chicago in 1949, John was 7 years old when Elvis made his first record. Over the next 10 years, John followed the music and movie career of the Rock and Roll star. It was ironic that John impersonated Elvis Presley on his show, Saturday Night Live, just three months before Elvis' death in 1977. The skit was called, Viva Las Vegas II, a sequel spoof of Elvis' original 1964 movie. In his 1980 movie *The Blues Brothers*, Belushi and fellow *Saturday Night Live* star actor Dan Aykroyd sang *Jailhouse Rock,* a song made famous by Elvis in 1957.

When John Belushi's life began to spiral down, Elvis arranged a meeting with the comic at his home in Los Angeles.

"This is quite a moment for me to meet you," John said to Elvis.

"Me too. I have been following your career. I loved your role in *Continental Divide*. It shows that you do have a serious side," Elvis said.

"Coming from you, that is quite a compliment," John said. After a pause, he asked the singer, "why are you here?"

"John, I am concerned about your drug abuse and am here to help. I want you to take a leave of absence from your movie career and come to my rehabilitation center," Elvis said.

"I can't do that sir. But don't worry about me, I can control this addiction at any time," John said. This was the typical denial of drug abusers regarding their illness. "Besides, Aykroyd and I are about to produce a new science fiction film called, *Ghostbusters.*"

"If you don't come with me now, you will never make that film," Elvis said. Somehow, Elvis knew that John was going to die.

Over the next several hours and well into the night, John and Elvis drank, talked about their lives, family, careers, and legacy. By the end of the evening, he convinced the comedian to come to

Memphis and be admitted to Elvis' rehabilitation center for a trial period.

"It is totally confidential, and if you don't like it, you can leave at any time," Elvis assured him. "I will be there every step of the way." John agreed and stayed 3 months. There, he was weaned off his dependency on heroin. He learned from the Center's psychiatrists about his abusive and destructive behavior. When he left, he was off drugs and ready to resume his movie career. Elvis and his center were successful in preventing the former *Saturday Night Live* star from his accidental overdose death the following year. Upon his discharge, Aykroyd was thrilled with the now recovered Belushi. They went on to make several more movies over the next 10 years. John received an Academy Award nomination for the Best Actor Award for his role in *Ghostbusters*. William Hurt won the award that year for his portrayer of Luis Molina in *The Kiss of the Spider Woman*.

A decade later, Elvis met with River Phoenix who was also suffering from this same combination of drugs and was to die in 1993. By then, Elvis had established the Presley Drug and Alcohol Rehabilitation Center in Memphis, and Phoenix became one of the Center's patients which led to his full recovery and abstinence. Both John Belushi and River Phoenix acknowledge the role that Elvis had in saving their lives and career. They donated much of their income to the Center. John and Elvis were also instrumental in preventing his fellow *Saturday Night Live* alumnus Chris Farley from his demise from drug abuse in 1997. Farley went on to have a great career making feature-length comedies.

Thirty years after his impromptu meeting with Richard Nixon, Elvis returned to Washington DC to meet President

George W. Bush. This time, he was invited to receive the Presidential Medal of Freedom, not for his music but for his humanitarian work. It was estimated that his rehab center saved hundreds of lives, celebrities and common people alike.

*

Elvis Presley died from a variety of medical problems. Elvis had a deficiency in the production of the protein alpha-1-antitrypsin. Patients with this abnormality develop pulmonary and liver disease, which were among the problems that Elvis faced. Because of his ailments, Elvis took many drugs to ease the pain, to fight his infections, reduce his anxiety, and promote sleep. Although not really appreciated by his doctors at the time, his regular use of opiate pain killers was slowly damaging his heart and cardiac rhythm. His obesity put an additional strain on his heart. Although it will not be fully known until 2027 when the final autopsy report is released, it is likely that Elvis died of cardiac complications brought on by poly-drug use. Upon his death, Elvis left 37 handguns and a number of other firearms.

Richard Nixon's popularity with the U.S. public helped him to get re-elected for a second term two years after his meeting with Elvis. But that was short lived, as he was forced into resignation of the office in 1974 for his role in cover-up of the Watergate burglary. Nixon never faced trial as he was pardoned by his successor, President Gerald R. Ford. Nixon's aide, Egil Krogh, who helped Elvis visit Nixon, was convicted for his role in burglarizing of the office of Daniel Ellsberg's psychiatrist. Known as the "Pentagon Papers," Ellsberg had leaked confidential military documents about the Viet Nam War to the press. Krogh was sentenced to 2-6 years, and served 18 weeks in prison. In 1991, Krogh wrote a book, The Day Elvis Met Nixon, *which chronicles the meeting between the two men. This was made into a Hollywood movie in 2016.*

iBrain

****

While they were born within a few days of each other and lived in the same part of California for most of their lives, they never had met. They both became experts in their chosen fields of clinical laboratory science and information technology science, respectively. But the two men took different paths towards arriving at the pinnacle of their professions. Amit Savjani followed a traditional route that included a private high school, four years of college, five years of graduate school to obtain a doctoral degree, two years of postdoctoral training, followed by an appointment as an Assistant Professor at a major University Medical Center by the age of 29. Robert was adopted, went public schools, and briefly took classes at a small liberal arts college before dropping out. It was ironic that Amit's father was in the high tech industry where Robert would later make his mark, and when Robert was young, he had traveled throughout India where Amit's family was from.

Robert and Amit were introduced to computer science while they were in their junior year of high school. Back then, mainframe computers were large pieces of equipment taking up an entire room. Programs were written into the early computer languages called FORTRAN or BASIC. Each line of code was punched into computer cards using a typewriter-like machine called a "key punch." The cards were assembled in the order of their intended execution within the program and delivered as a stack to the computer, which read and implemented each instruction. Since there were typically only one or two mainframe computers for the entire school, each student's program was batched processed, usually overnight. Results were printed out and made available the next day. If you made a mistake in a single line of code, the program would fail and the card would have to be reproduced with the correction and resubmitted for the programming run tomorrow. Today, a line of code can be tested and corrected immediately when mistakes are found.

Back in the late 1960s, science teachers taught students how to write computer programs and use them to solve problems. Amit wrote tools that would perform complex mathematically functions such as calculating a non-linear regression of data points. He used his program to simplify the calculations necessary for his chemistry experiments. Robert used the computer to entertain himself, so he wrote a Black-Jack program. Because the computer could quickly play thousands of hands in a short time, Robert developed and tested a card counting system and a playing strategy and that proved that under the current rules of gambling, he would consistently win. Robert was convinced that he could make a decent living as a professional black jack player. What he didn't know was that casinos carefully watched card counters through their pit bosses and overhead camera, and sometimes physically punished overly profitably cheaters. The good news for Robert and the rest of the world was that he was only 16, and was not old enough to even set foot into a casino, let alone gamble. He therefore set his sights on other goals.

*

As an Assistant Professor, Amit was responsible for teaching medical students, residents who wanted to be pathologists, and graduate students seeking a doctoral degree in clinical laboratory science. Amit was also the director of the University Hospital Chemistry Laboratory and he supervised the testing of samples sent from doctors practicing at his hospital to his clinical laboratory. While these were his "day" jobs, his promotion depended on making "scholarly" contributions to the profession of clinical chemistry. This meant writing and acquiring grants to conduct research in a specialty area. As a postdoctoral fellow, Amit selected cardiac markers as his area of investigation. During the course of 35 years, Amit helped identify and validate proteins that later became routine laboratory tests for the assessment of patients who had suffered a heart attack and others who had congestive heart failure. Amit had the satisfaction of knowing that the tests he had helped develop were now used in hospitals throughout the world helping patients. Amit received several awards and was well recognized by his colleagues within the field of laboratory medicine. However, few people in the general public were aware of his important contributions.

"The clinical laboratory field supports decisions made by doctors," he told his wife, Angie one night when they were lying in bed. "We generally don't have direct contact with patients and our work is more "behind the scenes."

"That's alright dear, I think what you are doing is great work," Angie responded.

"That is the only accolade that I ever need," Amit concluded. He reached to turn off the lamp on the night stand. *Tomorrow will yet be another busy day.*

*

After dropping out of college, Robert went on a prolonged trip to India to find himself. Upon returning Robert was unsure of his next move. He was friends with another man by the name of Steve, an engineer who graduated from the same high school a few years earlier. Together, they formed a company out of a garage. In 1908, Henry Ford built the first Model T automobile, believing that every family should be able to afford and have a personal horse-less carriage. Robert and Steve believed that every family should have and afford a personal computer. So just as Ford 80 years earlier, the two modern day entrepreneurs began mass-producing personal computers. Together, they revolutionized the information technology industry. Key to their early success was the development of the graphical user interface. Unlike their early competitors from IBM, Robert's computer made use of a device that make commands and navigate the interface more easily than through a keyboard.

Steve and Robert were having a discussion on what to call it. "I think we should call it a bug," Steve suggested.

"No, a lot of people are entomophobic," Robert said.

"Are you just showing off your vocab knowledge?" Steve asked. "I happen to know what entomophobia means. You could have just said you hate the idea. You have anything better?"

"What about calling it a mouse?" Robert said.

"And women are not afraid of mice?" Steve replied.

"Well........... maybe in the future if everyone uses a mouse, they won't be afraid of the critters." Robert concluded.

With the ubiquitous presence of mice as part of our personal computers today, maybe it has curbed the fear of these rodents.

*

Their computer with the mouse attachment was a big success and both became very wealthy. However, their competitive advantage was short lived because Microsoft was developing their own mouse-driven interface for IBM and other companies were producing personal computers. Bill Gates and Microsoft called their interface "Windows." In 1985, less than 10 years after its creation, Robert and Steve's company began losing the personal computer market share to IBM-based computers, and they both left the company.

Robert went on to form a new personal computer company that started out much slower than his first company. When it began to turn a profit after nearly ten years, it was bought out by Robert's original company, and he was soon back at the helm as CEO. By then, the personal computer industry was becoming saturated. So Robert began making other consumer electronic products. They were first to develop a portable digital music player, and distribute popular music to be used on the player. Later, they developed the next-generation of the cellular telephone that incorporated internet capabilities and digital photography. Electronic "tablets" became the next innovation where the power of a computer could be displayed on a small notebook. In releasing these innovations, his company became the world's most valuable company, exceeding the gross domestic product of many developed countries.

Robert's health began to unravel when he was diagnosed with islet-cell neuroendocrine pancreatic cancer in 2003. This is a slow growing rarer form of pancreatic cancer with better survival statistics. Robert first tried dietary means to curb his cancer development. When that didn't work, he underwent surgery to remove as much of the tumor as possible. Later, he went to Tennessee and received a liver transplant. He was in a period of remission for a few years and he returned to work full time. But then his cancer returned and Robert was forced to resign. He died in his home a few months later in October, 2011.

*

Amit like many in the world was greatly upset at Robert's passing. His leadership and vision led to products that altered how the world communicates, finds information, and listens to music today. Dead at the age of 56, many wondered what other innovations and inventions he might have brought about if he was still alive. Intrigued by this process, Amit did an investigation of neuroendocrine pancreatic tumors. If Robert's pancreatic cancer was diagnosed a little earlier in the course of his disease, it is possible that Robert could have survived his cancer with the appropriate treatment. But Robert was asymptomatic at the time of his diagnosis therefore there was no reason to do any testing. Furthermore, Amit acknowledged that even today, there is no effective screening test for early pancreatic cancer detection. So how could he use his mind portal to affect the future of this visionary?

The answer led Amit to genetic analysis. He knew that menin is a protein that is naturally produced in the body. It is responsible for keeping cells from growing too fast. Menin can suppress the development of cancer, since this disease is characterized by excessive and uncontrolled cell growth. The gene that encodes menin was discovered in 1997. Today there have been over 1300 mutations that have been identified with this gene. Individuals who are born with a genetic variance either produce a non-functional version of the menin protein or the protein is degraded faster than normal. As a result, individuals with a menin gene mutation are at risk for development of multiple endocrine neoplasia type 1 or MEN1. Between 20% and 70% of patients with MEN1 will develop a pancreatic neuroendocrine tumor.

Although Robert was a very public figure, he kept his personal life very private. And as would be expected, he kept his medical information even more confidential. When he was first diagnosed with pancreatic cancer, Robert withheld this information from his company, and he would be absent for weeks and months at a time seeking medical opinions and experimental therapies. Amit felt that there was only one person who could use the genetic information that he could implant, and that was Robert himself. Throughout his cancer, the inventor took charge of his own medial decisions, much to the disagreement of his doctors. Amit went into the portal and implanted a notion into Robert's brain in 2002, two years before he was diagnosed. Soon, Robert received the following message. *I might have cancer. I need to get a tube of blood collected and sent to this laboratory in Denver where a MEN1 gene mutation can be conducted.* Unlike California where most medical testing, especially for genetic disease, must be conducted with a physician's order, Colorado allows for direct access testing, i.e., patients and their families could order their own laboratory tests without a doctor's prescription.

Robert reviewed the result back after a few weeks. He was heterozygous for one of the common mutations in the MEN1 gene. He then made an appointment and traveled to Memorial Sloan

Kettering Hospital in New York City to be evaluated. Using state-of-the art radiological imaging, they located a small tumor growing in his pancreas. Surgery was scheduled later that week, and Robert had his tumor removed. Pathology showed that it was a non-secreting islet-cell neuroendocrine tumor of the pancreas. After a day of recovery, Robert and his wife met with the oncologist, a Dr. Jain.

"This form of pancreatic cancer is uncommon. It is not typically as aggressive as exocrine pancreatic cancer where the current 5-year survival rate is dismal. Your tumor is normally very slow growing, but small percentage of them can form metastatic disease. I am not sure how you knew to get genetic testing for multiple endocrine neoplasias, we have only recently begun testing for it, but it was a good thing you had it done," Dr. Jain explained.

"I don't know how I thought of this either. I was so busy with my company and the many projects that we are developing," Robert told the doctor. "I feel great and had no reason to suspect anything wrong, but something told me I needed to get this checked this out."

Robert returned to his company with a renewed sense of focus. *I dodged a bullet here. I am going to make the next few years really count. Just wait and see what we do next!*

His company completed the next generations of phones and tablets and was ready for the next big innovation. He asked the heads of each of his sections, electronics, engineering, software, hardware, and business development for a meeting without telling them of the objective. They assembled into the board room at the scheduled time and date but Robert was late in appearing. There was a buzz at the meeting.

"Why are we here?" one senior scientist asked.

"I don't know, the memo didn't say anything except that we needed to be here," another said. "When the boss says jump, we, well, you know."

"What does Robert have in mind?" was a third comment.

After 10 minutes, Robert waked into the door. Everyone stopped their conversation and the room became quiet. All eyes were on the CEO entrepreneur.

"I am taking you all off of your current projects and putting you on a new long range one. Please identify someone to succeed you in what you're doing so we can begin this new initiative," Robert said. The individuals in the boardroom looked at each other with puzzled looks but no one spoke.

"I want to disclose to you in the strictest confidence that I am a cancer survivor. I had surgery and radiation therapy last month, which was why I as away. My doctors believe I am now in remission. I am taking this opportunity to move our company in a neuroanatomy direction."

"But we make personal electronics," the senior vice president for research responded. "How does this new idea link to our existing core competency?"

"We're going to merge what we know and do best and apply it to human learning. We are going to hire behavioral scientists, psychologists, psychiatrists, neurologists, neuroscientists, biomedical engineers, neurosurgeons, and veterinarians to achieve this new goal" Robert said.

"What goal is that?" another of the chief executives asked.

"We're going to make iBrain." More puzzled looks appeared on the faces of his team. "We are going to learn how to interface pre-programmed digital electronic memory directly into the human brain. Our memory chip will be encoded to teach the recipient how to do things. Think of the possibilities. We can teach a child how to read by downloading a program directly into the child's brain. Our brain can connect directly with global position systems and instantly get directions to new locations. We can implant books so that we don't have to read them word by word. We can all learn new languages. Think of what THAT would do for the globalization of this planet! Even teaching muscle memory is not out of the realm of possibilities. We can teach ourselves to play a musical instrument, or hit a tennis ball. I don't think our product will be responsible for producing the next Yo Yo Ma or Roger Federer. But I hope we can lower the learning curve for these activities."

Many were skeptical. But Robert had shown time and time again how he could make his dreams and ideas into reality and in doing so, transform society with his products. Maybe this could work too if he could assemble the right team. They certainly had the money to invest, the electronic knowledge, and miniaturization skills. The team left the board room with a greater buzz than when they entered. Over the course of the next few months, Robert laid out a management and R&D strategy to create iBrain.

The initial development of iBrain was conducted tested first on monkey brains. A maze was created at the company's newly created animal facility. Through trial and error, it took on the average 15 minutes for the monkeys to enter and exit the maze. Then the iBrain chip was implanted into the brain of other monkeys that contained an aerial view of the maze. When these maze-naive animals entered, they made all correct turns without guessing and were able to exit the maze on an average of 5 minutes. Clearly these monkeys could see the path based on the image that was implanted into their brains. The behavioral scientists monitoring the trial all cheered and iBrain was born.

Robert's cancer was in remission for nearly 15 years before he his cancer returned. He lived long enough to witness the first animal experiment and saw that their invention might work. Robert passed at the age of 62, several years before human studies of iBrain would be initiated. Amit met Robert for the first time a few months before the inventor passed. Amit was asked to measure some specific brain proteins from the spinal fluid as a marker of cerebral injury during chip implantation. Little did Robert know the role that Amit played in his medical survival?

*

Steve Jobs and Steve Wozniak created Apple Inc. in Cupertino California, in 1976 and released Apple I, one of the first personal computers. Years later under Job's leadership, Apple diversified the business in creating iTunes and iStore, and various generations of the iPod, iPhone, and iPad. Separate from Apple's achievements, Jobs was also instrumental in digitizing animated movies and desk publishing. He contributed to over 450 patents. Apple today ranks as either first or second among the most valuable companies in the world.

The iBrain does not exist nor is it likely a current project with Apple. iBrain, however, is a portable brain device developed by neuroscientist Dr. Philip Low. It is hoped that brain wave activities from human thoughts can be interpreted by an algorithm. Dr. Low is working with physicist Steven Hawkins in hopes that his thoughts can be translated in real time by iBrain.

TBI

****

Amit Savjani was both an avid participant and spectator of sports. The games he played at the local level included tennis, slow-pitch softball, and indoor volleyball. These were rather "safe" sports in that it would be highly unusual for anyone to suffer a major debilitating or life threatening injury while participating. Once in a great while, there may be an emergency department visit for a softball pitcher who might have gotten hit in the head or chest by a batted ball. Given the close proximity of the batter's box to the mound, this is not a rare event. When playing college volleyball, Amit once witnessed a teammate who suffered a mild concussion and hospitalized when he was struck by a hard driven spike. Amit's believed that the physical fitness benefit of being athletically active far outweighed the risks of any serious injury, and he continued to participate in sports activity, despite now being in his mid-60s.

As a spectator, Amit enjoyed watching professional football, major league baseball, hockey, boxing, and soccer. He recognized that these sports were sometimes associated with significant injuries to the extent that they could threaten an athlete's career. Injuries to the head and spinal cord are the most devastating. Examples of significant brain injury include blows to the head by an opposing player's helmet, a baseball thrown at speeds great than 90 miles per hour, a puck that is accelerated by the low frictional surface of ice, a punch of a fist even from a padded glove, and from a soccer ball where the head is purposely used as the manner for striking it.

Once, Amit was watching a high school soccer game where his niece was playing as a defense-man. The goalie made a save and then kicked the ball high into the air near mid-field. Amit's niece, Anitha, positioned herself directly under the ball and jumped just as it was coming down. She struck the ball with the top of head back into direction it came from. It was a spectacular soccer shot that was marveled by the coaches and spectators alike. A forward on Anitha's team took the pass, dribbled the ball towards the goal, and kicked it past the goalie for a score. The team and their fans cheered. But when they looked back at Anitha, she was lying face-down on the field. In the excitement of the play, nobody but Amit noticed that after the "header," Anitha took two staggered steps and fell forward, and was unconscious. The referees stopped the game, and the coaches and players ran over to their fallen teammate. A doctor, who was the parent of another player, told everyone that Anitha was not to be touched or moved. An ambulance was called and arrived a few minutes later. The emergency vehicle drove directly onto the field to where Anitha lay. It had rained that morning and the tires were making track marks onto the field, but nobody cared about that. When the paramedics arrived, Anitha had regained consciousness. While supporting her neck, paramedics lifted her body onto the stretcher and into the ambulance where she was taken to the General Hospital. The girls from both teams were crying. The remainder of the game was called off and everyone left the field in a somber and very concerned mood.

At the General, the emergency department staff examined Anitha using their concussion protocol. Although Amit was the chemistry lab director at the General, he was told to stay in the waiting room along with his brother and sister-in-law. Anitha complained of a headache and double vision. She was asked a series of questions to test her recall.

"Where are you?"

"At a hospital," she responded.

"What happened to you?"

"I was playing soccer and hit the ball with my head. Then I passed out."

"How do you feel now?"

"I have a headache. I am dizzy. And I am very tired."

Anitha was diagnosed as having suffered a mild concussion, or "traumatic brain injury." She was kept in the emergency department overnight for observations and discharged on the following day. All of her teammates came to the ER to wish her well. Anitha did not suffer from any further complications from her TBI and was in school the next week. But her brief amateur soccer career was over.

Anitha moved on from her injury and became a successful neurologist. She selected this profession because of her childhood injury. Anitha married and had several children. Her son plays in an under 8-year-old soccer league and was one of the first kids to wear a soft protective helmet. Amit changed the direction of his research after Anitha's injury, focusing on proteins release into the blood from TBI. They worked together in developing a prototype blood test to detect cerebral injury following a mild concussion. This test measures markers such as S100B, neuron enolase, and glial fibrillary acidic protein.

Amit wondered how traumatic brain injury might have affected the lives of other individuals. Muhammad Ali suffers from Parkinson's disease that may have been brought on by his prolonged boxing career. Brittanie Cecil was watching a professional hockey game when she was hit in the head by a puck, and died two days later from a torn vertebral artery. There have been several ex-professional football players who died of brain injury including Mike Webster and Terry Long. Dave Duerson committed suicide rather than face the slow cognitive decline due to traumatic brain injury. In a suicide note to his family, Duerson wrote, "Please see that my brain is given to the NFL's brain bank." Autopsies from each of these men confirmed that they suffered from a newly defined injury called chronic traumatic encephalopathy. The death of these and other individuals have led the National Football League to institute new playing rules to protect players from brain injury, largely caused by collisions with hard helmets. But Amit wanted to know if there was another prominent figure in history, whose life may have changed with the knowledge of TBI. A recent report of a prominent figure in history by a behavioral neurologist led Amit to enter his mid portal.

*

Henry was the second son of the king and was therefore not next in line for the throne. Arthur, who was Henry's older brother, married Catherine at the age of 15 but before the marriage could be consummated, he died a few months later. Henry became the heir to the kingdom. His father wanted him to marry his sister-in-law after Arthur's death, but he was only 11 years old at the time. When his father died 6 years later, Henry became king, and to everyone's surprise, he married Catherine. The Queen became pregnant several times with Henry, but the children were either stillborn or died within a few months of live. Only daughter Mary survived into adulthood, but was not the first heir because of her gender.

Henry was a virile man who had many affairs as the young king. He was well educated, an avid reader, and spoke and wrote in English, French and Latin. He stood over six feet tall and was very athletic. One of his hobbies was jousting and hunting. A few years into his reign, at the age of 26, he organized a jousting tournament where he wore gilded armor, pearls and jewels. It was quite a spectacle for foreign ambassadors to watch the young king galloping at full speed on horseback toward another equally armed competitor, each carrying a long wooden lance that was aimed at their adversary's armored shield. The winner of each round would be one who could the knock the other off of their steed onto the soft ground.

But it was another jousting event, some years later that would change the course of history for the king, his reign and his country. At 33 years old, Henry, was now losing to younger and stronger competitors. His advisors told him that he should quit the sport as it was endangering his health. Henry would not admit to being less than capable and continues participating in the sport.

The competitors stood on their horses ready for the signal to advance. When it was given, Henry lowered the visor of his helmet and signaled his horse to gallop towards his rival. The other knight did likewise. They both lowered their lance and aimed at the other's shield. Henry's opponent was quicker and struck Henry's shield first. It was a glancing blow that slid off the shield and up into the King's helmet. His visor popped open. The lance shattered, but not before it struck the king in the head and face, knocking him off his horse. The King lay on the ground dazed. There was a sudden hush among the crowd. There was sort of a reverse hush as he slowly got up from his fall.

"I'm fine, everybody," he told the crowd as they all cheered. The king saluted his opponent who'd made the successful hit. The king did not want to show any weakness to his subjects. His head ached but he jumped back on his horse and continued to joust against other opponents for the remainder of the day. The knight who won that round was banished from further competition.

A year later, the king had another fall when was hunting. He attempted to vault over a brook with a long pole but it broke and he fell into ditch. His advisers told him that he should stop participating in these high risk physical sports, as he was the king, but he adamantly refused. Over the next decade, the King would have several additional episodes of TBI while jousting.

Henry's head injuries began to affect his personality and demeanor. His marriage to Catherine began to fall apart. The King was frustrated that she had so many miscarriages and stillborn deaths and was unable to produce a male heir. Of course, he thought that there could not be anything wrong with his royal sperm. He had extra-marital affairs with many women including Catherine's lady-in-waiting. Because the official religion of his country was Catholic, divorce was not an option. Instead, Henry petitioned the Pope to have his marriage with Catherine annulled.

Because Henry married his brother's wife, he cited Leviticus 20:21 as the basis for this annulment:

"If a man marries his brother's wife, it is an act of impurity; he has dishonored his brother. They will be childless."

Unfortunately, the Pope ruled that this was insufficient grounds for an annulment. This left Henry with no options, if he wanted out of the marriage. So he did what any progressive leader might do to get his way: he changed the rules. He broke away from the church and formed new leadership for their religion.

King Henry VIII was now the "Supreme Head on Earth of the Church of England." Anyone who refused the Oath of Supremacy was committing treason, punishable by death. After denouncing the Pope, Henry VIII removed all of the monasteries and priests loyal to the Catholics. This was a revolutionary event as nearly 100 religious houses in England were destroyed and monks, canons, friars, and nuns were displaced from their profession. Their assets were turned over to Henry VIII and used to sponsor the King's wars with Scotland and France.

Henry VIII self-annulled his marriage to Catherine of Aragon in 1533, in order to marry Anne Boleyn. The new Queen delivered a baby girl they named Elizabeth, but bore no sons that survived. By then, Henry's personality and temperament began to change and he was less tolerant. Anne was much more independent than Catherine which angered Henry further. Shortly after her last miscarriage, Henry VIII accused her of treasonous adultery and incest. She and her brother were found guilty and beheaded at the Tower of London just three years after their marriage. Henry VIII wedded Jane Seymour 10 days later.

*

Amit studied the medical accounts that described Henry VIII's demeanor before and after his episodes of TBI. He understood that like post-traumatic stress disorder, victims of TBI suffer from significant emotional disturbances. Victims experience extreme mood swings, anxiety, and depression. Damage to the cerebral cortex will also affect memory. Henry VIII exhibited all of these symptoms beginning at the age of 40. How would England's history be changed if someone was able to convince him to stop the activities that cause traumatic brain injury? Amit went into his mind portal and showed Henry when he was in his early 20s, that unless he stopped participating in activities that resulted in head injuries, his future would consist of denouncing his Catholic religion, marrying six times, and be responsible for beheading two of his wives. Henry was appalled that he would become this person. He immediately dropped his case for annulment and Catherine remained Queen until her death in 1536. Henry did not marry Anne Boleyn and the future Queen Elizabeth I was never born. Instead, he married Jane Seymour as his second wife and she delivered Edward VI. In history, Edward became King upon Henry's death in 1547. But because he didn't suffer TBI, Henry went on to live and rule England for 8 more years, past the death of his only son Edward in 1553. His daughter with Catherine, Mary, became Queen of England in 1555, two years later than in history. Queen Mary died in 1558. Without another heir, the Tudor line ended with her death instead of with Queen Elizabeth's death in 1603.

King Henry VIII's marriage with Catherine of Aragon improved with his avoidance of traumatic brain injury and change in the family outlook. He now had no desire to divorce her and there was no need or thought for the King to break away from the Catholic Church. England remained a papal state and there was no creation of a separate Church of England. King Edward VI was more pro-Protestant but he never made it to the throne. Queen Mary was very much pro-Catholic and rebelled against the Protestants. She had many of their leaders exiled or executed, earning her the nickname "Bloody Mary." With no Church of England and the ties with the Pope being strong under Queen Mary, the English Protestant Reformation did not take place, and today, England is largely Catholic today. After the death of Pope John Paul II, the Arch Bishop of Canterbury became the second English Pope, after Adrian IV who occupied the throne from 1154 to 1159. The new Pope renamed himself Henry I.

Henry VIII's milder demeanor prevented many of the conflicts he engaged with against neighboring countries. Instead, he took the lead in overseas exploration. During the 15th and 16th Centuries, Spain and Portugal ruled the seas and colonized South and North America. The "British Empire" didn't begin in earnest until Queen Elizabeth I rein in the late 1580s. Instead, many of the countries today that are Spanish speaking such as Mexico, and Portuguese speaking such as Brazil, now speak English. In the U.S., Catholicism became the dominant religion from the very beginning. John F. Kennedy was not the first Catholic American President, but one of many.

The day after Amit entered his Portal to affect Henry VIII's past, he noticed rosary beads in his bedroom bureau, a small crucifix hanging on his wall in the living room, and a bumper sticker of an ichthys on his car. There were other signs that he, indeed, had converted to Catholicism at some point in his past.

*

Henry VIII traumatic brain injury may have been responsible for a major shift in his personality that has been documented by historians for centuries. There is ample evidence that he suffered bouts of depression, headaches, memory loss, and irascibility. TBI may have contributed to many of his other significant medical issues that contributed to his death at the age of 56. In retrospect, many of these issues could have been explained by his traumatic brain injury. Modern day physicians opined that the King's brain injury from jousting may have also damaged his pituitary gland, located at the base of the brain. Among other hormones, the anterior pituitary produces human growth hormone and its absence can cause visceral obesity. A decline in the release of pituitary gonadotropic hormones may have led to a decreased libido, a significant departure from his early years. While he Henry had many wives, there were no apparent pregnancies after Jane Seymour and his sex drive was diminished. For example, he failed to consummate with his fourth wife, Anne of Cleves, and his fifth wife, Catherine Howard was not satisfied with Henry and had an affair with a courtier while married to the King.

Pope John Paul II was the first non-Italian Pope in over 450 years. After his death, his successors were from Germany and Argentina. Not surprisingly, there have been no Popes from the United Kingdom since the establishment of the Church of England. To this day, the Catholic church prohibits divorce, according to Mark 10:9: "Therefore what God has joined together, no human being must separate."

The laboratory detection of traumatic brain injury remains a hot topic of clinical laboratory research today. If a biomarker or series of blood-based markers can be validated for use in detecting mild concussions, it will likely be used in many areas such as emergency medicine, sports medicine, pediatrics, geriatrics, critical care medicine, and family medicine.

Passage of proteins from the brain and central nervous system across the blood brain barrier is against a concentration gradient, such as swimming against the current. Therefore testing used for measurements must have high analytical sensitivity.

Sweat Shop

****

On January 1, 1988, the US Food and Drug Administration required manufacturers to supplement their cereal grain products with folic acid. The objective of this mandate was to reduce neural tube defects among newborns. These are birth defects that affect the development of the brain or spinal cord. One of these defects is spina bifida, caused by the incomplete closing of the backbone and membranes around the spinal cord. Increasing the dietary folate concentration also reduced neurologic symptoms of pernicious anemia. Today, the practice of adding folic acid to cereal grains has been extended to over 75 countries

Folate deficiency is also a cause of megaloblastic anemia. In this disease, there is a reduction in the number of red blood cells, essential for the delivery of oxygen from the lungs to peripheral tissues. The cells themselves are larger than normal, hence the term, "mega." The size of red cells is routinely measured when a hematology panel is ordered on an individual. The red cell volume is determined by calculating the mean corpuscular volume, abbreviated as MCV. Patients with megaloblastic anemia are overly tired, may have difficulty breathing and suffer from tingling or numbness around their extremities.

Years after the folic acid mandate, Amit Savjani

conducted an epidemiologic study at his hospital. He and his colleagues showed that the incidence of megaloblastic anemia had decreased. Amit was especially interested in conducting this study because of the large homeless population that his hospital served. His research showed that the number of megaloblastic anemia cases had declined since the folate mandate, even in his homeless population.

"But what about vitamin B12?" one of his students asked. Vitamin B12 works closely with folate in producing healthy red blood cells. "Did folate supplementation affect megaloblastic anemia in patients who were deficient in vitamin B12?"

"Possibly, but the studies are inconclusive. There are reports that folic acid supplementation masks the symptoms of anemia caused by a vitamin B12 deficiency. If a patient is asymptomatic, doctors may not know that they have this deficiency and may not think about checking blood levels," Amit remarked.

"But a blood test for B12 is so inexpensive, why not routinely test it on everybody?" the student asked.

"Because B12 deficiency is reasonably rare today, it is not cost effective to test everyone, especially if they appear healthy. If someone is identified as having a deficiency, treatment begins with recommending food that contains high levels of B12 such as read meat, salmon, and fortified cereals. Some people have an intestinal infection that can block B12 absorption and they must be treated with antibiotics."

In the process of performing the epidemiology study, Amit spoke to some of the older hematologists regarding their treatment of anemic patients.

"Prior to the discovery of the biochemical role for B12 in

megaloblastic anemia and the existence of a clinical laboratory test, a deficiency of this enzyme was characterized by a high rate of mortality," on doctor told Amit. The discussion prompted Amit to do some additional reading. He had been taught that pernicious anemia was a readily treatable disease and fatalities were rare. He was surprised to learn that many people died of this disease before the biochemistry was elucidated.

*

One such person was Inez Milholand. Inez was born in Brooklyn New York in 1886. Her father, John Milholand, was a newspaper reporter who also owned a successful business that made pneumatic tubes. Because of their wealth, Inez was able to attended college and law school, and she eventually became a successful attorney specializing in labor law. Inez was particularly interested in the working conditions at companies that primarily used female laborers. New York City's Garment District in 1910 had many clothing manufacturing facilities that employed thousands of seamstresses.

One day, John was asked by his editor to write a story on New York City's sweat shops in Manhattan. He asked Inez to accompany him given her emerging expertise in labor law. John called Max Harris, the owner of the Triangle Shirtwaist Factory and they scheduled a visit. On the appointed day, one of the owners, Max Blanck met the pair at the main entrance on the ground floor. Together, they walked to the elevator where Gaspar Mortillalo the lift operator met them.

"Good morning Mr. Harris," Gaspar said. "Eighth floor?"

"Yes, Gaspar. We have some special visitors today," Max replied.

When they reached the floor, Gaspar opened the hand-operated door and the three of them walked towards Max's office.

Seated in the office, Max introduced everyone to his products. "We make blouses that are attractive and colorful, as well as being very affordable" he told them. "Our workers take pride in producing the highest quality garments anywhere." Max had arranged for some of his more attractive workers to model samples of the blouses they make. "Would you like to see our showroom?" he asked.

"Actually, I would like to visit the production floor and talk to some of your workers if I may?" Inez said.

"Well, they're very busy, but I suppose we can spare one or two for a minute or two."

The office was set high above the office floor. In this way, Max and his factory foreman could watch the workers. As they walked down the stairs, Inez asked Max about wages and hours. She found out that the women worked six days a week, 52 hours total, and were paid 50 cents per hour. The Triangle Shirtwaist Factory also employed children as young as 12 to work in their factory.

When questioned about these low salaries, Max stated that they were in line with all of the other factories in the area and they were not breaking any labor laws. "We pass the labor savings onto the customer by offering lower prices," was his explanation.

When Inez and John reached the factory floor, Max called Rosie Weiner to talk with them. Inez asked Rosie how she liked working for Triangle.

"Oh, I just love working here," Rosie said. "Everyone is so nice. I used to work across town but this factory is so much better." Max, who was standing right next to the woman, nodded, smiled and patted the woman on her shoulder. Inez could tell that Rosie was intimidated by the owner's presence and dare not say anything negative for fear of losing her job. Rosie was only 16 years old. There were dozens of other workers who could replace her.

Max and the group walked to another station where Max began bragging about their modern sewing machines. "These are the latest Singer models," He said. "They can do cross stitch, double stitch, and just about anything else a designer could want."

John knew that Inez wanted to ask questions of the workers without Max present. So he distracted the owner by asking a series of inane questions. "But what about your threads? How many colors do you have?"

We dye our own thread with the most vibrant colors. As they walked towards the supply cabinet, Inez stayed back from the pair and snuck away. Oxana was working next to Rosie. She was watching the proceedings carefully took the opportunity to catch Inez's attention.

"They lock us in here," Oxana said quietly while looking to see if Max had noticed them talking. "They don't trust us. They think we will steal the blouses. I would never wear their stinking blouses anyways. They also think if the doors are open that we'll slip out for a break or a cigarette. They want us to be always working. It's not safe. What if there was a fire?"

Inez looked at the exit and saw that the door was ajar. "What do you mean? It looks open now?"

"That's because you're here today. But tomorrow, it will be locked up like a prison," Oxana said. "I have to go back before he sees me, but can you help us?"

John and Max returned from their tour of the factory floor. Inez rejoined the group. John thanked Max for his hospitality, and reporter and attorney left. Once outside, Inez told her father about the terrible working conditions. "These women work like dogs," she said. "These women work their fingers to the bone under unbearable conditions. They put their blood and sweat into that shop."

"Hmmm. Sweat shop," John said. "I like that alliteration. Can I use it in my report? "

"Hold off Dad. I need to find out more about the industry standards and if they are breaking the law or not. I don't trust that owner."

"OK Inez, tell me when you finish your investigation. I have no specific deadline. I want to get the full story."

He kissed his daughter on the forehead. "I love you too Dad," she said and they went their separate ways to their respective offices in the city.

Over the next few weeks, Inez investigated the labor conditions of the sweat shop that they had visited. She spent many hours in the law library looking to see if there were any violations. One of her classmates was an Assistant Attorney for New York City and she wanted to know if there was evidence for criminal endangerment. Word spread from within the law office. One of the partners called her into the office.

"I hear you are investigating the Triangle Shirtwaist Factory. Who assigned you to this case?"

"Well, nobody. I went there with my Father and found the working conditions were appalling," Inez said. "These women need help."

"Inez, we are a private law firm. We do not do *pro bono* work. If you don't have paying clients, we cannot have you spend time on this case at the expense of the other ones you are assigned. Do I make myself absolutely clear?"

"I understand. I will get back to work immediately on my assignments," Inez said.

Soon after her encounter with her boss, Inez's health suddenly started to decline. She started to complain of weakness in her extremities. She was depressed and had difficulty concentrating. Her father called Dr. Horatio Kleinfelter, their family doctor to perform a complete physical examination. Unfortunately, he could not find out what was wrong. John told the doctor that Inez's boss was unhappy with her spending time on the shirtwaist case. "Her depression could be causing the peripheral neuropathy that she is suffering from," Dr. Klein said. "I think she should take a leave of absence from her job. After a few weeks of bed rest, she will be back to the driven girl we all know."

Unfortunately, Inez's health continued to deteriorate. Dr. Klein ordered a complete blood count and concluded that she suffered from pernicious anemia. There was no cure for this form of anemia, and Inez died a few months later. John blamed himself for taking her to the Triangle Shirtwaist factory.

*

On Saturday afternoon, March 25, 1911, a few months after Inez's death, fire broke out at 23-29 Washington Place in Greenwich Village. One of the women was secretly smoking in the back. She extinguished her cigarette onto the floor, then picked it up and threw the butt into a bin containing discarded scrap cutting. She did not want to leave any evidence of her smoking activity. She went back to her station not realizing that her cigarette had not extinguished completely, and the clothing bin was on fire. Before anyone knew it, the fire spread to the clothes hanging above the bin. The smoke quickly filled the room and the workers started to panic. The factory did not have fire extinguishers or running water. There were no fire alarms in the building. Within minutes, the entire floor was ablaze. Many of the workers rushed to the exits only to find that they were locked. When they realized that there was only one way out, they all rushed toward the open door. Gaspar, the elevator man, was on the eighth floor and crammed as many women as possible into his tiny elevator to evacuate them. When the workers emptied out of the elevator on the ground floor, Gaspar risked his own life by repeatedly returning the elevator back to the 8th floor to retrieve more women. But soon the rails to his elevators buckled under the heat of the fire and the elevator stopped operating. Rosie and some of the other workers climbed onto the small fire escape. But the iron escape was not designed to hold that many people and it collapsed sending all of them to their deaths. Others climbed up the stairs to the roof of the building hoping to be rescued by firemen. But the fire truck ladders could not reach that high. Oxana saw that the firemen were holding a tarp and signaled them to jump one at a time to their safety. But when she jumped, five others jumped at the same time, and the tarp ripped open and they all died. Many more voluntarily jumped to their deaths rather than be burned alive. In total, 123 women and 23 men died in the Triangle Shirtwaist Factory fire that day. There were several survivors, including Max Harris, the owner, who was one of the first the escape. Unknown to anyone then or later, the key to the locked doors was in his pocket.

*

While doing research for his paper on folate supplementation, Amit learned about the Triangle Shirtwaist Factory and the aftermath from John Milholland's newspaper article. Max Harris was charged with first- and second-degree manslaughter for having the doors locked during working hours. But the prosecution could not prove that the owner ordered the door locked. He was acquitted of the criminal charge. There was a civil trial the following year, where the Triangle Shirtwaist factory was found liable for the wrongful death of its employees and was ordered to pay $75 for each victim. Triangle actually profited from the lawsuit because their insurance company returned $400 per casualty back to the company. Amit also learned that John's daughter had been a labor lawyer and had visited the factory some months earlier. The newspaper's obituary stated that Inez died of pernicious anemia. In examining NYC death records, Amit discovered that Dr. Horatio Klein had signed the death warrant and had been Inez's personal physician.

Amit went into his mind portal and brought up the image and spirit of Dr. Klein. Without transferring the idea that Inez had a vitamin B12 deficiency, he simply implanted that it was vitally important that Inez change her diet to contain red meat, salmon, and liver. *We know today that these foods are rich in vitamin B12,* Amit reasoned to himself. There were no blood tests at the time that Dr. Klein could order to check on this so let's see what this idea might do. After this encounter, Dr. Klein went to see his patient and told her of his dietary recommendations. Inez asked him why that was helpful. She was a vegetarian. Dr. Klein could not provide a cogent explanation but simply said that this change in diet would work. Inez suffered from partial malabsorption. The altered diet was sufficient to overcome the reduced dietary absorption.

When Inez felt better, she was more committed than ever to help the women at the Triangle Shirtwaist factory. She told the NYC fire marshal about the dangers of locking exit doors and together they obtained a court order to demand that Max keep all of them open. Max reluctantly complied. On March 25, 1911, fire broke out at the Triangle Shirtwaist factory. All survived except Oxana and two other women. Inez lobbied for better working and safety conditions, working closely with The International Ladies' Garment Workers' Union to improve conditions, increase wages and benefits, and reduce working hours. Children were no longer permitted to work.

Rosie escaped the fire. Having seen the death of her friend and co-worker, she quit the factory. With Inez's help, Rosie finished high school, was admitted into New York University, majored in chemistry, and upon completion of her studies, she became a laboratory technologist at the NYU hospital. She worked at the campus that was very near to the Triangle Shirtwaist Factory. She was a research technologist under Dr. Arthur Karmen, when in 1955, as a medical student, Karmen co-discovered the first enzyme test for the diagnosis of heart attacks. The next day, Amit went to the internet to learn about the Triangle Shirtwaist fire and learned that only three people died.

*

Inez Milholland was a labor lawyer. She made significant contributions for the women's right to vote movement in the U.S. She also helped to improve working conditions for factory workers and prisoners alike. While speaking in Los Angeles on women's rights, she collapsed and died a month later at the age of 30 of pernicious anemia. Who knows what more she could have accomplished for gender equality had she lived?

Inez had not yet finished law school and was not involved with the Triangle Shirtwaist factory before its fire as told in this story. Nevertheless, her work of improving conditions in sweat shops may have prevented other tragedies from occurring. The last survivor of the Triangle fire was Ms. Rose Freedman, who died in in 2001 at 107 years. There was a remembrance of the fire on its 100-year anniversary. A ceremony was held in front of the building in New York City where the fire occurred, and bells rang throughout cities in the U.S. on the moment the first fire alarm was sounded in 1911.

Along with John Ladue, Arthur Karmen discovered alanine aminotransferase as the first test for heart attacks and liver disease. He is still living in New York City. Rosie was not an assistant of Dr. Karmen as she died in the fire before her destiny could be fulfilled.

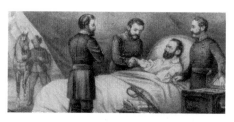

A Wall of Stone

****

Thomas was born in Clarksburg, Virginia on January 21, 1824. Some 37 years later, this small town would be part of a new state called West Virginia. Had Thomas been born just a few miles north into the Union state of Pennsylvania, his adult life would have been very different. Instead of a hero with statues and parks named after him, his life and career would likely be just a footnote today.

Thomas' father died when he was 2 and he was only 7 when his mother died. For the next few years, he, his younger sister and older brother were separated and lived with various relatives in the area. Thomas attended school where he could but mostly he was self-taught. He was an avid reader and read anything he could get his hands on. By the time he was a teenager, Thomas had become a school teacher in his small town. This helped him get into U.S. Military Academy at West Point when he turned 18. Because his formal education was spotty during his youth, he was initially at the bottom of his class academically. But by the time he graduated, he was in the top third. Some felt that he could have been at the top of his class if West Point's program had been five years instead of four.

Thomas left West Point as a second lieutenant in the U.S.

Artillery and fought in the Mexican-American War for the next two years. It was there that he first showed the talents of a brilliant leader in battle. He was promoted in the field twice, ultimately to the rank of major. It was also there that Thomas met is future boss, a man who was second in his class at West Point some 17 years earlier.

*

Amit Savjani participated in one of the earliest trials of d-dimer. "This is a breakdown product of fibrin, the stuff that clots are made of," he told his wife Angie one day at home. There was a puzzled look on her face, so he knew he had to explain further. "When blood clots dissolve, they form smaller degradation products. D-dimer is one of those products." Angie knew from her years of marriage to Amit that there he would eventually tell her why this test was clinically important. She kept silent waiting patiently for him to finish.

"When blood clots, soluble fibrinogen is converted to a fibrin where it binds to other fibrin to form an insoluble matrix. This keeps us from excessive bleeding when we cut ourselves," Amit continued. "The protein consists of two "d" subunits and one "e" subunit. When fibrin degrades, the d subunits combine to form a dimer. Get it?"

Angie knew what Amit was saying. "I know, you scientists try to make it easier to understand the biochemistry by naming proteins based on their structure. Whoopie doo." She twirls her index finger in the air in the form of a circle.

Amit paused for a second then proceeded. "The REASON this is important, sweetie, is that the d-dimer test when negative, tells us that someone has not suffered a blood clot in one of their veins. This is a serious medical condition, and we can now rule this out with a blood test. Pretty neat, uh?"

Angie was actually interested in the medical science that Amit brought home with him. She knew he was doing important work to help mankind. She also saw that people who work in the laboratory hardly ever received credit for many of the medical discoveries that are made each year. "You know I am just pulling your chain. I think this is really great and your test should help a lot of people."

*

After the Mexican War, Thomas returned to Virginia and received a faculty position at the Virginia Military Institute in Lexington Virginia. He was not particularly well liked by his students because of his stern teaching style. In contrast, Thomas was well liked among the slaves and free black community around Lexington. He and his wife taught at their Sunday school classes. While he owned several slaves, he and his family provided good homes for them and treated them like family members. He allowed some of the better educated slaves to work for their freedom.

When the War Between the States broke out in 1861, Thomas became a Colonel in the Confederate Army and was assigned by the Virginia Governor to command a brigade at Harpers Ferry. It was ironic that he was fighting to keep the institution of slavery when he had personal doubts about its morality. As with the Mexican campaign, Thomas' brilliance as a strategist and leader became evident. In the First Battle of Bull Run, the rebels were losing to the Union forces as he watched them disassemble and retreat. These men were not yet professional soldiers and were experiencing battle for the first time. Thomas stood tall on his horse and rallied his troops to stand firm and committed to the cause. The Confederates regrouped and mounted a counter attack against the Union troops, who also had inexperienced soldiers that were easily panicked. The attack resulted in a resounding victory for the Confederates. From that day on, Thomas became known as Stonewall. General Thomas "Stonewall" Jackson.

*

Amit's clinical lab was one of the first to implement the d-dimer test in the emergency department. It was used in patients who presented with leg pain and swelling. One of the causes of this inflammation is a "deep vein thrombosis" or DVT, a blood clot in the leg. "A piece of a blood clot can break away and be carried away by the circulation of blood," Amit explained to one of his students. "When it lodges in an artery or arteriole of the lungs, it can cause blockage and respiratory problems. This is known as a "pulmonary embolus" or PE, and has a significant mortality. Our d-dimer test when negative tells an ED doc that a DVT or PE has not occurred."

"What are the causes of DVT or PE?" the student asked.

"There are many including obesity, heart disease especially of the valves, cancer, genetic factors, pregnancy, trauma, smoking, and prolonged bed rest or immobilization," Amit said. "That is why you should always get up out of your seat and walk around an airplane during a long flight to get your blood flowing. If you sit too long, your blood pools into your legs and this stagnation can produce a blood clot."

*

Stonewall Jackson continued his military brilliance in the

battles following Bull Run. He defeated the Union Army at several locations despite having inferior forces. The Confederate forces were commanded by General Robert E. Lee whom Jackson served under during the Mexican War. Stonewall became General Lee's most reliable leader in battle. Then on May 2nd, 1863, Stonewall Jackson and his staff were returning to his camp after the Battle of Chancellorsville. His own soldiers mistook the group as a Union cavalry force and fired into the group. Several of Jackson's aides were killed. Jackson took two shots in his left arm and one in his right hand. Due to the darkness and chaos, there was a delay in getting Jackson any medical treatment. Dr. Hunter McGuire was at the medical tent and decided to amputate the General's wounded arm. Jackson was moved to a local Virginia plantation for recovery of his wounds. All appeared well after the amputation until he began to complain of chest pain.

*

Many years after Amit launched his d-dimer test, Amit became interested in the Civil War and was especially interested in reading about the death of Stonewall Jackson. The General had breathing problems shortly after his arm amputation for several days before he died. Dr. McGuire attributed his death due to pneumonia. However, Dr. Philip Mackowiak of the University of Maryland suggested that Jackson died of a pulmonary embolus. In reviewing Dr. McGuire's medical notes, there was no mention of Jackson having a fever or cough, key features in patients suffering from pneumonia. Jackson had many of the risk factors for blood clotting including surgery, fractures, and immobilization. The d-dimer test would not be available for over a century so there was no way that Amit could get doctors to test Jackson's blood to rule out a PE. Nevertheless, he found an image of Dr. McGuire and planted an idea into his brain…

*

A few days after Jackson's arm amputation, the General was feeling better and was anxious to be up and about, but his nurses refused to allow him to rise.

"I have to see where my troops are relative to Union forces. Send for my commanders!"

One of the nurses responded. "Dr. McGuire has strict orders that you are to stay in bed. There is no way we can allow you to return to duty. A dead general is of no use to us, sir."

Dr. McGuire was standing to the side listening to the conversation and nodding his head in agreement. Then all of a sudden, his head turned askew and is facial expression changed from confident to one who was puzzled. He started blinking uncontrollable for a few seconds. Then, unexpectedly, he approached the nurse and their patient. "Get him up. I want him to begin to resume normal activity, now."

"Now you're talking Doc," the General spoke as he tried to lift himself up with his only remaining arm.

"Doctor, what are you doing??" the nurse asked. "This patient needs rest. You are countermanding your own order! I can't allow this."

"Step aside," Dr. McGuire said to the nurse. There is nothing wrong with this man's legs."

"But doctor!" The nurse was pleading.

The nurse stopped her argument when she saw that the doctor had a determined glaze on his face. The General arose from his bed and sat down in a chair nearby. Dr. McGuire ordered one

73

of his aides to massage the General's leg. Within a few hours, the patient was walking around the room. Someone handed him a pair of binoculars and he peered out on the horizon towards his headquarters using his only arm. It was difficult to hold the binoculars steady. *I'll have to get used to this,* he thought. Then he commanded to an aide. "Call my commanders to assemble at the headquarter tent. I need to get back to the front," he said. The nurse left the room totally convinced that the General was given his freedom to move about.

The next day, the General who was heavily bandaged, return to his men. There was a loud cheer among his troops as they saw their leader pass by on his horse. The General was in intense pain due to his amputated arm. But he did not show any sign of discomfort. *My men must see me as a strong and invincible leader.*

"We got them now," one of the Rebs was heard to say.

"Yea, those Yanks won't know what hit them." another said.

General Stonewall Jackson survived his injury and returned to full duty within a few days. Two weeks after the decisive victory at Chancellorsville, Jackson met with General Lee to strategize the future.

General Lee spoke first. "I want to march directly into Union territory. We need to take these battles onto the front doors of Union States and see how they like being invaded. We need to show Lincoln that we are strong and that we are not going away. His re-election is coming up next year and we want to put doubts into the minds of Northern voters about keeping this war going."

"I support this idea completely. My men are ready to

attack. We are sick of defending. Let's hit them with everything we've got," Jackson said with perhaps more bravado than what he had seen before his injury. Lee loved this attitude and wished more of his generals had this fearlessness.

"We also need to show Britain and France that we can be a powerful independent nation. They need our cotton for their textile industry," General Lee said.

In late June, 1863, Confederate forces marched into Pennsylvania. There, they were met with strong resistance at a small town. A critical event occurred on the second day. Lee ordered Jackson to attack the Union forces who were defending Culp's Hill and Cemetery Hill. These were key positions as roads leading to these spots supplied the Union army and provided a direct access to Washington DC and Baltimore. Jackson recognized the importance of this location and threw his entire division into taking it. It took two days but Jackson' troops overtook the Union defenders forcing them to retreat to Maryland. With it, the Battle of Gettysburg was won by the Confederates. In history, Abraham Lincoln gave an address at the National Cemetery in Gettysburg four months after the Union victory. In Amit's altered world, the Confederates occupied Gettysburg and Lincoln's famous address was never delivered or even written. While the nation was deprived on Lincoln's great address, the individuals who would have attended were spared the two-hour, 13,607-word oration by former Secretary of State Edward Everett.

There would be more battles between the Union and Confederates over the ensuing months. Lee knew that the South, being largely agricultural, could not compete against Northern factories that were feverously producing war goods. But the victory of Gettysburg bought him time and hope for a peaceful resolution.

*

In the summer of 1864, John Wilkes Booth was making plans to kidnap President Lincoln. Booth was an educated man and an actor. His sympathy for the Confederate cause was fueled when he witnessed the hanging of abolitionist John Brown in December 1859. Coincidentally, Thomas Jackson commanded a detail of cadets who were ordered to provide military support at the execution, but he and Booth did not meet. Initially, Booth wanted an exchange of the President for captured confederate soldiers but his plans soon changed to assignation. Lincoln was inaugurated for his second term as President on March 4, 1865. Booth was there with finance Lucy Hale, daughter New Hampshire Senator John Parker Hale. During the middle of Lincoln's address, Booth walked to the front of the audience, pulled out his gun and shot Lincoln in the chest. Guards at the inauguration wrestled Booth's gun from his hand and arrested him. Lincoln was taken to the Petersen house, a private home across the street from Ford's theater, where the President died on the following morning.

Vice President Andrew Johnson was quickly sworn in as President. Johnson was born in North Carolina and moved to Tennessee where he became a Congressman, Senator and Governor before the Civil War. When Tennessee succeeded from the Union, Johnson remained on the side of the Union. He was appointed Military Governor of Tennessee by President Lincoln. In 1864, he was selected by the Democratic Party over the incumbent, Vice President Hannibal Hamlin to be Lincoln's running mate for this second term. Sensing that the war could drag out for many more months and possibly years, Johnson contacted the Confederate President Jefferson Davis and they met at the Appomattox Court House in Virginia to talk about peace. The two settled on a mutual end to the war without one declaring victory over the other. The Union allowed the Confederate States of American to operate as a separate nation.

Jefferson Davis completed his 4-year term as President of the Confederacy in 1865. Robert E. Lee was the hero of the Civil War for the South and was elected President. Thomas Jackson became the Vice President. Together, they served two terms. Their immediate mission was to reconstruct the South to a position of strength equal to that of the North. Both were against the institution of slavery. To them, the Civil War was more about States' Right and not the right to own slaves. Toward the end of their second term, they convinced enough legislators to put into a 10-year plan to educate slaves and to enable them to purchase their freedom. The plan also called for the end of slavery in all states by the end of the century.

In 1914, during the outbreak of World War I, President Wilson called for the reunification of Union and Confederate States. Slavery had already been abolished and the South had equal economic strength to the North. Wilson saw threats from countries outside the United States, particularly Germany, and rallied the two countries back into one so that the U.S. could better protect itself from foreign threats. Congress ratified the reunification in 1916, just before the U.S.'s entry into the First World War

*

Stonewall Jackson remained bedridden after accidently being shot by friendly fire and died 8 days later. The cause of death was pneumonia.

Could his death have been prevented by early mobilization? If pulmonary embolus the cause of death, it is possible that he could have lived. He was a young a fit man of only 39 years. Following his death, Robert E. Lee acknowledged that the Confederacy lost their best General. During the critical Battle of Gettysburg, Lee instructed one of his new commanders, Richard Ewell to take Cemetery Hill. But this General did not take the initiative to attack at a key moment in the battle as General Jackson would have, had he lived, and the Union took the upper hand. Historians have suggested that the South could have won Gettysburg had Stonewall Jackson been in command instead of Ewell.

John Wilkes Booth assassinated President Abraham Lincoln after the Confederacy surrendered at the Appomattox Court House. Andrew Johnson became the 17th President of the U.S. but his Presidency was marred with controversy and was the first president to be impeached. The Union attempted to reconstruct the South. However, much of the wealth and resources of the Southern states was taken by Northern businessmen termed "Carpetbaggers." The Carpetbaggers did not re-invest their profits back into the Southern industries and the people who had generated them. Some of the invaders achieved political office, which led to further corrupt administrations. To this day, many states in the Deep South, such as Alabama and Mississippi are well behind the Northern States in regard to income, living standards, civil rights and the potential for prosperity.

The hypothetical election of Robert E. Lee and Thomas Jackson to the Confederacy led to economic development that did not occur during the Reconstruction years. Therefore, foreign investments made by Britain and France went to the Carpetbaggers and to the Northern States.

From imagining the alternate history, Amit saw that his implantation of a notion to Stonewall Jackson's doctor to get the general up and move about had an impact today in the productivity of the former Confederate States. Starting with the Lee/Jackson administration, the African American population received civil rights and liberties decades before the real history. There was little racial segregation then, and wages were approaching more equality with Whites than today. The civil rights era of the 1960s with President Johnson, Robert Kennedy, and Martin Luther King Jr. did not occur in this alternate history.

If it did happen, the U.S. would not the only country to separate into two nations and then reunify years later. In the 20th Century alone, the reunification of East and West Germany and North and South Vietnam are prime examples. It is hoped that someday, Korea will become one again, but under the rule of the South Koreans.

Ashwood

****

They had very different backgrounds. Chowder grew up in liberal San Francisco where his father was a well-known drag queen. Chowder's nickname was "Soup." As Soup's father divorced his wife when the boy was 5, he had little influence on his son's upbringing. Ashwood had been raised in conservative and racially segregated Richmond Virginia, the former capital of the Confederacy. His father had been a strict disciplinarian. Both men grew up to stand six foot one inches tall. But Soup was muscular and powerful. He was confident and brash and at one time was in a neighborhood gang. Ashwood was thin, slight of build, as such, his father forbade him to participate in football and so he chose tennis instead. He was reserved, thoughtful and highly intelligent. What they had in common was that both men were black, gifted athletes, and reached the pinnacle of their chosen sports.

Ashwood broke racial barriers during his rise in tennis. As a junior player, he was prohibited from playing in most of the regional tennis tournaments. At the time, there were no other prominent black male tennis professionals. There was only Althea Gibson who had excelled in women's tennis over a decade earlier. While most of the top players learned the game from country club tutors and coaches, Ashwood learned on the public courts of Richmond. When tennis talent was exhibited at an early age, Althea' coach, Walter Johnson, began to train young Ashwood. Within a few years, Ashwood won the National Indoor Junior Tennis Championship, and he received a scholarship to attend the University of California, Los Angeles.

Soup excelled in all sports, but particularly football as a youth. Because of the success of running back Jim Brown of the Cleveland Browns, Soup did not face the same level of discrimination that Ashwood confronted. Soup played two years at a junior college before joining University of Southern California on a football scholarship. During both years, Soup led the nation in rushing yardage among NCAA Division IA schools, and at the end of the season, he won College Football's most prestigious award. While both men attended schools in Southern California, Ashwood finished a year before Soup's arrival, and their paths did not cross.

Ashwood and Soup's professional careers were highly successful during the 10 plus years of their participation. Ashwood won Wimbledon, the U.S. Open, and the Australian Open championships and is still the only black male player to have done so. Soup led the NFL in rushing yardage on 4 occasions, and was All Pro for 5 years. His career rushing totals were second in the history of the game to that date.

Amit Savjani was a few years younger than either Ashwood or Soup. As a youth he was an avid sports fan and he followed the success of these two men on television. During the 1970s, there were only three major TV networks. With limited view options, tennis and football became highly popular, and Ashwood and Soup were among the first TV superstars of their sports. When they retired from competition, television network executives hired them as "color analysts" for broadcasts. At different times, both men worked alongside Sal Michaels, who was the "play-by-play" announcer. In the early 1980s, Ashwood and Soup met for the first time during an event hosted by Sal.

"My father wouldn't let me play football," Ashwood told Soup. "He thought it was a little too rough for a guy with my build. When I was small, they used to call me "bones.""

"I really envy you, Ashwood," Soup remarked. "I have this recurrent nightmare about this one line-backer from the Chicago Bears. His name was Butt Dickas. He would knock me out of bounds so hard that I would crash into the retaining wall and fall unconscious. I then wake up and realize that it was just a dream." Like most football players, but especially running backs, Soup had his share of concussions and traumatic brain injuries. While there was no such diagnosis at the time, it is highly likely that Soup suffered from post-traumatic stress disorder. "I get angry at my wife over the smallest most insignificant things. She is the love of my life, and I can't understand why I say nor do some of the things that I have done."

At the time of their meeting, Ashwood was nearing the end of writing a book on the history and difficulties of being an African American Athlete. He didn't want to tell Soup, but Ashwood himself had significant health issues. A few years earlier, he had suffered a heart attack and endured several cardiac surgeries to repair his ailing heart. A blood transfusion from his second heart surgery would ultimately lead to his premature mortality.

*

Amit took his students on ward rounds one day very early in his clinical chemistry career. They met an infectious disease doctor outside the room of one of his patients. "This man is suffering from an infection with pneumocystis pneumonia or "PCP." This man does not fit the pattern of a PCP infection, which is not common around here. There is something very different about this patient." This was Amit's first encounter with a patient who had AIDS, or acquired immune deficiency disorder. It would be a few more years before the human immunodeficiency virus or HIV would be discovered as the offending agent and the discovery of how AIDS was transmitted from one infected patient to another. As a blood-borne pathogen, HIV can be transmitted through transfusions of tainted blood. In 1985, the first laboratory test was approved by the FDA for diagnosis of AIDS. Soon thereafter, blood banks were testing donated units for the presence of antibodies to HIV. A mandate for testing of all donor blood units by blood banking laboratories lead to a great reduction in HIV cases.

Ashwood had been given blood as part of his open heart surgery two years before the introduction of the HIV test and the testing of the blood supply for the presence of the virus. One of the units given to him was tainted by HIV, and Ashwood acquired the virus. Symptoms of AIDS became evident a few years later. After exhibiting some neurologic problems, tests revealed that he had *toxoplasmosis*, a common opportunistic infection among AIDS patients. An HIV test revealed that Ashwood had AIDS. He and his wife kept this information private for the next four years. When his declining physical appearance became evident, Ashwood revealed to the media that he acquired AIDS, and he died a year later of pneumonia brought on by his weakened medical condition.

Amit imagined how the world would be different had Ashwood lived. After retirement from tennis, Ashwood used his fame to support civil rights. He visited South Africa to protest against apartheid. He was arrested on several occasions for demonstrating in Washington DC. Ashwood was well respected among both the Caucasian and African American communities, and Amit believed his calming demeanour could defuse confrontational situations. Perhaps he could have been a mediator between sides as he had experienced both American social culture and the world of country clubs through his tennis success.

Through his mind portal, Amit convinced Ashwood to have his open heart surgery performed at Stanford University Hospital in Palo Alto. Years before a laboratory test for HIV was implemented to screen blood products, the Blood Bank at Stanford was measuring CD4 and CD8 cells in donated blood. High numbers of CD4 white cells in blood help fight infection. CD8 white cells help kill cancer cells and other invaders. It was known that a low ratio of these circulating cells was characteristic of individuals infected with HIV, and these units were discarded. Stanford was ahead of other blood banks, which were not performing these tests in 1983. But at Stanford, use of this surrogate test prevented the HIV infection that Ashwood had acquired. Since Amit prevented the tennis star's HIV infection, Ashwood did not go on to establish an AIDS Foundation for educating people about HIV transmission, a negative consequence of Amit's portal suggestion. Instead, Ashwood continued to focus his attention towards domestic and international social issues.

*

In the initial real meeting with Soup, Ashwood was already infected with HIV. He knew his time was short and he wanted to devote it to his AIDS foundation. Now that history had been altered and that his blood was not infected, Ashwood became interested in Soup's plight of that of other football player's health issues. There were several prominent NFL players who suffered significant neurologic problems that we now know were likely due to concussions suffered while playing. Ashwood convinced Soup to work with him in studying the health and social history of other football players once they had retired from the game. They found that like Soup, many of these athletes had multiple divorces, complained of continuing health issues and had a high incidence of drug and alcohol abuse, and domestic violence.

"I am guilty of verbal and physical spousal abuse just as the other men we have interviewed," Soup confided. Ashwood knew all about it. Soup's wife placed multiple calls to 911 and to the Los Angeles Police Department because of her husband's attacks on her. Each time, the Officers would issue a warning but there were no arrests. After all, this was Soup, football hero and overall good guy. Sometimes the Officers would even ask for pictures with Soup and his autograph.

"I don't understand why I get into these rages, and I wish there was a way to control these impulses. At your suggestion, I regularly see a psychiatrist."

"Soup, I am here to help you in whatever way I can. I am going to give you the number to my personal long-range beeper. If you feel these negative urges, all you have to do is call me, and no matter where I am, or what I'm doing, I will get to a phone and get back to you. You have my promise."

Ashwood was true to his word. One day, Soup was visiting his young children from his second marriage. When he arrived at his former house, he saw that his ex-wife, Nicollette had spent the night with Donald, a young and highly attractive man. *That boy has to be 10 years younger than Nicollette.* Soup started to clench his teeth and his hands formed a fist. He was seething. *How can she be with that boy with my children in the room next door? Is there no decency?* When Donald left the room, Soup and Nicollette had a heated argument.

"I forbid you to see that man. You are a bad influence on my children," Soup yelled.

"Your children?? I bore them and I alone am raising them now. We're not married any more, remember? You have no right to tell me what I can do and can't do in my own fucking house. If you can't deal with this, then get out. Leave now!" Nicollette shouted, as she turned to leave the room.

Soup's emotions were totally out of control and he was not thinking rationally. He had a medium sized pocket knife attached to his car keys. He pulled them out and started slowly after Nicollette. *I'll fix them both. They are not going to make a fool out of me.* But as he pulled the blade out of his knife, a small piece of paper fell out. There was a telephone number written on the slip. Without Soup's knowledge, Ashwood had put it there thinking it might be important someday. Soup stopped, recognized that this was the number to Ashwood's beeper, and he sat down. He bent over and put his hands over his face. *Take a deep breath. What am I doing? Calm down. Ashwood is right, this is not me behaving in this way. I have a sickness. I need help.* Soup stood up, put his knife away, and headed for the front door.

Nicollete had called the police who arrived just as Soup was stepping out. Soup put his hands up and stopped in this tracks. "Don't worry, guys. I'm leaving. Nicollette is safe and in the house with the kids."

The police could see that Soup was calm and that there were probably no issues. "Soup, we have to check this out. We need for you to stay with this officer," one of them said. When the other officer left, the remaining older policeman questioned Soup about the UCLA-USC football game that Soup had played in some decades earlier. The officer was just a teenage then and Soup was one of his heroes.

Nicollette and Donald were watching from the window and they both came outside. They could also see that Soup was no longer inflamed. The officers nevertheless went into the home and saw that the children were fine and playing in their room and there was no sign of any violence. The officer went back outside and told Soup he could leave. When he arrived back at his house, Soup beeped Ashwood who was in town. Ashwood came over to Soup's house and stayed over that night. They had a long talk about what could have happened. Overcome with emotions, Soup openly wept at what could have happened that night.

There were no more confrontations after that evening. Nicollette considered filing a restraining order but Donald convinced her not to do it. They married a few years later and Donald became a stepfather to Soup's children. Soup could see that Donald was a good man, and was very kind to Soup's kids.

*

In 1991, Rodney King, an African American male, was involved in a high speed chase through the city of Los Angeles. When he stopped and got out of the car, police officers assaulted King. The incident was caught on film by a bystander. Four officers were tried and acquitted of criminal charges. This verdict led to riots in the city resulting in the deaths of 53 individuals. There was a tenuous relationship between the LA Police Department and African American citizens. Soup and Ashwood became strong advocates for the police department. With their sports celebrity status, they participated in community activities and education against prejudice. Through their efforts, the relationship of the police to minority groups gradually improved. The success of these programs spread to police departments at other cities.

The first case of HIV infection was thought to have occurred in 1959 in the Democratic Republic of the Congo. The first case in the U.S. occurred in 1981. The term "Acquired Immune Deficiency Disorder" was coined by the Centers for Disease Control a year later. The underlying etiology of AIDS was simultaneously discovered in 1984 by investigators at the Pasteur Institute, National Institute of Health, and the University of California, San Francisco. Within a year, a clinical laboratory test was developed that identified the presence of antibodies to the virus responsible for AIDS. *Laboratory testing for CD4 (T helper) and CD8 (T killer) cells is performed today to evaluate the medical status of AIDS patients but they are not used for screening the donated blood supply. Today, there are newer assays, termed "HIV Combination Tests" that can detect the presence of tainted blood earlier than the original assays launched in 1985.*

This is an alternate reality story about Arthur Ashe and Orenthal James ("O.J.") Simpson. Both highly successful athletes had a significant role in popular culture during their playing days and especially immediately after their retirement. Simpson made several Hollywood movies including the Naked Gun *series while Ashe wrote articles for several magazines and newspapers and spent $300,000 of his own money to pen the three-part book,* A Hard Road to Glory: A History of the African American Athlete. *Simpson's conversion from athlete to a well-paid advertising icon, the earliest example for an African American athlete, is discussed in Ashe's "Since 1946" volume. OJ's endorsement success set the stage for other African American athletes to reach new financial heights, such as what was achieved by Tiger Woods.*

As both men were broadcasters for their respective sports, they might have met through their mutual acquaintance with Al Michaels, who worked with both men at various times during the 1980s. The relationship between Ashe and Simpson is not documented, and their introduction through Michaels is fictitious. Given their similar accomplishments in sports, it is plausible that they could have become close friends and confidants.

Prior to Nicole Brown Simpson's divorce to OJ, there were several complaints filed by her with the local police regarding spousal abuse and domestic violence. The notion that Simpson suffered from chronic traumatic encephalopathy from concussions suffered as a running back is very possible but has not yet been documented. If OJ Simpson was responsible for the murders of Nicole and Ron Goldman, perhaps their deaths could have been avoided with the calming influence of Arthur Ashe. However, the international tennis star died of AIDS one year before Nicole's death.

The relationship between the police and minorities in America continues to be strained today. The recent events in Ferguson, Missouri, Baltimore, Maryland, and Dallas Texas attest to this fact. Part of the problem is the absence of an ambassador for peace, the role that Martin Luther King Jr. provided during the 1950s and 1960s. Perhaps if Arthur Ashe had avoided his HIV infection, he could have been this person, and our race relations might be better today.

Point-of-Care

****

He was born into a family of Georgian sharecroppers, the youngest of five. His parents named him Jack. His middle name was Roosevelt, name after Teddy, the former President of the United States. Nobody in his family or community could ever dream what this man would eventually achieve in his lifetime. This was especially true since his father left when Jack was just an infant. But perhaps that was a good thing, because his Mom moved the family to Southern California hoping for a better life. His mom worked as a housekeeper in an affluent area of Pasadena. While there were gangs, Jack's older brothers kept the boy out of trouble by making him concentrate on playing different sports. His brother Mack was an Olympic track sprinter. In Nazi Germany in 1936, Jesse Owens and Mack won the gold and silver medals in the 200-meter dash. As they stood on the winner's podium, both men glanced up at Adolf Hitler while listening to the US National Anthem and saluting the American flag as it was being raised.

As a teenager, Jack excelled in tennis winning the Pacific Coast Tournament and when he went to Pasadena Junior College, Jack was a star on the baseball team, and he was selected as the league's Most Valuable Player. Jack later transferred to UCLA where he excelled in football and was the NCAA long jump champion in track and field. A year later, Japan attacked Pearl Harbor in Hawaii and Jack was drafted into the U.S. Army soon thereafter.

*

Two thousand miles away in the small town of Elkhart Indiana, Anton Clemens was born on the same day as Jack. Anton was the third son of immigrants from Austria. His early life was largely unremarkable, until he turned 7 years old. His parents noticed that he was constantly thirsty. In kindergarten, his parents Robert and Sarah told his teachers that Anton had special needs and they asked that he be allowed to keep a water bottle with him at all times. Accompanied with excess water consumption was the need for frequent urination. It seemed that Anton had to go to the bathroom almost every hour.

"If he didn't drink so much, he wouldn't have to pee so often," Robert said to Sarah. "None of our other kids ever went through this."

"He can't help it. There is something different about his metabolism," Sarah said. "You should be satisfied that he is a happy boy who never complains."

"I know. But it is an annoyance that we always have to be near a bathroom for the kid."

One day, Robert and Anton went on a long walk in a park. After 20 minutes, Anton spoke up. "I have to pee Daddy."

"The bathroom is just a little further down this path," Robert said.

"No, Daddy, I have to go now. I'm going to wet my pants."

93

"Alright, alright. Don't pee your pants. Let's go over to the side where nobody can see and you can go there." Anton opened his pants zipper and started to urinate on the sidewalk. A large amount of urine came out forming a large puddle. *How could so much urine come out of this little kid?* Robert thought to himself. When Anton was done, he zipped his pants and the two were back on their way.

Twenty minutes later, Robert and Anton returned to the parking lot retracing their steps. As they passed the spot where Anton had urinated, the young boy made an observation.

"Look Dad, there are ton of ants all over where I peed." Indeed, a large hoard of ants hovered over the dried urine stain. They appeared to be busy taking crystals down the path and into their ant hill. *Something is wrong with Anton,* Robert thought. *This should not happen.* "Let's go home Anton," was all Robert said.

On Monday, Robert called Anton's pediatrician and requested an appointment. But before the date of that scheduled visit, Anton became very sick. Robert noticed an unusual fruity aroma emanating from his son's body. He and Sarah rushed their youngest child to the emergency room. The doctors seemed to know what was wrong, and immediately started an intravenous infusion. They called for a porter and the child was transferred to the hospital. There were no pediatric intensive care units back then. Anton's pediatrician was alerted and was at the hospital within an hour of his patient's admission. Once Anton's medical condition stabilized, the doctor met with Robert and Sarah privately in the ICU waiting room.

"Your son has juvenile diabetes. He is currently in a diabetic ketoacidosis crisis." Sara started to sob quietly. "Not to worry, we have his condition under control. We gave him an injection of insulin and he will be fine. But we need to keep him here for a few days just to be sure."

It was only a few years earlier in 1921 that Drs. Frederick Banting and Charles Best isolated insulin and conducted their sentinel studies on diabetes while at the University of Toronto. Amazingly, the University immediately gave permission for pharmaceutical companies to produce and use insulin to treat diabetic patients without royalties. Within a year, insulin was in use therapeutically. Now, in 1926, insulin was widely available for treatment. Anton made a full recovery and had a healthy childhood.

*

Jack was assigned to a segregated Army cavalry unit in Fort Riley, Kansas. Being black, he was denied entry to the Officer Candidate School. But heavy weight boxing champion Joe Lewis was also assigned to the Fort. This would not be the first time that Jack would befriend a world class athlete. With Lewis' help, Jack and other African Americans were admitted to the school and were commissioned as second lieutenants upon completion. Jack was scheduled to be deployed overseas to fight in World War II, when he was arrested and court-martialed for insubordination for refusing to go to the back of an Army bus. This would not be the first time that Jack would confront racism and prejudice. Jack did not see military action and was honorably discharged in 1944. In early 1945, he wrote to the Kansas City Monarchs of the Negro Baseball League about playing for them. After they reviewed his college baseball career statistics, they offered Jack a $400/month contract to play shortstop. A few years later, another team offered him a somewhat larger contract. That man was Branch Rickey, club president of the Brooklyn Dodgers.

"We relish the aggressive manner by which you play the game and would like for you to play for our team," Rickey told Jack and then handed him a copy of the contract. "We will offer you $5000 contract for the first season. Beyond that you have to prove yourself," Ricky said and gave Jack a pen to sign.

On April 15, 1947, the man now known as Jackie Robinson became the first black man to play in the major leagues. Jackie was subjected to racial slurs and insults throughout his time in the game. Nevertheless, he had a stellar baseball career and went on to play 10 seasons for the Dodgers and was selected to six All-Star Games.

*

Because of Anton's diabetes, he was denied entry to the military during World War II. Instead he went to graduate school at Indiana University in Bloomington, and earned a doctoral degree in analytical chemistry. Upon completion of his studies he became a research scientist at Ames Laboratories in his Indiana hometown. It was there in 1956 that the husband and wife team of Helen and Al Free had been in the processes of developing the first urine dipstick test for diagnostic purposes. A few years later in 1963, Ames issued a patent for the first blood glucose dipstick. Anton joined Ames shortly thereafter, and was given the opportunity to develop a meter that would convert the color produced from dipstick to an actual glucose concentration. He naturally jumped at this opportunity given his own medical problems.

"If we can develop a simple test for blood glucose, it is

conceivable that diabetics can monitor their own blood sugar levels," Dr. Helen Free told Anton.

"I get light headed if I skip a meal or don't eat right," Anton remarked to his colleague. This is a typical physiologic reaction for someone with a low blood glucose concentration. "When it happens, I take out my roll of Life Savers and eat a few of the candies." Little did the Life Saver candy company know in 1912 when it first started selling their hard lozenge with a hole in the center and shaped like a boat lifesaver, that their candy would restore blood sugar concentration and was indeed a lifesaver for Anton and the others who have the same affliction? During the early 1970s with Anton's help, the first portable battery operated glucose meter became commercially available for use in doctor's offices.

*

Jackie Robinson left baseball in 1957 and began a career in business as Vice President of Personnel at the coffee company, Chock full o'Nuts. Robinson was now a public figure and soon became active in national politics. He supported Richard Nixon's 1960 Presidential Campaign and Nelson Rockefeller's unsuccessful campaign to be the Republican nominee for President in 1964. When Rockefeller lost the nomination to Senator Barry Goldwater of Arizona, Robinson helped the New York Governor get re-elected in 1966.

Jackie Robinson retired from baseball partly because he began to suffer from numerous physical ailments. He complained of arm and leg soreness during his last few seasons. Shortly after leaving baseball, he was diagnosed with diabetes mellitus. He was taught how to inject himself with insulin. Unfortunately,

Robinson was not able to control his blood glucose levels to any acceptable level. He traveled a lot and had a very irregular dietary schedule. He also had a sweet tooth for ice cream, cakes, and pies. As a result, he began to suffer even more serious complications of uncontrolled diabetes including heart disease and neurologic problems including near blindness. On October 24, 1972, Jackie Robison died of a heart attack at this home in Connecticut. He was just 53 years old.

*

Amit Savjani was an avid sports fan and loved to watch baseball. In 1997, all of the Major League baseball teams retired Jackie Robinson's jersey number, 42. Ten years later, a policy was instituted so that every player would wear number 42 on games played on April 15, the day that Robinson became the first African American to play in the major leagues. Amit reviewed Robinson's medical record and learned that the slugger died of complications due to diabetes. At that time, portable blood glucose meters were just being introduced into the market. *What if the glucose dipstick had been made available to Robinson and he had been better able to titrate his insulin dose?*

Amit entered his mind portal and planted an idea into Anton's brain that he should contact Jackie's doctors about his revolutionary new product. Then Anton met with Jackie and his doctors in 1963, explaining their new technology to him and how it might help him with his medical care. Soon Robinson was regularly testing himself with this device. Whenever his blood sugar showed a high result, he gave himself an injection of insulin. Ames used this opportunity to advertise their new blood glucose test that could help millions of diabetics just like it was helping

Jackie Robinson, who became a spokesman for the company. With this publicity, Anton received a bolus of funding, and they were able to develop the first glucose test strip meter several years earlier than in actual history.

Jackie Robinson was the beneficiary of this new glucose monitoring device. With a quantitative reading of the dipstick, Robinson was better able to control his insulin injections and ultimately his blood glucose concentrations. This had a dramatic effect on diminishing the complications of his diabetes. Instead of slowing down, his improved health led him to have a renewed enthusiasm and vigor for his various causes. In 1968, Richard Nixon ran again for the Presidency, and Jackie Robinson again, played a big part of his campaign. Nixon and his Vice President candidate Spiro Agnew defeated Hubert Humphrey to become the 37th President. Because of Robinson's interest in inner city America, he became the Secretary of Housing and Urban Development (HUD) in Nixon's cabinet. He succeeded Robert C. Weber, who was the first African American to serve in any cabinet, when Weber was HUD's Secretary under President Lyndon Johnson.

Nixon and Agnew were re-elected for a second term in 1972, defeating George McGovern and Sargent Shriver. Then in 1973, Agnew was charged with extortion, tax fraud, bribery and conspiracy. He plead no contest, was convicted of failure to report income under the condition that he resign as the Vice President. To everyone's great surprise, Richard Nixon nominated Jackie Robinson as the new Vice President to serve out Agnew's remaining term. Nixon hoped that his appointment of a well-known sports hero would ease racial tensions that plagued the

1960s and early 1970s. This nomination had to be approved by the U.S. House and Senate. There was significant national debate over this nomination.

Was America in the mid-1970s ready for an African American President? What qualifications did this man have? What did he know about foreign policy? He would be only a heartbeat away from the top office in the nation. These were the issues debated in congress and in the media. The Congressional votes were extremely close and largely divided along party lines. Nevertheless, Robinson received the necessary endorsement, and he became the next Vice President.

A year later, Nixon resigned from the Presidency because of his role to cover up a break-in at the Democratic Party's Headquarters at the Watergate Complex office buildings in Washington DC. As next in line, Jackie Robinson became the first African American President of the United States. He also became the first person to reach the nation's highest office without being elected by the public. President Robinson nominated Nelson Rockefeller as his Vice President. Unlike his own nomination as the vice president, this time, there was little debate in Congress over the selection of Rockefeller. Robinson served two years as the Commander-in-Chief. During his short tenure in office, he made significant reforms in mandating employment quality for minorities. He was nominated by the Republicans as their candidate in 1976. However, the stigma of the Nixon administration led to their defeat, and the election of Jimmy Carter and Walter Mondale. Several decades later, Barack Obama would become the second African American President. Since he was no longer the first, his presidential campaign was focused more on the issues of the day.

After his presidency, the Robinson Presidential Library was established in Brooklyn on the site of Ebbets Field, the old ball park where Robinson had started his baseball career. The field demolished in 1960, three years after the Dodgers had moved to Los Angeles. An apartment building on the site was purchased and renovated for the library. With better control of his diabetes, Jackie Robinson lived until 1983.

Amit could not anticipate this outcome with his mind portal. He was just hoping to prolong the life of a decent man and pioneer. Was there a significant ripple effect from having Robinson at the helm instead of Gerald R. Ford? As with Ford, Robinson pardoned Richard Nixon for his role in the Watergate cover up. "Our country needs to move on from this scandal," Robinson wrote in his memoirs years later.

*

The incidence of diabetes is increasing with advancing age and the global epidemic of obesity. Type II diabetes is characterized by insulin resistance and affects adults more often than children. Often this disease can be controlled by improvements in diet and exercise. It is likely that Robinson had type II diabetes given his age of disease onset. Type I diabetes is a destruction of the pancreatic islet cells and was previously known as juvenile diabetes because of the age of onset. Most patients with this form require life-long insulin injections. Anton's was a type I diabetic. His disease was first manifested by a sudden drop in insulin and development of a diabetic ketoacidosis. This was a life-threatening medical emergency that required immediate emergency department and intensive care unit hospitalization and treatment with insulin.

Blood glucose testing has become the mainstay for managing patients with diabetes since the very first meter was released by the Ames Corporation. These devices have become highly accurate, very easy to use and inexpensive. Devices and test strips are sold in any drug store. Over a number of years, controlling glucose concentrations to within tight limits retards the development of complications. These diabetics can live normal and productive lives.

In actual history, from the time of Jackie Robinson's retirement from baseball until his death in 1972, his support waivered between the Republicans and Democrats. During his life, he lobbied for civil rights at a most difficult time in U.S. history. While he did support Nixon in his first bid for the presidential office in 1960, he did not support Nixon eight years later. Gerald Ford became Vice President under Nixon after Agnew's resignation and became President upon Nixon's resignation. Ford selected Rockefeller as Vice President and together, they lost the 1976 election to Carter and Mondale.

Bladder Control

****

It was Sunday night in Washington DC. A man who had aged dramatically over the past 4 years stepped in front of the television camera. He was addressing the nation from behind the desk of his office.

He spoke about peace in a region that had suffered civil war for 20 years. He spoke about his efforts to stop the bombardment of a country and its people. He spoke about his need to devote his time toward the duties of his office and not his responsibilities to his political party, in this election year. The date was March 31, 1968. The man from Texas then stunned the nation with his concluding remarks:

"Accordingly, I shall not seek, and I will not accept, the nomination of my party for another term as your President."

After he finished the remainder of the speech, he stepped away from his desk at the Oval Office and away from camera view. There, he met and hugged his wife, Lady Bird. She could see that a big burden was lifted from his shoulders. A tear came to her eye as she knew it was the beginning of the end of a long career in public service. She recalled the sacrifices that he and their family made. There were many hours of negotiations with his colleagues from both parties. She remembered the criticism he and his administration suffered. The man knew, however, that there would be difficult months ahead for him and his country. There was some satisfaction that somebody else would be making these difficult decisions soon. The burden of responsibility was simply too much for him and it was time to pass the torch.

As can be imagined, this speech immediately sent shock waves to key members of both political parties. This was especially true for the incumbent party, as they naturally assumed that President Lyndon Baines Johnson would seek a second full term. Nevertheless, several prominent members of the Democratic Party indicated their desire to run for president and they entered state election primaries prior to the President's March 31st speech. These candidates campaigned on an anti-Vietnam War platform, given that the President's approval rating for the war effort was at an all-time low. But in reality, these candidates were simply positioning themselves for the 1972 election.

Notably absent from candidate considerations in 1968 was the incumbent vice president, Hubert H. Humphrey. Humphrey was a liberal democrat who sought the Democratic nomination in 1960 but failed then because he didn't have the financial assets that Kennedy had. Now as the Vice President, his liberal followers were dismayed that he did not publicly oppose the President's policies on the war. While not widely known at the time, Johnson threatened to withdraw his support of Humphrey's future presidential aspirations if he didn't support the current administration's foreign policies. When Johnson withdrew from the 1968 election, Humphrey needed to decide if he was going to enter his name as a candidate for the Democratic Party, and if so, would he pledge to continue the current Administration's commitment to the Vietnam War effort or withdraw the troops from the conflict once elected. Humphrey waited a month before formally announcing his candidacy. He also decided not to break with the President's policy on Vietnam.

Humphrey was well behind the other candidates, notably Eugene McCarthy who won the Oregon and Pennsylvania primaries, and Robert Kennedy who won in Indiana and Nebraska prior to Johnson's announcement. Four days later, Kennedy won the California primary and was well on his way to the Democratic nomination.

Humphrey was at his apartment in Chevy Chase Maryland watching the returns on the television. When he learned that Kennedy won, he turned off the set not wanting to hear his victory speech. Humphrey was awakened by an aide in early morning telling him that RFK had been shot and killed in Los Angeles. The nation was recovering from the assassination of Martin Luther King Jr. in Memphis just two months earlier. Humphrey went to the bathroom and just before flushing the toilet, he noticed a red color in the bowl. He didn't know what this meant, but he didn't bother to tell his wife or any of his staff. *Today is going to be a very busy day,* he thought to himself, *and I don't have time to worry about what this means.* He met with his campaign staff to discuss the length of mourning that was appropriate for the death of Robert Kennedy. That night before going to bed, he noticed that his urine was no longer red. *This morning it must have something I ate,* he thought to himself.

The campaign resumed in earnest in late June, as the candidates were preparing for their party's nominating conventions. At that point, Humphrey was second in the polls for the Democratic nomination. From the Republican Party, Richard Nixon was nominated in early August. The Republican convention was uneventful compared to the Democratic Convention held in Chicago later that month. There were demonstrations and riots in the streets by students and dissidents protesting the war. Humphrey succeeded in capturing the Party's nomination over McCarthy amidst the chaos of the convention. That night, he noticed blood in his urine for the second time. When he returned to Washington, he called Dr. John Wagner, his private physician, and asked to be examined.

While at the doctor's office, Humphrey provided another urine sample that was as bloody as the one from the previous evening. Dr. Wagner told him that there were dozens of reasons why blood can be present in urine and that the laboratory would need to do some testing. Satisfied, Humphrey dressed and his driver took him back to his office in the Executive Office Building.

The urine sample was sent to the National Cancer Institute in Bethesda. Privacy laws referring to medical histories were not as they are now, and everyone in the lab knew that the sample was from the Vice President. It was not uncommon to receive samples from noted politicians in Washington. It was quickly confirmed by the laboratory that Humphrey's urine contained blood and other cellular substances. The sample was centrifuged and the cells were sent to Dr. Lloyd Dubois, a noted expert in urine cytology.

In 1979, 11 years after the election and 1 year after Humphrey died, Dr. Dubois and colleagues at NCI discovered p53, the tumor suppressor gene that produces a protein that helps in repairing DNA. His studies showed that a high number of individuals with mutations to the p53 gene have a genetic predisposition to acquiring cancer. Amit Savjani learned of this history and went to visit the now retired Dr. Dubois in his home. During long discussion with him about his discovery, Amit decided to plant the notion of the p53 gene to when Dr. Dubois first began his gene discovery work in 1966. It was the only time that Amit tried to change history by implanting an idea to someone who had already made their contributions through history but was still alive.

By the time Hubert Humphrey urine was sent to the NCI, Dr. Dubois and his scientists already knew the importance of the p53 gene. This together with the presence of blood in the urine with this mutation suggested that Humphrey was in the earliest stage of bladder cancer. When the results were confirmed, Dubois called Dr. Wagner. When the Vice President received the news from his doctor, he was in denial.

"I feel fine. There have been no other episodes of bloody urine since," Humphrey told Wagner. It was a lie. Humphrey would occasionally see blood but this was not a time to be worried about his own health.

"Nevertheless, I'd like to start you on some experimental chemotherapy that is being tested at Memorial Sloan Kettering in New York. Some of these doctors were involved with the initial discovery of p53," Dr. Wagner pleaded.

"What will this do to my stamina?" Humphrey asked.

"It will make you tired. You will likely lose your hair. You may need to take some time off to have this done," Dr. Wagner stated.

"John, I'm running for the Presidency of the United States. We are less than 7 weeks from the election and I am 15 points behind Richard Nixon. This is not the time for me to step away from the campaign. I must make a final push for the White House. There is no time for the Democratic Party to find a replacement. We are the incumbent party!" Humphrey said.

"I know, Hubert. But as your doctor, I am obligated to tell you that your best chance of survival is to get treated for the tumor now, while it is in its early stage. You are no good to the country if you are dead," Wagner pleaded.

"We're in crisis right now. Students are protesting in college campuses across America. Fanatics have killed Martin Luther King Jr. and Bobby Kennedy. George Wallace is threatening to bring back school segregation. We started this, I cannot stop now." With that, Humphrey started to get dressed to leave. As he was departing he said, "I expect you to maintain our patient-doctor confidentiality. I will see you after the election."

"Of course," Dr. Wagner said as the Vice President was leaving. "God be with you, Hubert" Wagner said after Humphrey left the office.

With the potential diagnosis of bladder cancer, Hubert Humphrey saw his own mortality right before his eyes. He had devoted most of his life to public service, starting as the mayor of Minneapolis in 1945. Shortly after his visit with Dr. Wagner, Humphrey assembled his campaign team. They urged him to denounce Johnson's Vietnam policies in favor of de-escalation and ending the war. In the past, he consistently told them that he would not back-stab his friend and colleague. But on this day, his aides could see that he showed a new resolve. He informed them that they were to change their campaign. He was throwing caution to the wind because of his imminent mortality and returning to his roots of pacifism.

In his first campaign speech after this meeting with his staff, he told the stunned audience that if he was elected president, he would immediately stop the bombing of Hanoi. He also devised a plan to gradually withdraw American troops from Vietnam. Win or lose, he was going to end the war once and for all and he repeated this at all of his campaign stops from that point forward. Humphrey was more energetic and driven than ever before.

November 5th was Election Day in 1968. The real history saw that Humphrey lost the popular vote to Richard Nixon by just 500,000 votes. But in Amit's altered history, Humphrey distanced himself from LBJ earlier, history was changed. Humphrey and Edmond Muskie from Maine took office in January of 1969. True to his word, the Humphrey administration stopped the bombing of North Vietnam and negotiated peace terms which led to the withdrawal of troops. The last soldiers left in August 1971.

It was a year after his first meeting with Dr. Wagner that he returned to his office for a checkup. At that point, his bladder cancer had progressed to Stage III. Humphrey underwent radiation and chemotherapy but it was insufficient to stop the spread of cancer to his liver. Doctors at the National Cancer Institute opined that the stress of the President's office had led to an accelerated progression of the disease. Humphrey died in June, 1971. Like Franklin D. Roosevelt, he did not live long enough to see the end of the Vietnam conflict. Muskie was sworn into the presidency and completed Humphrey's term. In 1972, Humphrey's cancer prevented him from running for a second term. George McGovern from South Dakota was nominated by the Democratic Party. This time, Richard Nixon and Spiral Agnew from the Republican Party won the election.

*

This story diverged from the true history at the point when Humphrey's urine was being analyzed for cancer. It is accurate that the Vice President did have blood in his urine, but it was in 1967, a year before he announced his candidacy for the 1968 presidency. While the cells from his urine did reveal a mutation in p53 and a diagnosis of bladder cancer was evident from that test, the protein was not discovered until one year after his actual death in 1978. With permission from Murial Humphrey, laboratory testing was conducted in 1994 from samples that were taken in 1967 and were archived by the pathology laboratory. History showed that Humphrey lost the 1968 election by the narrowest of margins in history to that date, a difference of only 500,000 votes. This was largely because he waited until the end of September to distance himself from LBJ. Even with only 5 weeks to go, the Democrats closed the gap with Nixon and on Election Day, the polls were even. Political analysts have stated that if the election was a week later, he would have been voted into office.

In this story, because a laboratory test revealed a high likelihood of bladder cancer, Humphrey departed from Johnson's policies two weeks earlier. This was sufficient time to tip the balance in his favor during the 1968 election. A change of just 177,000 votes out of 73 million that were cast that year in 4 key states (Illinois, Missouri, Ohio and New Jersey) enabled him receive the required electoral votes to win the election, despite still losing the popular vote. This story highlights how the course of American history from the Vietnam War to modern day may have been altered if this single lab test had been available. The withdrawal of troops by the Humphrey administration in 1969 would have resulted in the savings of over 10,000 American lives.

Dishwashing Liquid

****

Jacqueline was young and very pretty. She came from a privileged world. She went to an exclusive private all-girls school in Connecticut. She spent her summers on the cool waters of the North Atlantic Coast. There she sailed aboard her family's yacht and rode horses. Outsiders didn't know it but she was also very well read and highly intelligent. But she was never asked for her opinions on the issues of the day. It just wasn't done back then. She lived in a white male dominated world. To most, she was just eye candy. But she would soon be the face of the nation. Jacqueline married a war hero who was from a rich and influential family. She knew that much of the motivation for their marriage was to advance his career and to give him heirs. Like most male-dominated families, John wanted a son. So when she became pregnant for the first time, the couple was thrilled. In her day, there were no medical means to determine the gender of a fetus in the womb. They would just have to wait until the child was born to find out, just like every other couple. When that day arrived, there were tears, but they were not tears of happiness. The infant, a girl, was stillborn.

The couple did not stop trying. Jacqueline was still young and fertile. A few years later, Jacqueline became pregnant again.

This time, she delivered a healthy baby girl. They named her Caroline. By then, Jacqueline's husband was the junior Senator from the State of Massachusetts. Within three years, Caroline had a baby brother. They named him John Junior. At that time, his father had just been elected as the Supreme Commander of the nation.

Having come from a large family, John Senior wanted to have more children. So when John Junior was three years old, Jacqueline became pregnant for the fourth time. At that point, Jacqueline was 34 years old and her husband was focused on the nation's mid-term elections. There were several key senatorial and house of representative races that could be swayed in favor of the president's party if he was willing to campaign on their behalf. Jacqueline was very popular with the voters so he asked her to accompany him on some of these campaign stops. Jacqueline's obstetrician was concerned for her health given her advancing age and her history of difficult pregnancies. Therefore, the First Lady's travel schedule was heavily restricted. This was welcome news to her. While she had always been supportive of her husband's politics, she was very happy to stay behind and spend time with her young children, and take care of herself during her new pregnancy.

*

Dr. Mary Allen Avery completed her residency in pediatrics at Johns Hopkins in the late 1950s and moved to Boston to become an Assistant Professor at Harvard and attending physician at Massachusetts General Hospital. Her research interest was in diseases of the newborn that develop respiratory distress. Her interest in this field stemmed from her own struggles with tuberculosis and her own difficulties in breathing. When she was a first year medical student, she had to drop out of her spring semester because she tested positive for tuberculosis. Her chest x-ray revealed an infiltrate in her left lower lung. She was quarantined for 4 months and could not attend class. Mary Allen finished her training one year after her classmates. Mary Ellen did not have any symptoms of TB and felt retrospectively that she didn't have this infection. Nevertheless, she was isolated from the others as a protective measure.

While at Mass General, Mary Ellen saw many babies who were born prematurely. A large number of these infants died of respiratory failure within the first few days of life. When this happened to a child of one of her former classmates, she vowed to study this problem, in hopes of finding a cure. With each new case, Dr. Avery talked to the parents and asked them for permission to perform an autopsy. Many grieving parents granted permission in hopes of finding out why their children had died, which could lead to better treatment. Mary Ellen began working closely with Dr. Ghani, a pediatric pathologist. After a few months of investigation, Dr. Ghani made a critically important observation and called Dr. Avery to his office to show her what he found.

"This dish contains fresh lung tissue from a child who died of a congenital heart malformation." Dr. Avery knew that this group of infants was the comparative or 'control group,' that is, they didn't die of respiratory disease. Dr. Ghani continued, "The second dish contains lung tissue from a child who died of respiratory distress. Look at what happens when I rinse each of these tissues with a saline solution."

Mary Ellen looked closely at the dish as Dr. Ghani squirted the solution into and around the tissue. "Foam and bubbles are produced in the first dish. However, when I do the same thing to the second dish, there is no foam produced," the pathologist stated.

"What does this means?" Mary Ellen asked her colleague.

"The foam we see in the control tissue is produced by surfactants, a substance that is similar to our dish washing detergents. In infants who die with respiratory distress, there appears to be a deficiency of these chemicals. I don't know how or why, but I think this absence may be related to the death of these children," Dr. Ghani concluded.

Over the next several months, and then years, Dr. Avery learned whatever she could about these surfactants. She consulted with experts in the field of physical chemistry, biochemistry, and engineers from Harvard and the Massachusetts Institute of Technology. They told her that water has a high surface tension that causes it to form a bead when a drop is placed on a smooth surface. The introduction of surfactants reduces the surface tension enabling the liquid drop to spread more evenly over the surface. Dr. Avery felt that there was a connection between the surfactant concentration and the coating of lung tissue with fluid. Without this coating, the neonatal lung is unable to maintain normal shape and integrity, and it collapses. The child cannot breathe without assistance and suffocates. To demonstrate the importance of surfactants, Mary Ellen and her colleague created a device that could measure the surface tension of thin films. Lung extracts containing surfactants were able to lower the surface tension whereas the physical property remained high in lung extracts missing this critical ingredient.

This discovery led to the development of a routine clinical

laboratory test. The surfactant concentration can be measured from amniotic fluid and reflects the concentration seen in fetal lungs. Amniotic fluid can be removed from a woman in her third trimester through a procedure called "amniocentesis," the insertion of a long needle into the abdomen. Dr. Avery found that high surfactant concentrations in amniotic fluid predicted that the lungs of a newborn will not collapse when the infant takes his first breath of life. In contrast, respiratory distress leading to infant death can occur when the surfactant concentrations are low. In this situation, the delivery of the child should be postponed as long as possible, assuming that the mother's life is not in any imminent danger.

Amit Savjani knew he did not need to influence Dr. Avery's understanding of the pathophysiology of hyaline membrane disease. Dr. Avery was well on her way to this medical discovery. History did show, however, that the test for fetal lung maturity would not be available for a few years after Patrick Kennedy's death. So through his mind portal, Amit accelerated the development of the clinical laboratory test by implanting the idea of how the test could be conducted and interpreted some years earlier. By the time Patrick was born, Jacqueline Kennedy's doctors would be able to use the information to make the decision to prolong her labor....

*

When Jacqueline began to experience pre-mature labor, Dr. Avery was in her office at Mass General in Boston. She received a call from one of the White House doctors regarding the pregnancy of the President's wife. Dr. Avery was the recognized expert on neonatal respiratory distress syndrome and the First

Lady's doctor wanted the best medical opinion available. She was flown to DC on Air Force One and immediately taken to Jacqueline's hospital bedside. During the early 1960s, Dr. Avery's lab was the only one in the world doing surfactant analysis on amniotic fluid. She personally performed an amniocentesis on Jacqueline and had the sample flown back to her lab in Boston on Air Force One. She and the other doctors eagerly waited outside Jackie's hospital room for the result of the test. Six agonizing hours later, Dr. Avery's lab called with their findings.

"Based on our lab results, there is a high likelihood that if Jacqueline delivers her baby now, the child will develop respiratory distress," she told the medical team. They had already discussed the consequence of this possible outcome. The patient's condition was sufficiently stable to the point that they could delay delivery of the baby.

While the First Lady had some hypertension and mild bleeding, the doctors felt that with careful monitoring around the clock, a one-day postponement in delivery of her child could be tolerated. Dr. Avery had convinced them that the risk to the baby was greater than the risk to the mother, so they delayed the scheduled Caesarian-section operation. A press conference was called and the media was updated regarding Jacqueline's medical condition.

After a few days passed, a repeat amniotic fluid collection and analysis was performed on the President's wife. This time, the surfactant concentration was within acceptable safe limits. Jacqueline was sent to the operating room for her Caesarean section and her next child was born. A few minutes after delivery, doctors spanked the child, and a healthy cry was heard throughout the corridor. The baby turned pink and was breathing on his own! The parents named him Patrick.

*

Patrick's father was shot and killed a few months later while campaigning in Dallas Texas. Jacqueline was no longer the First Lady. Nevertheless, there was still a lot of interest by the press in the lives of the former First Family. She therefore moved out of the Washington DC area in an attempt to be less in the eye of the public. As a result, Patrick and his older brother and sister experienced a relatively normal childhood. Patrick's sibling became attorneys. Patrick became a writer. During their early adulthood, none of the former President's children expressed any interest in entering politics. But that changed when tragedy struck the family yet again. John Junior had his pilot's license, and was a reasonably inexperienced pilot. While flying to a cousin's wedding, John Junior, his wife, and wife's sister died in a plane crash that night. John Junior was 40 years old. This event changed Patrick's outlook on life. While his older brother denied interest in politics, Patrick thought that he would have followed in their footsteps. That idea came to an abrupt halt when John Junior died in a plane crash. Patrick felt the burden of his family's legacy had passed onto him the weekend of his brother's death. The media could not help acknowledging a similar situation that occurred in their family decades early. JFK entered politics after his older brother, Joseph Kennedy Junior, Patrick's Uncle, also died in a plane crash during World War II. Now Patrick, the only surviving male in JFK's family, felt the torch had passed to him.

With the help of his Uncle, the senior senator from Massachusetts, Patrick entered local politics and became mayor of

Boston, just as his great grandfather had done nearly a century earlier. This led to several terms as the Junior Senator from Massachusetts, the first time the two senators from the same state were uncle and nephew. Eventually, Patrick would run for the Presidency of the U.S. He hoped to follow in the footsteps of John Quincy Adams and George W. Bush as the third set of father and son presidents. Patrick competed against Hillary Clinton to be their party's nominee.

*

During the early years, testing amniotic fluid for surfactant content took 4 to 5 hours. The "L/S ratio" measured the lecithin content, which increases during the course of the third trimester, and the sphingomyelin content, which remains consistent. A ratio exceeding 2.0 indicated fetal lung maturity. Only highly trained technologists were allowed to do the test. Sometimes we had to call someone at home to come in and perform the test. Other times someone had to stay overtime to complete it. Today, we measure something called "lamellar bodies." Surfactants aggregate into a "micelle," a spherical particle that forms and circulates within the amniotic fluid. The higher the lamellar body count, the more surfactant is available for fetal lungs to use. The test now takes 5 minutes to conduct, requires no reagents, and is measured on the platelet channel of a hematology analyzer, an instrument clinical labs use to measure the complete blood count. Thus, the technology has advanced from a highly complex, time and labor-consuming test only available during certain times of the day, to one that is available 24 hours a day, 7 days a week, requires no special training, and uses existing equipment present in clinical laboratories worldwide. This is quite an advancement from the test that I saw as a student visiting while Portland, Oregon, some 35 years ago.

Mary Ellen Avery is credited with discovering the role of

surfactants in fetal lung disease. Her work has been credited in saving over 1,000,000 lives. In 1991, George H.W. Bush awarded Dr. Avery the National Medal of Science for her work. Dr. Avery died in 2011 at the age of 84 years.

In August of 1963, Jacqueline Kennedy gave birth by Caesarean section to Patrick Bouvier Kennedy, who was 5 ½ weeks premature and weighed only 4 pounds and 10.5 ounces. The infant suffered from respiratory distress syndrome, known as hyaline membrane disease then, and he began having breathing problems immediately after birth. Despite efforts by the child's pediatricians, Patrick died 39 hours after his birth. Patrick's death stimulated the medical community to conduct more research on how to keep premature infants alive. This led to the creation of the subspecialty of neonatology. Today, most children born with hyaline membrane disease survive and can lead normal lives. Through the miracles of modern medicine, infants that weigh only 1 pound have survived.

Some 100 days after Patrick's death, the president was assassinated in Dallas, Texas. The President was laid to rest in Arlington Cemetery. Patrick's body and that of his older sister were moved to Arlington a few months later. Caroline Kennedy was appointed by President Barack Obama as the U.S. Ambassador to Japan. John Junior became an attorney and publisher of the magazine, George. John Junior was not politically active but he never ruled out the possibility. Some historians believe that John Junior was just about to enter politics around the time that his plane went down.

In this story, it was the second son, just like JFK, who survived and became president of the United States. Only in this case, the second son never lived beyond the first few hours of birth. This tale shows how the existence of a clinical laboratory test, on the verge of its discovery in real history, i.e., when Patrick Kennedy was born, could have changed the face of American history had it been available to Jacqueline. Could his survival at birth have altered any of the events surrounding the President's assassination? Would Jacqueline have accompanied the President on his trip to Dallas having an infant to nurse and care for back in Washington DC? Would the President have even gone on the trip? Of course, no one can answer these questions. It is likely, however, that Patrick's survival could have changed the face of American history.

George's Last Legacy

****

They assembled in the oval office. There was a sense of urgency and desperation. In the room were the President and members of his cabinet. The date was June, 1811. The location was the President's Mansion, not yet called the "White House." It would be a century later before Theodore Roosevelt would formally establish this iconic label. James Madison was the President of the United States. They were contemplating another war between the United States and Britain. It had only been 30 years since the last conflict.

The secretary of war, William Eustis spoke up first. "We are unprepared for another war," he told the President. "We need strong leadership. I don't have confidence in General Hampton and Wilkinson." Both men fought in the Revolutionary War. History would show that Eustis fear was correct. Hampton was commanding the American forces in 1813 Battle of the Chateneauguay in present day Quebec. Although Hampton's army was more than twice the size, they were defeated by the British and Mohawk Indians. His army then proceeded to get lost in the woods while retreating. Wilkinson also lost the Battle of Crysler's Farm despite his superior forces in terms of troop numbers. Both men were relieved of their commission a year later.

"Who did you have in mind?" President Madison asked.

"We need George back," Eustis calmly stated.

Madison was taken aback by this comment. *Certainly he didn't mean George Washington*, he thought. He looked at Eustis who nodded his head indicating that that was exactly whom he meant. Then Madison spoke. "Are you insane? The man is 79 years old. He is living a quiet life in Mt. Vernon. What makes you think he will come back?" The President was flabbergasted.

"Hey, Benjamin Franklin was 79 when he was our Ambassador to France, and he was President of Pennsylvania well into his 80s. We really need someone that everyone respects and will rally behind."

*

As most schoolchildren know, George Washington was Commander-in-Chief of the Continental Army President of the U.S. during the Revolutionary War. Although he was defeated in New York, and nearly captured by the British, Washington subsequently won key battles at Trenton, Princeton, Saratoga, and Yorktown. After the war, he presided over the Constitutional Convention in 1787, and two years later, he was elected as the nation's first President. Washington served two terms and retired from public office in 1797.

On a cold and wintery day in December, 1799, Washington told his wife Martha that he was going to inspect his plantation. The temperature was 30°F.

"George, let one of the men do that. It is hailing and freezing rain. You'll catch a cold," she pleaded with him. "You're not getting any younger."

"Martha, you older than me, so you shouldn't talk about that," George said as he was putting on his winter coat and hat.

"I am not the one heading outside in this weather, General." But Martha could not dissuade her husband from leaving the house. Washington worked outside for 5 straight hours. When he returned that evening, he was very hungry and sat down to eat his supper before getting out of his wet clothes. Martha had retreated to her bedroom and was not there at the time to scold her stubborn husband. The next day, Washington complained of a sore throat, but he still went out into the heavy snow to mark trees that needed to be cut for firewood. The next morning, his condition worsened with him having difficulty speaking and swallowing. He motioned to one of the men who managed his estate to cut him and remove a cup of blood. Washington believed that this medical practice was useful in treating illnesses. In the meantime, Martha sent for Washington's personal doctor. Under Washington's orders, Dr. James Craik continue to remove copious amounts of blood from the ex-President, both men hoping that this would help him recover.

Martha was never in favor of this medical procedure. "Should we really be doing this?" she asked both the doctor and George. Washington had previously directed the use of this blood-letting procedure to treat his slaves when they were ill, with some success.

"We have no choice," Dr. Craik said to Martha. "We tried to give him some molasses, vinegar and butter, but he couldn't swallow it and he nearly suffocated." Unfortunately, the massive loss of blood, estimated to be about half his total blood volume was removed over a period of less than 24 hours. This resulted in his death due to hypovolemic shock. George Washington was only a few weeks away from living to see the turn of the century. According to his will, the 123 slaves that were directly owned by Washington were freed.

Martha was devastated by George's death. She warned him about not going out in the cold and about her doubts on blood-letting. She now had to bury her second husband. Her first, Daniel Curtis, died when Martha was just 25. Together, she and Daniel had four children, but all of them died before they reached the age of 30. George was her true love, but now she was all alone. *If I could have stopped this damn blood-letting, maybe he would still be alive today,* Martha thought during the General's funeral. Martha's health began to decline rapidly, and she passed away a few years later at the age of 70. Her remains were interred in George's tomb at Mt. Vernon. Before she died, she had all of her private letters between her and George burned to protect their privacy. However, five letters are known to survive between the Nation's first First Couple.

*

One of Amit's responsibilities at the General Hospital was the phlebotomy service. Each morning, a portion of his technical staff would don their personal protective equipment, including lab coats and gloves and head out to the inpatient wards. Blood was collected from these patients on a routine basis for clinical laboratory testing. Medical technologists are specifically trained, licensed, and qualified for phlebotomy. Amit and the other faculty taught their staff the correct manner to draw blood from the arm vein and finger sticks.

"Improper techniques can lead to hemolysis, or a

breakdown in the red cells from the blood after it has been collected into the tubes," he told his students during one of the very first lectures of the new semester. Years ago, blood was collected into syringes whereby the plunger was withdrawn to create suction. "Before there were phlebotomists, some attending doctors were in a rush and withdrew the plunger too quickly. This creates a turbulence within the tube causing cells to lyse," Amit explained. "Today we use a tube that is already evacuated. So there is an even and steady negative pressure that draws blood from the vein and into the blood collection tube."

The concept of phlebotomy for testing blood for diagnostic purposes is relatively new to medical science. One of the first clinical laboratory tests was for creatinine, a kidney function marker, first described by Dr. Jaffe in 1886. A test for blood glucose was described during the 1920s. In contrast, the medical practice of blood-letting dates back to the ancient Egyptians and Greeks who believed that toxins and poisons build up in the blood, and that regular bleeding was useful to cleanse the circulation. The blood was discarded as it was not recognized that there was substantial medical value contained with the fluid itself. "Fortunately, these old civilizations did not believe in transfusion, replacing lost blood from someone else," Amit said during class. "With ABO incompatibility, this would have led to transfusion reactions and many deaths."

In reviewing the history of phlebotomy, Amit learned that George Washington was the victim of his own blood-letting practices and he wondered what other accomplishments Washington could have made if he survived longer. It was then that Amit decided to reach out to Dr. Craik while the doctor was tending to George Washington's illness back in 1799, through his mind portal. Instead of the extensive blood-letting, Amit instructed the doctor to have Washington gargle with salt water without swallowing. Then he instructed Martha to boil water and to let Washington breathe in steam. Martha then heated a soft towel and placed it on Washington throat. The home remedy worked. Washington felt much better and there was no further talk about blood-letting. Dr. Craik stayed a few more days to ensure that his patient was well before he left Mt. Vernon.

*

William Eustis sent a messenger to Mt. Vernon asking George Washington to come to the President's mansion, some 12 years after the day he should have died. It was only 18 miles and took about an hour by his horse-driven carriage. After the customary pleasantries and introduction of his staff, President Madison got down to business.

"We are having trouble with the British again, and I think war is inevitable," Madison said.

"Is there no peaceful solution possible? I think you will find little interest among your constituents to take up arms again," George said. "They, like me, are now farmers and ranchers. I believe the New Englanders will especially be against this idea."

"We have run out of diplomatic options. The British have imposed trade restrictions with France which is crippling our economy," Madison said.

"I know, Britain is fighting with Napoleon, and they don't want us to send the French our supplies," Washington said.

"They have forced 10,000 of our merchant sailors into their Navy to fight the French. The British also want to block our expansion in the western frontier through their support of Native American Indians," Madison said. "That is really none of their damn business, but I guess they don't us to get that big and strong."

"What do you want me to do about this?" Washington asked.

"George, I want you to take command of the Army and prepare our nation against the British. They have enlisted the American Indians, and their other North American colonies outside of the U.S." James Madison said. The President was referring to the colonies north of the St. Lawrence Seaway.

"But James, I am an old man. I don't have the energy I once had. I cannot be on the combat field leading our troops," George said. "Martha will never let me do this."

"You don't have to actually deploy in the field. Just your name as the Commanding Officer will spark confidence in the current generation of soldiers. Your experience in battle tactics will be invaluable to our inexperienced generals. I think you can also help organize our war supplies. The head of our Quartermaster Corps has said that many farmers who are opposed to the war are not allowing us to buy the supplies needed to do the job."

The War of 1812 was fought in three theaters. There was a naval battle between British and American warships in the Atlantic Ocean and off the coast of the U.S. War waged in the Southern part of the United States and the Gulf Coast. Fighting also occurred at the U.S. and Canadian borders. George Washington returned to active duty and commanded the American forces that attacked Canada and defended the Northern cities. His impact was immediate. In the actual history, the War of 1812 lasted three years. This included an invasion of

Washington DC in 1814, and the burning of city buildings including the President's Mansion. Under George Washington, the American troops were better trained, better equipped, and outmanned the enemy. Just as in the Revolutionary War, George's leadership was the deciding factor. Instead of a stalemate after three years of war, America defeated the British during the War of 1812 within 18 months. At the armistice, the vanquished British conceded additional land to America. Today, Montreal and parts of the southern half of the Quebec Province is now part of the U.S.

*

After Amit entered his mind portal, he went into the living room at his home and turned on the television to watch the 49ers and Cowboys football game. All of the players were standing with their helmets off in preparation for the national anthem. Then the PA announcer came on the air. "Ladies and gentlemen, please welcome country and western megastar Carrie Underwood, who will sing our national anthem." She then proceeded to sing "God Bless America." Amit started to hum along and then he made a startling realization. *What? This is not the national anthem! Something is wrong.* He arose from the couch and went to his computer. Under a Google search, he typed in "The Star Spangled Banner." The top entry was about the Star Spangled Banner Incorporated, printing company out of Lexington Massachusetts. "We print large banners for patriotic celebrations. Use our services when planning your next Fourth of July parade." The second entry was the Star Spangled Hot Dog Company. "We put the best meat in our dogs." Then Amit went into Google Scholar and then typed in the title of the national anthem in parentheses. The computer returned the message, "Your search did not match any articles." When he typed in "American national anthem", indeed, the song *God Bless America* was listed. Amit had changed this segment of history. The original anthem was penned by Francis Scott Key in 1814, as he witnessed the bombardment of Fort McHenry by the British. Despite the onslaught, the next day, Key noted that the American flag was still flying over the fort, "And the rocket's red glare, the bombs bursting in air, gave proof through the night that our flag was still there." But it would not be until 1931 that the *Star Spangled Banner* would officially become America's national anthem. Because Amit altered the course of the War of 1812, Fort McHenry was never attacked, and the national anthem was never written by Francis Key. *Ah, that is ok*, Amit thought. *I like this song better anyway.*

*

It is hard to image today that people in olden times believed that blood-letting was therapeutic. The average healthy adult has about 5 liters of blood circulating in their veins and arteries. New cellular elements are continuously being produced by organs such as the bone marrow, while old cells are removed from the circulation by the spleen and other organs. Toxic constituents are removed by the liver and kidneys. Unless there is significant blood loss, it is unnecessary to replace blood on a regular basis. Individuals who have reduced red cell mass are anemic. Excess bleeding is a major cause of death for trauma patients. Hypovolemic shock is defined as the loss of 20% of a person's blood volume. A severe loss of fluid causes a drop in the blood pressure. Under this condition, the heart is unable to pump enough blood to meet metabolic needs and organs begin to fail. In addition to extensive external bleeding, internal bleeding or hemorrhage is a major cause of mortality today.

There are some blood-letting practices that continue today. Patients with iron overload are regularly bled. Individuals undergoing plastic reconstructive surgery are treated with blood sucking leeches to remove excess blood. Because of a concern for infections, there is work being conducted to developing artificial leeches. Some individuals such as Olympic swimmer Michael Phelps believe that "cupping" is health benefits. This involves placing suction cups on the skin and evacuating the air under the cup such that the skin rises and reddens due to the expansion of blood vessels. Cupping is thought to help circulation, relieve pain and remove heat. Puncturing the skin with acupuncture needles causes bleeding and is a mild form of bloodletting.

In the absence of modern drugs such as antihistamines and cough suppressants, there were natural remedies available to doctors during Washington life. In addition to gargling with salt water, gargling with licorice root, drinking Chamomile tea and extracts of slippery elm and marshmallow root, and the use of honey and peppermint, can ease the symptoms of a sore throat. These remedies contain antihistamines and other compounds that have anti-bacterial properties.

The song, God Bless America was written by Irving Berlin in 1918 while he was serving in the U.S. army. In 1938, Berlin revised it to be a peace song in response to the rise of Adolf Hitler in Germany. Berlin, whose birth name was Israel Baline, was a Jewish Russian immigrant who came to the U.S. in 1893 at the age of five. On Armistice Day, Kate Smith sang this song on her radio show and made it famous. Incidentally, Berlin lived for 101 years. Ever since the attack on America on September 11, 2011, the song God Bless America is song as part of the "seventh inning stretch." Now that this is the national anthem, the song, American the Beautiful is song during this part of baseball games instead.

You Vee to the Rescue

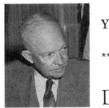

****

Darryl Shapiro was born in the summer of 1915 in Washington DC, a few miles from the Washington Monument. As a child, Darryl's family belonged to a country club where his Bar Mitzvah was held. It was also there that he honed his golf skills. After high school, Darryl received acceptance to attend the University of Pennsylvania and to play on their golf team. During one of the summers, Darryl was invited to compete in the Hershey Open Golf Tournament as an amateur. There, he met Milton Hershey, founder of the chocolate empire. He also played against Ben Hogan, who in 1941, became the head pro of the Hershey Country Club, and Harry Barrow, who in 1942, would go on to become the first Jewish player to win a PGA golf event. After college, Darryl realized how difficult it was to be a professional golfer as a career, so he attended Harvard and later received a medical degree. Darryl was in a pathology residency program at the Massachusetts General Hospital on the day the Japanese attacked Pearl Harbor on December 7th, 1941. A few weeks after, Darryl joined the Army Medical Corp and was stationed in England.

On that same day that Darryl was born, a cadet ranked 65th out of 287, was graduating from the U.S. Military Academy at

West Point. This cadet would rise through the ranks of the US Army, becoming a five-star General. Later, he was promoted to Supreme Commander of the Allied Forces in Europe during World War II. General Dwight Eisenhower commanded "Operation Overload;" the D-day invasion of France. On June 5, 1944, Eisenhower met with army paratroopers just before they boarded the plane for the invasion. Darryl was not a paratrooper, but was present when the General gave his motivational speech. It was the first time he met the future US President.

Darryl arrived in Northern France a few days after D-day to attend to the medical needs of Allied soldiers. When the war ended, Darryl returned to Boston so he could complete his pathology residency training at Mass General. After completion, he accepted a job at the Armed Forces Institute of Pathology and the Walter Reed Army Medical Center.

With the success of the D-day invasion and the defeat of Nazi Germany, Dwight Eisenhower returned home as a war hero. Many in Washington wanted Eisenhower to run for president. Amazingly, during the Potsdam Convention after the war, President Harry Truman told Eisenhower, that he could help him run for the highest office, and that Truman himself could step back to become his vice presidential candidate. When Eisenhower declined to run, Truman was selected by the Democratoc party and he went on to defeated Thomas Dewey in 1948 for his second term. Four years later Eisenhower ran on the republican ticket and was elected as the 34th President of the United States. He would serve two full terms before retiring in 1961. Another war veteran, this time a Navy man, would succeed him as the Commander-in-Chief.

Throughout his life, Eisenhower suffered from a variety

of medical problems. In 1923, he underwent an appendectomy after several episodes of abdominal pain. In 1947, the General had a diagnosis of partial small bowel obstruction, although it resolved spontaneously. Nine year later during his first term as President, he was diagnosed with regional enteritis or Crohn's disease. This disease, named after Dr. Burrill Crohn, was first recognized as a medical condition in 1932. Given that the disease was only recently known at the time, was it possible that Eisenhower's doctors did not recognize that he was suffering from this disease during his early abdominal problems?

*

In reading about Eisenhower's medical history, Amit Savjani had this same question. Like others, he assumed that this disease was autoimmune in nature, the development of his own antibodies attacking his gastrointestinal organs. But when Amit attended a medical conference, he learned that Crohn's disease might be caused by the presence of a common bacteria, *Mycobacterium avium*, subspecies, *paratuberculosis*. This bacterium is slow growing and it's existence can be easily missed. In 1998, Dr. David Relman, a microbiologist and immunologist at Stanford University, suggested that chronic inflammatory diseases, including those of the bowel, had a microbial etiology. Dr. Barry Marshall's work on *H. pylori* opened the door for others to link bugs as the cause of other diseases. But *paratuberculosis* was a different because clinical trials had shown that treatment with antibiotics infected with *paratuberculosis* was usually ineffective against Crohn's disease.

Amit understood that *paratuberculosis* infections occur in sheep, goats, and cattle, and appears in their milk. Given that

Eisenhower was born in rural Texas and raised in Kansas, Amit reasoned that it was entirely possible that he was exposed to the bacterium of these domestic livestock during his youth, and he continued to have a latent infection into his adulthood. Amit wondered how Eisenhower's life could have been improved with knowledge of his medical illness, but in the absence of effective therapies of that day, the medical knowledge might be just be an academic exercise. Amit's interest changed when he read about ultraviolet light blood irradiation therapy or UVBI. He was fascinated to learn about the work of Dr. Niels Finsen, a Danish physician who in 1895, successfully treated some 900 patients with skin tuberculosis. UVBI involves removing blood of infected patients under sterile conditions, subjecting it to UV light, and then returning the blood back into the patient. Dr. Finsen concluded that the UV light was effective in killing bacteria. He used the power of the sun on himself, as he suffered from Niemann-Pick disease, a congenital disease that produces excess lipids and fatty substances. For his work, Dr. Finsen received the Nobel Prize for physiology and Medicine in 1903. His success was short lived, however, as he died just a year after receiving the award at the age of 43. With the development of antibiotics, UVBI treatment was abandoned.

In trying to alter Eisenhower's medical history, Amit debated on whether or not to implant the idea of *paratuberculosis* infection as the causative agent in Crohn's disease into the mind of Eisenhower's personal physician, Dr. Howard Snyder. Dr. Snyder was trained as a surgeon with a rank of Major General during World War II. After Eisenhower's inauguration as President, Dr. Snyder became Eisenhower's personal physician and was 76 years old in 1956, when the President's Crohn's disease was diagnosed. Due to his advancing age, Amit felt that Snyder would not be the appropriate recipient of his current medical knowledge on Crohn's disease. Instead, he chose Dr. Darryl Shapiro, who was 30 years younger and more likely to accept Amit's implanted ideas.

*

After returning from the war, Darryl resumed his interest in golf. The second time he met General Eisenhower in his life was at the Congressional Country Club in Bethesda, Maryland. One day, when Eisenhower was told that there was a scratch golfer who was a former member of his battalion playing, he came over to meet the doctor. Over the ensuing months, Darryl became the President's a regular golf partner. Darryl would give tips to the former Allied Commander.

Although he wasn't Eisenhower's personal physician, Amit felt he would be in the best position to learn about *paratuberculosis* and UVBI, and influence Dr. Synder. But Amit knew that it would not be easy to alter the course of Eisenhower's medical care without direct evidence. He taught Dr. Shapiro through repeated visits through his mind portal on how to grow the pesky *tuberculosis* bacteria in a culture. *Paratuberculosis* is extremely slow growing and difficult to detect. While it took months, Darryl perfected the technique and isolated the bacterium of patients suffering from Crohn's disease.

Amit then taught Darryl how to perform UVBI treatment. They withdrew 60 ccs of blood from Crohn's disease patients through a venous catheter, and subjected it to ultraviolet radiation before returning the blood back to the patient. Dr.

Shapiro was taught that this had to be done weekly for 3 months. It was also necessary to initiate combination antibiotic therapy to all of the patients, including penicillin, streptomyocin, and para-aminosalicylic acid, drugs available since the 1940s to treat tuberculosis. Shortly thereafter completing this treatment cycle, symptoms for most of these patients began to subside. They all gained weight and were more energetic.

He was now ready to discuss his findings with Dr. Synder and convince him to test the President's blood for the presence of a *paratuberculosis* infection. In the early months of 1955, Dr. Darryl Shapiro contacted Eisenhower's doctor.

"You want to do what with the President's blood? He is 65 years old and strong as an ox. There is nothing wrong with him, especially since I got him to stop smoking 6 years ago," Dr. Synder said.

"You haven't seen him on the golf course like I have. Sometimes he doubles over in stomach pain. Other times he has to rush off to the bathroom. That is very inconvenient when you are on a golf course," Darryl said. "The President is a proud man and doesn't always reveal his weaknesses. But I have seen this first hand."

"Well I see no harm in getting you a blood sample from him. Of course, all of this must remain strictly confidential," Dr. Synder concluded.

A blood sample was delivered directly from Dr. Synder's office to Dr. Shapiro at the Institute. After a few weeks, Darryl successful isolated *parabacterium* from Eisenhower's blood and called Dr. Synder with the news. It was now time to discuss UVBI therapy with the President. Dr. Synder arranged a meeting with him and Darryl.

"Ike, you know Dr. Darryl Shapiro, right?" Dr. Snyder asked.

"Of course. How's your short game? You were having trouble getting out of the bunkers last time we played," the President remarked.

"I got a new wedge, sir," was Darryl's response. "Actually, sir, we're here to discuss your intestinal problems. My lab found a bacterium in your blood that we think is causing your stomach cramps. We are here to suggest some novel treatments." Darryl said. They started to explain the UVBI procedure.

Midway through, Eisenhower interrupted them. "This isn't blood letting is it?" He was referring to the practice of permanently removing liters of blood as a means to remove the bacteria. "George Washington had this done and he succumbed to it," he said.

"No, we not suggesting that! We will be returning the blood back to you when we have treated it. You will not become anemic," Dr. Synder said.

Surprisingly to both men, Eisenhower said to proceed. "I trust both of you with my life," he said. Then he went off on a tangent. "Your task will not be an easy one. You are well trained, well equipped, and battle-hardened. I will fight savagely." These were revised statements from his talk to the British and American paratroopers some 22 years earlier. "I hope I can continue to eat some of my favorite foods, like pig knuckles and sauerkraut."

Eisenhower's UVBI treatment was initiated, and like the other patients, his intestinal health improved dramatically. Over the next few months, he had more stamina, gained weight, was more attentive at meetings, and even lowered his handicap by 5 strokes. Amit went back into the history books and learned that Eisenhower's medical history had changed as the result of his intervention. The history of Eisenhower having a heart attack in 1955 and abdominal surgery in 1956 was erased from the history books. He was healthier and lived an additional 5 years from this original date of death in 1969.

But Amit was unsatisfied with simply prolonging Eisenhower's life. *What was a key mistake that he made during his Presidency that could be reversed with his improved medical condition?* he asked himself. Amit learned that Eisenhower's biggest misstep made while in office was his handling of the Suez Canal Crisis. In 1956, Egyptian President Gamal Nasser decided to nationalize the Suez Canal, which was built by the French in 1869 and controlled by the French and English. Together with Israel, the three countries began attacking Egypt and occupying the Canal Zone. Egypt's ally, Russia, threatened nuclear weapons. To everyone's surprise, Eisenhower sided with the Russians and threatened economic sanctions against the Israel and the U.S.'s former western allies. Within a few weeks, British and French forces were compelled to withdraw. This signaled the beginning of the end for these illustrative empires.

Amit wanted to know how the Middle East could be different today if Eisenhower had a reversal of this position. To answer this question, he went back to his mind portal and summoned Darryl Shapiro again. As a devout Jew, Darryl was naturally supportive of Israel. In discussions with the President on the golf course, he subtly implanted the notion that Nasser could not be trusted and supporting Egypt would lead to ongoing instability in the region. When the Suez Canal Crisis occurred, this time President Eisenhower took a neutral stance and allowed the France, England, and Israel maintain control, and Egypt withdrew its intent to nationalize. In the actual history of the Middle East, Egyptian President Nassar rode Eisenhower's endorsement to great popularity within his country, a popularity that remained intact until his death in 1970. This is despite the fact that the American Foreign Policies subsequently backed off of the support of Egypt. Now, Amit saw that Nasser was not as firmly supplanted as Egypt's leader, resulting in the earlier emergence of Egyptian President Anwar Sadat. The subsequent wars between Israel and Egypt, namely the 6-Day, War, War of Attrition and the Yom Kippur War did not occur in Amit's altered world, resulting in thousands of lives saved on both sides. Eventually the control of Suez Canal was turned over to Egypt without a conflict. While the Middle East is still volatile today, and Israel continues to be in conflict with their neighboring countries, two of the main combatants, Israel and Egypt have a stabilizing influence on the other countries due to a better understanding of each other than they did in history. Amit was pleased that he had a small role easing this ongoing troublesome region.

*

The incidence of Crohn's disease cases is roughly 200 cases per 100,000 adults. The etiology that it is due to an Mycobacterium avium *ssp.* paratuberculosis *infection has not been established by medical societies. The cause is still listed today as "unknown." It is recognized that environmental factors are important in addition to immune system dysfunction and genetics. It has been stated that an individual who has a parent with this disease faces a 20% change of acquiring it. Given that* paratuberculosis *is present in milk and meat of domestic animals,* *wouldn't it appear to be logical that the increased prevalence within* *families is due to a common diet? To address this issue, there was* Mycobacterium avium *ssp .*paratuberculosis *conference held in 2017.* *Seventy-eight percent of the conference attendees concluded that the* *bacterium causes human disease. Some of the evidence in favor of this* *hypothesis is the increasing prevalence of* paratuberculosis *in US dairy* *herds. The incidence of Crohn's disease as also increased during this time* *interval.*

Opponents to this hypothesis cite an Australian trial that *showed the failure of anti-paratuberculosis antibiotics to treat patients* *with Crohn's disease. However, a re-analysis of the data showed that those* *patients given a combination of antibiotics performed significantly better* *than the standard of care. Others doubters cite the lack of compliance to* *the Koch's postulate. (In 1890, Dr. Robert Koch wrote that in order to* *demonstrate causation the microorganism must be present in all cases, can* *be grown in culture, produces the disease when inoculated into a healthy* *susceptible laboratory animal, and can be re-isolated in the newly infected* *host.) Presenters of this conference noted that the difficulty of culturing* paratuberculosis *has been a deterrent in accepting* the paratuberculosis *hypothesis. The pharmacology industry may also be disbelievers of this* *approach, given their investment in drug approaches for Crohn's disease* *treatment.*

Despite the long history, ultraviolet blood irradiation therapy, *also known as photoluminescence therapy, it is considered experimental and* *is currently not reimbursed by the Centers for Medicare and Medicaid or* *private insurance companies. There are no FDA approved UV treatment* *devices. There are however, clinics across the U.S. where UVBI treatment* *is available. The procedure requires about 1 hour and can be used for a variety of medical conditions. .*

In 2016, author Michael Doran, a Hudson Institute senior fellow, published a book entitled, "Ike's Gamble: American Rise to Dominance in the Middle East." This describes the mistake that Eisenhower made regarding the support of Egypt during the Suez Canal Crisis. The subsequent actions taken by Egypt and other Middle East Countries caused Eisenhower to reverse his policies and a return to the support of Israel and the Western Allies. Doran concludes that supporting countries that are unfriendly to American ideals rarely reaps benefits.

Purple Reign

****

An individual that played a large role in the formative years of American history is George III, who became the King of Great Britain and Ireland at the age of 22 years and ruled from 1760 until his death in 1820. King George was a central figure in the Revolutionary War which began in 1775. King George was 37 years old at the time. The war was started by the American colonists who were being taxed by the British government but had no representation within Parliament. Colonists felt that they were simply pawns being played according to the will and whim of bureaucrats across the Atlantic. As the war continued and casualties mounted, King George's cabinet ministers thought that the King should consider the colonist's demands. However, George III was adamant in fighting the rebels until ultimate victory was achieved by the Empire. He felt that giving in to the colonies might spark revolution and independence among the other British colonies. Of course, Britain lost the war and the colonists gained independence from the British in 1783. With the loss of the 13 colonies, the British Empire set their sights on securing neighboring Canada and the exploration of the Pacific. Just before the Revolutionary War, James Cook discovered the eastern coast of Australia. A few years after the end of the war, Britain established "Botany Bay," and sent exiled English convicts to New South Wales in Australia. There were no wars of independence between Britain and Canada or Britain and Australia. They eventually formed their own Parliaments. However, both Canada and Australia remain members of the British Commonwealth and are ceremoniously ruled by the Queen of England.

History has shown that King George suffered from recurrent mental illness. He became seriously ill in 1788 to the point that he was unable to fulfill many of his royal duties. Granted that this was after the war, but if he had a genetic disease that caused this illness, he may have been sick a decade earlier. Centuries later, psychiatrists and physicians have suggested that George suffered from an inherited metabolic disease. Did ill health cloud his judgment during critical times of his reign? How might the world look today had he been diagnosed and treated appropriately? The following is an account of history re-written with the availability of modern clinical laboratory diagnostics and therapy.

*

George succeeded to the throne when his grandfather, George II died in 1760. Within a year, he married Charlotte of Mecklenberg-Strelitz, whom he met on their wedding day. It was not likely a situation of love at first sight. Within a year, their first son was born who was heir to the throne and later became King George IV. George III and Charlotte ultimately produced 15 children. Their marriage was a happy one. Unlike his predecessors and descendants, George did not have any mistresses.

George's health was good until he began suffering from attacks when he was in his early 40s. His symptoms included severe abdominal pain, muscle weakness, and numbness in various parts of his body. There were also skin lesions and blisters on his arms and legs. The King was also agitated, depressed and suffered from hallucinations. These attacks would coincide with upsetting news regarding the 13 colonies in America that he was getting from his foreign ministers on a weekly basis. They thought that the King was having panic attacks. This didn't make sense to his chief physician, Dr. Henry Beauregard, because King George was used to political instability, and regularly dealt with issues within his government and abroad. The Royal physicians suspected a medical problem and did a thorough physical exam of the king, which included a regular analysis of his urine. The doctors knew that sugar in the urine was a sign of diabetes and had laboratory workers whose job it was to taste the King's urine to see if it was sweet. His urine was clear and devoid of any glucose. In contrast, when he went into one of his psychotic fits, his urine would be a bluish purple in color. Dr. Tarpley Cox was one of the Royal doctors involved in the King's care.

Amit Savjani found a drawing of Dr. Tarpley Cox in the royal archives. After a careful plan, Amit conjured up his mind portal and implanted an idea into Cox's brain that King George was suffering from a porphyria. Even though the disease had not yet been discovered, he transferred information to Cox about the underlying biochemistry of the disease and how it might be treated with 18th century medicine. Knowing that Dr. Cox was very cleaver, Amit reasoned that the young Royal doctor would find the knowledge and resources needed to treat the King's ailment. He only needed some subtle direction.

Dr. Cox had just given a lecture on urine testing to his

students at the London Royal Academy of Medicine. "Normally, urine has a yellow colour due to the presence of urobilinogen, a pigment produced in the liver by the breakdown of hemoglobin. Red-colored urine can be caused by kidney injury or disease and is due to the release of red blood cells and/or hemoglobin. Red urine can also be caused by eating certain vegetables such as beets or rhubarb. Dark urine can be caused by extensive muscle injury and is due to the presence of myoglobin, which is another oxygen-bearing protein containing heme. When the urine is white or cloudy, it may be due to the presence of bacteria which can be the result of a urinary infection."

Dr. Tarpley had never seen purple urine before. So he went to the archives to find out if anyone had published on this before. While searching the medical literature is a simple matter today, back in the 1760s, there were no computers, internet, search engines, or printed catalogs. There were only a few medical journals. But after several days of searching, he was successful in finding an article in the "Philosophical Transactions of the Royal Society," a journal first published in 1665 by the Royal Society of London. The article described a patient with purple urine, just like the King. The article further described the investigation as to the cause of this pigment. Dr. Cox also read about Vlad Tepes III Dracula, the Prince of Wallachia in Transylvania, who lived some 300 years earlier. Dracula was most healthy when he stayed out of the sunlight and in the dark of night. He had a thirst for liquids. Modern day folklore suggests that this liquid was blood *Hmmm,* Cox thought. *Perhaps the King and Dracula have the same affliction?*

A few days later, Dr. Cox met with Dr. Beauregard and his staff met to discuss what his research showed.

"Heme is an iron binding molecule that is the active part of hemoglobin," Dr. Cox remarked. "This is essential for red blood cells to transport both oxygen to the tissues and carry away carbon dioxide as a byproduct. Heme is produced from porphobilinogen through a series of enzyme-catalyzed reactions. If any of these enzymes are defective, high levels of porphobilinogen are excreted into urine. Because this molecule is reddish-purple in colour, individuals with acute porphyrias produce urine that has this hue. There is a simple test that we can conduct to determine if the King's urine contains this metabolite. We add a solvent and chemical known as the Ehrlich's reagent. If porphobilinogen is present, the solution will turn a red rose color."

Impressed by his investigation, Dr. Beauregard granted permission to Dr. Cox to have this test done on King George's fresh urine sample. The extraction of the urine by the organic solvent produced a colorless liquid. When the Ehrlich's reagent was added, the red color instantly appeared indicating a positive result. Dr. Cox rushed to report his finding to Dr. Beauregard. Satisfied that the King was suffering from the same disease as Dracula, the next logical question was how should George be treated? Dr. Cox noticed that the lesions on the King's skin looked worse when he was exposed to the sunlight. He told Dr. Beauregard that the King should avoid direct sunlight exposure unless it was absolutely necessary. When he was outdoors, he should have as much of his skin covered as possible.

"We can't expect the King to be a hermit inside his own castle," was Dr. Beauregard's response. "He has duties to the kingdom and his subjects."

"Then let me keep track of the times and days when he is

outside and what the weather conditions are on those specific days." Back then as today, London had periods of many days and even weeks without significant sunshine. "If his lesions improve during the rainy weeks corresponding to less sunlight exposure, this might corroborate my theory," Cox concluded. Dr. Beauregard saw no harm in this plan and agreed. The young doctor's time was not as valuable as his.

After one month of observation, Dr. Cox's theory proved to be correct. Skin lesions appeared on days when the King was exposed to sunlight, and resolved during long periods of overcast skies. His demeanor also appeared better on rainy days. When Dr. Beauregard, who took sole credit for this observation, told the King of the potential dangers to his health from the sun, the Royal Highness opted to reduce his outdoor exposure. When it was necessary, he wore ceremonial clothing that covered as much of his skin as possible.

The king was also instructed to drink as much fluid as possible. Dr. Cox reasoned that the porphobilinogen was a poison and that it should be flushed from his body as quickly and efficiently as possible. Drinking water that contained sugar also facilitated thirst and more frequent urination. While he didn't know why, the King's diet rich in carbohydrates also reduced the frequency and severity of his attacks. Fortunately, he did not crave for blood as Dracula had. All of these measures appeared to work. The King was more relaxed and exhibited far fewer symptoms than before and he was back to his happy self. As a result, the King fathered several more children during this time.

Ultimately, King George's personality and outlook changed from one of aggression to one of peace and calm. When the colonists begin to complain about their treatment by his cabinet, the King took a very different approach toward them rather than what actually occurred in history. The King decided to negotiate with the colonists rather than wage war. All but a few of the militant colonists, who wanted independence from Britain, were thrilled. Most of the colonists were simple farmers and merchants and did not want war with the mother country. The decision by the King to negotiate rather than fight dramatically changed history from that point forward.

Within 6 months, Benjamin Franklin, who was 71 at the time, sailed to England to become the first representative to the British Parliament. General George Washington, who was the hero of the Revolutionary War, was the head of the colonial army. But since there was no war, he did not become the first President of the United States and his name was not significant in the history of the country. Four years later, Thomas Jefferson replaced the aging Franklin in Parliament. By then, the 13 colonies were known as the "United States of New Britain." The name of the town of New Britain, Connecticut, which predated the formation of the USA, was changed to "America", Connecticut.

Eventually the United States of New Britain became a nation separate from Great Britain. The New Britainers elected their own prime minister instead of a president, and created their own parliament instead of a congress. The U.S. of N.B. remained a commonwealth of the United Kingdom, along with Canada, India, and South Africa. With an emphasis on maintaining relations with U.S. of N.B., England did not explore or colonize Australia. It became a separate country and continent unrelated to the British Commonwealth. It was first part of the Dutch East

Indies that occupied present day Indonesia since the 16th Century until their independence in 1945. It was later inhabited by the Japanese instead and was called "Australasia." As a commonwealth nation, the New Britainers entered World War I at its inception in 1914, instead of a few years later in 1917. This infusion of solders ended this war two years earlier. Not only did this save millions of lives, but the blame and reparations that Germany felt after the war were minimized accordingly. Rampant inflation did not occur, and as a result, Adolf Hitler did not rise to power, and there was no World War II. There was no need to develop rockets or nuclear weapons. The absence of German rocket scientists delayed the development of the US and Russian space programs for a half century. Nuclear power as an energy source was also delayed.

Even popular culture changed dramatically as the result of the singular decision made by King George to keep the peace. The two American pastimes of football and baseball became soccer and cricket. In Australasia, instead of rugby, Sumo wrestling became popular under the Japanese influence. Words such as "apartment" and "elevator" were replaced with the British words "flat" and "lift."

*

The suggestion that King George III suffered from acute porphyria was made in the 1960s by two psychiatrists Dr. Ida Macalpine and her son Richard Hunter, who examined medical records and other documents relating to the period when the King became ill in 1788. According to the records, the King experienced bizarre behavior, peripheral neuropathy, muscular weakness, vocal hoarseness, abdominal pain, and he excreted urine that was discolored. These investigators also corroborated their opinion by citing that current descendants of the King have evidence of porphyrias. In 2005, scientists found a high concentration of arsenic in the King's hair and they suggested that this metal disturbs heme synthesis thereby precipitating the porphyria attacks. The King's hair was provided by the Science Museum of London. The source of the arsenic was thought to be the medications his physicians were giving him. Recently, other scientists have reviewed the Macalpine and Hunter data and refuted their findings.

The Watson-Schwartz screening test for the detection of porphyrin disease is one of the older clinical laboratory tests in existence and was developed in 1941. The test is still used today. The Ehrlich reagent that is used in this test was first discovered in the 1880s to stain hemoglobin. Naturally, neither this reagent nor the lab test existed in the mid-1700s at the time of King George III's reign. Porphyrias, as a disease was not described until 1874 by Dr. Schultz. The term "porphyrin" comes from the Greek word "porphyrus," a reddish-purple color. Today, we have genetic and precise biochemical tests that can identify the specific cause of porphyria in any given patient.

Cursed

****

It was an arranged marriage to Prince Phillip of Denmark. Lady Catherine was 19 years old at the time and the Prince was 12 years older. It was important to her family that she wed the right man if their ancestral line was to continue in power. Her uncle was the King but he had no legitimate children. Upon the King's death a few years later, Lady Catherine's father inherited the throne. Because of religious differences, she was a Protestant and he was a Catholic, she and her older sister conspired to overthrow the new King. Fearful for his life, the King fled to France and in doing so, abdicated the throne. Lady Catherine's sister Elizabeth and her husband Harry became the new King and Queen. They too had trouble conceiving children. Because Lady Catherine was next in line, she and her new husband desperately wanted to have heirs in the event that she became the Queen.

As a member of the royal family, Lady Catherine led a life of privilege. Mrs. Sarah Paddington was her governess when Lady Catherine was a child. After her marriage to Prince Philip, Sarah became a Lady's Maid to Lady Catherine. Sarah was married to Robert, a senior footman in the household. She privately confided to her husband about Lady Catherine's health and wellbeing, even though it was strictly forbidden. They were both happy that Phillip was chosen as Lady Catherine's mate, even though the couple met just a few weeks before the marriage. Sarah could see that they grew to love and devote themselves to each other. When Lady Catherine became pregnant for the first time, there was hope and excitement in the manor.

"I am sure it is a boy," Sarah told Robert. "I have a feeling about these things."

Robert replied. "It's looking like the King and Queen might not be able to have children. If that is the case, this boy could become King someday."

But during the last trimester of the pregnancy, things were not going well for Lady Catherine. "I have seen a lot of pregnant women in my day" Sarah remarked to Robert. "My lady appears small for this stage of pregnancy."

"I wouldn't worry, she looks healthy to me," Robert said.

But she wasn't. Lady Catherine did not disclose to her doctors that the baby stopped kicking a few weeks earlier. Lady Catherine was young and didn't know that this was highly unusual. A few weeks later, she went into labor. The royal doctors and midwives were busy delivering her baby. Lady Catherine never experienced any kind of pain before, and she screamed out loudly. When the baby appeared, the doctors saw that it was a girl. Lady Catherine and Phillip had predetermined her name to be Victoria, named after Lady Catherine's great grandmother. But the girl was ashen in color and was still born. They concluded that she died several weeks earlier in the womb before her birth. Lady Catherine cried uncontrollably upon seeing her lifeless baby. There was a quiet ceremony and Victoria was buried in the Abbey. Lady Catherine could not bear to attend. For the next several weeks, she stayed in bed and refused to see anyone except her husband and Sarah.   "She is really sad," Sarah told Horace.   "She appears to be strong, having helped drive her father from the throne, but deep inside, she is still just a young girl."

"That's the good part," Horace remarked. "There will be plenty of time for her have other children."

Horace was correct. After a period of mourning, Lady Catherine became pregnant again and this time a healthy baby girl named Anne was delivered. A year later, another child was born who was named Mary. The nursery was filled with the joyous sounds of infants wanting to be fed, held, and changed. This was the happiest time of Lady Catherine's life. Unlike most royals, she took a lot of responsibility in caring for her daughters.

But tragedy was soon to strike the Royal family again. During a visit to Africa, Prince Phillip contracted a smallpox infection. Upon his return home, he inadvertently infected his daughters. There was no cure for variola infection then. The disease either runs its course or causes death. Prince Phillip survived his infection and lived for another 20 years. However, the death rate for children with smallpox was nearly 80%. Little Anne at age 2, and Mary aged 1 died within 6 days of each other. They were buried alongside Victoria in the Abbey. A month before their death, Lady Catherine had a miscarriage. This was followed by the delivery of a second stillborn child, this time a son. Some 10 months later, yet another miscarriage occurred, then 6 months later another, after that one more followed.

"There must be a curse on that family," Sarah told her husband. "Maybe she should see a mystic or a wizard."

Marlin was known throughout the countryside as an

herbalist. He was brought in and he met with the couple on a regular basis. He prepared private chants and incantations in an attempt to chase the curse away. He also prescribed special herbs and concoctions for them to eat and drink. The Royal doctors tried to dismiss the mystic as a quack, but the royal couple would not listen. Lady Catherine in particular was desperate to change her fortunes by whatever means possible. The herbalist appeared to be doing something right. During Lady Catherine's next pregnancy, she delivered a healthy baby boy, who they named Charles.

News spread around the kingdom that Marlin had lifted the curse that tormented Lady Catherine's family. Marlin was hailed as a miracle worker. His services were in demand for other members of the royal family both at home and abroad. He treated Princes, Earls, and Dukes in France, The Netherlands, and Germany. Much of what he accomplished may have been the "placebo effect." No real therapeutics, just belief by the patient that they were getting better.

Then one day, he was found dead in his home at the age of 35. The cause of death was never determined. There appeared to be no sign of an intrusion or any violence. Royal doctors suspected that he accidently poisoned himself with some of his own concoctions. Whatever the reason, it had a dramatic effect on Lady Catherine. A few months after Marlin's death, she gave birth to another daughter who only lived for a few hours. The next year, a son was born but he lived for only a few minutes. Over the next few years, Lady Catherine had several more miscarriages and more stillborn children.

Then the worst thing imaginable happened. Her only

surviving child Charles died at the age of 8. Lady Catherine went into hysterics and became paranoid. She fired all of the Royal doctors and Charles' caretakers. When Sarah tried to convince her to reconsider this decision, Lady Catherine accused her of talking behind her back and conspiracy. Catherine discharged her and Horace too.

Lady Catherine was alone and her health began to decline. Her weight doubled from her first pregnancy. She was only 29 years old. Due to her sedentary lifestyle, Lady Catherine started to get swelling and inflammation in her legs. They were very painful and inhibited her walking even further. Everyone remaining in Lady Catherine's household believed that the curse had returned with Marlin's passing and there was a gloom throughout the palace.

*

Thaddeus Collinson III was a young physician who studied at the Royal Medical Academy. He was one of the doctors who took over caring for Lady Catherine after she terminated the employment of her other doctors. Thaddeus did not believe in curses and witchcraft and he sought a medical reason for Lady Catherine's medical and obstetrical problems. In doing so, Dr. Collinson peppered Lady Catherine with many questions. She was very reluctant to disclose any information about herself, as she considered her health was a private matter. But Dr. Collinson was persistent and convinced her that he could help her get well. They had many conversations about a variety of subjects. Thaddeus had a soothing and calming bedside manner. Over time, Lady Catherine developed affection for the young doctor. Quietly and without fanfare, he provided important psychological help to the heir of the kingdom. Prince Philip saw a rapport between the doctor and patient that he didn't have as husband. When confronted, Lady Catherine reassured Philip that this was strictly a professional relationship.

Amit Savjani understood why Lady Catherine was having so many terminated pregnancies. He implanted an idea through his mind portal into Dr. Collinson's head so that he would ask the right questions of Lady Catherine and eventually learn why she had miscarriages and what to do about it.

During one of their weekly sessions, Lady Catherine said something to Dr. Collinson that particularly piqued his scientific interest.

"Do you bleed when you cut your finger?" she asked the doctor on this day.

"Of course, everybody bleeds. Why do you ask?" Dr. Collinson said.

Lady Catherine responded. "When I accidently cut myself last week, the bleeding stops almost immediately. This has happened before. There is never any blood flow. What do you think of that?"

"That is highly unusual. Normally you would think that this was a good thing, because nobody wants to lose blood. But in your case, maybe this is part of the root of your medical problems. Everything in medicine is about balance. You don't want to be too weak or too strong in anything. Let me do some research on this."

"I can't keep going on like this. Year after year, getting pregnant, only to lose my child." Lady Catherine was starting to cry. "My sister apparently can't have babies either. This could be the end of our family line. Please help me Doctor. I am begging you." The doctor said nothing more. He bowed his head to the Lady and left the room, determined to help her. He went to the Royal Library to read about blood clots. Dr. Collinson found the answer in a very unusual place.

Thaddeus was taught that Hippocrates, the father of medicine who lived in Greek times wrote that the blood of a wounded soldier congealed as it cooled. Aristotle also made an observation that when "fibers" are removed from a blood sample, clotting can be prevented. There wasn't a lot of work done on coagulation for many centuries until an English physician, Dr. Mercurialis, showed that blood clots can form in the blood vessels of humans. Thaddeus met with Mercurialis to discuss Lady Catherine's case.

Could this be what's wrong with my patient?

Thaddeus asked Mercurialis. "Could a blood clot in the vein of Lady Catherine's leg be the cause of her swelling?"

Mercurialis wasn't sure. "Even if this is the case, what can you do about her condition?"

Thaddeus shrugged his shoulders. *I have to come up with something to help the Lady.* He left Dr. Mercurialis' office with more questions than answers.

*

Edmund Stone was a scholar in nearby Cambridge. He came from a long line of farmers. But unlike his ancestors, he studied at Cambridge University and upon completion of his studies, he became a chaplain at a nearby abbey. When people in the village became sick, they sought out Edmund because they thought he could heal them through prayer. But Edmund thought he could also help them with therapeutics. *Doctors are beginning to use medicines derived from plants* he thought to himself. Edmund knew from ancient cultures that chewing the bitter bark of the cinchona tree relieved fevers due to malaria. One day when he was suffering from a mild headache, he took a walk into the woods hoping that fresh air would be therapeutic. Edmund came to a white willow tree and unexplainably and without a specific purpose, he took a piece of the bark and started chewing. He quickly noticed that it was very bitter tasting, just like cinchona tree bark. Within a few minutes, his headache went away. *Was this a coincidence, or could there be some chemical in the bark of this tree that relieves pain?*

Edmund collected several large pieces of bark from this tree and took it back to his home. After drying the bark in the sun, he took a hammer and pounded the material into a fine white powder. He then placed small amounts of the material into bottles and began using it on his patients who complained of headaches. He justified his actions by arguing to himself that nobody had ever died from chewing the bark of a tree. Sometimes there was some stomach irritation, but his patients said it was better than the splitting headache they suffered. Edmund sent a letter to the Royal Academy of London documenting these observations.

Thaddeus Collinson learned about this work and went to see Edmund Stone. "Lady Catherine is my patient," he told Edmund. "You had indicated in your writing that some of your patients complain of bruises when they take your medication and that they didn't bruise so easily before. Do you think willow bark could help her?"

"Does she suffer from headaches?" He asked.

"No, but she has the opposite problem of bruising. I

believe her blood forms too many clots and I want to see if something can be done about her problem," Thaddeus said. There was silence for a few minutes while both men contemplated Lady's Catherine's medical problem. In retrospect, Thaddeus was one of the first doctors to think that bruising and clotting were the opposite end of the same physiologic process of coagulation.

"Hmm, let's try an experiment." Thaddeus then took his pants off. Edmund had a puzzled look. He was not sure what this young doctor was doing. "Hit me with your fist on my left thigh," he told Edmund.

"What? I don't want to hit you," he said.

"Edmund, this is a controlled experiment. Hit me here," pointing to his leg. "But not real hard."

Reluctantly, Edmund struck the doctor. "Again" Dr. Collinson commanded. After five punches, he instructed Edmund to stop. Dr. Collinson put his pants back on and explained to the rector what they were doing. "We are going to repeat this tomorrow but on my other leg. I want you to prepare some willow bark for me to consume." Edmund understood the experiment they were conducting but wasn't sure how this was going to help Lady Catherine.

The next day, they met again. Dr. Collinson removed his pants and showed Edmund that the punches he gave to the doctor did not result in any bruising or marks. "Give me some of your powder now." Dr. Collinson swallowed a solution of the powder and they waited 30 minutes. "Ok, now, hit me again, but this time on my right thigh." He complied by striking the young doctor another five times with approximately the same force. They waited another 30 minutes. The skin was forming a dark bruise where he was struck.

"Does it hurt," inquired Edmund.

"No, I feel no different on this side as the other side that doesn't have a bruise." That part didn't surprise Edmund. The powder was blocking his pain. He then asked, "What does all this mean?"

"By hitting me, you have injured my muscle. Like an open wound, this attracts blood to the area to form a clot as part of the normal healing process. The willow bark is temporarily inhibiting my body's ability to clot. What you see is blood forming just under the skin. I am going to try this medicine on Lady Catherine in hopes of preventing some of her clotting problems."

"Do you think that is a good idea? We don't want to form bruises on the poor woman. She has suffered a lot already," Edmund said.

"If my theory is correct, she won't bruise because she doesn't bleed now. I am hoping that this reduces the ability to clot to the point where she is more like a normal person." Edmund gave Dr. Collinson a month's supply of extract, thanking his colleague as he left the abbey. Dr. Collinson met with Lady Catherine and gave her the medication on a daily basis. He then carefully monitored her for any side effects. There were none, although Thaddeus didn't experiment on her by striking the Lady in the manner that Edmund had done to him.

Remarkably, Lady Catherine stated after taking this medication for a week, she felt better and more energetic than ever before. Her leg swelling gradually went away. She did have more color in her face and extremities. Dr. Collinson theorized that her blood was flowing more easily. She started walking more regularly and gradually began losing weight.

"This is a miracle cure, Doctor. Thank you so much," she said to Thaddeus.

"We need to keep a close watch but I am hopeful things are going to turnaround for you," he remarked.

Catherine took the willow extract each day for the rest of her life. Within a few months, she became pregnant again. This time, she delivered a healthy baby boy, that she and Prince Philip named Henry. A few years later, her sister the Queen died. Although the King remarried and had a son, he was not the Queen's child, therefore the boy was not the heir to the throne. Upon the death of the King, Lady Catherine became the new Queen. Queen Catherine went on to have several more children. She was one of the most popular Queens in British history. She died of natural causes at the age of 75 after a reign of 38 years. Upon her death, the throne passed to her son Henry. Both he and the next King, Henry II, treated the American colonists fairly and provided them representation in Parliament. The hostilities that ignited the Revolutionary War in history did not occur under the Stuart family leadership.

*

This is an alternate reality story of Queen Anne who had 17 known pregnancies with the majority of them resulting in miscarriages and still born births. Three of her children lived beyond 1 year, but her two daughters died of a smallpox infection. One son, Prince William, Duke of Glouchester, died at the age of 11 years. He would have been the King of England. The cause of death is disputed but like his sisters, he could have died of a smallpox infection. This infection is caused by the variola virus. Back in the 17th century, there was no vaccination or cure, so the death rate was extremely high, especially among children. With the development of an effective vaccine, smallpox disease has largely been eradicated throughout the world.

Queen Anne died of a stroke at the age of 49 years. The failure of Anne and her husband Prince George of Denmark to produce an adult heir led to the end of the House of Stuart as monarchs of England. George I of Hanover became the next King. His grandson, King George III was responsible for the Revolutionary War against America, detailed in my previous story, "Purple Reign." This story would not have happened at all if Anne had heirs.

Some scientists and medical historians today believe that Anne suffered from "antiphospholipid antibody syndrome." First described in the 1980s by Dr. Graham Hughes of St. Thomas' Hospital in London, this syndrome is an autoimmune disease that is associated with episodes of arterial and venous clots and one or more unexplained deaths of a morphologically normal fetus or unexplained consecutive spontaneous abortions. Blood clots within the placenta of women with this disease cause their fetus to be starved of blood and oxygen. The diagnosis is also dependent on finding abnormal autoimmune antibodies in the blood such as anti-cardiolipin, anti-beta-2-glycoprotein, and the lupus anticoagulant antibody. These tests are regularly performed on patients suspected of phospholipid syndrome. These patients are treated with blood thinners such as aspirin and low molecular weight heparin. When pregnant, women with phospholipid syndrome do not suffer from the miscarriages and still born pregnancies such as Princess Anne did.

The analgesic effect of white willow tree bark extract is due to salicin, a compound closely related to salicylic acid, the active ingredient in today's aspirin. Its use to treat pain and inflammation was discovered by Edward Stone of England. In actual history, Stone's discovery did not occur for another 50 years after Anne's death. It would be another 100 years (in the 1890s) before the Bayer Company produced aspirin as a commercial analgesic drug. The effect of aspirin on blood clotting and as an inhibitor of platelet function was not known until the 1970s. Today, aspirin is used to prevent heart disease.

Libertadore del Liberador!

****

Simón Bolívar was born in 1783 in Caracas, a region known as the "Captaincy General of Venezuela." The region was under the rule of the Spanish empire. He came from a wealthy family. From his mother's side, they owned numerous mines harvesting gold, silver, but especially copper. His father died when Simón was two years old, and his mother passed away just before he turned 9. Thereafter, he was largely raised by a black slave woman named Hipólita. He had numerous instructors and mentors, including Don Simón, who taught the boy about liberty, freedom, human rights and human decency. At the age of 14, Simón entered *Milicias de Aragua*, a military academy. There he learned about battle field tactics, armaments, and discipline. Both his intellectual and military training would serve him well in the coming years.

*

As a clinical laboratory director, Amit Savjani and his staff underwent annual tests for the presence of tuberculosis or TB. The test, also known as the Mantoux technique, involves the intradermal injection of tuberculin, a protein derived from *Mycobacterium tuberculosis*, the bacterial agent responsible for some of the cases of tuberculosis. Within 48 to 72 hours, an individual infected with TB will produce a bump or a raised hardened area on the skin where the injection took place. Tuberculosis is transmitted from human to human through inhalation of airborne droplets. Technologists within the clinical laboratory have direct exposure to patients because many of them are responsible for collecting patient's blood. Hospitalized patients are susceptible to a TB infection due to their weakened immune system. The microbiology laboratory identifies a TB infection from the demonstration of bacillus in a sputum specimen. A suspected infected patient coughs up a mucus material from the upper respiratory track into a cup. The sample is examined under the microscope for the presence of acid-fast bacillus. Tuberculosis is a rod-shaped bacterium that remains stained after it is washed with acid. Tuberculosis can also be detected by growing the bacteria in an appropriate culture media, or through the identification of specific DNA sequences belonging to the *Mycobacterium*.

"In the 1900s, tuberculosis infection was among the leading cause of death in America," Amit was explaining to a group of high school students visiting the clinical laboratory. "Today, there are about 4 cases per 100,000 individuals in the U.S. Most of them are from people who come from other countries where the incidence of TB is still high."

*

Shortly after completing military school, Simón traveled to Spain for additional education. While in Spain, he met and courted Maria Teresa Rodriguez. After two years, they were married in 1802. Unfortunately, Maria contracted yellow fever and died just 8 months later. Simón was devastated and vowed to never marry again. He was true to his word, but this didn't stop him from having numerous mistresses.

There were other events occurring around him that would change Simón's destiny. Europe was in the middle of their "Enlighten Period." Beginning in the late 17th century, this was an era when the philosophers and political leaders began to challenge the traditional authority of autonomic rule by the various European monarchs. By the time Simón arrived in 1799, both France and America had revolted against their Kings to form new leadership. Simón believed that his country should also break away from Spanish rule and he returned to his home country in 1807 to initiate independence. Over the next dozen years or so, Simón was involved in numerous battles against the Spaniards for control over Venezuela and neighboring lands. He became known as "El Libertado" the Liberator. In 1819, Simón and his troops won the Battle of Boyacá, a key battle against the Spanish royalists in New Granada, the present day Columbia. He declared a new state that was named "Grand Columbia" and he became their President. There would be many other battles, including a decisive victory for the revolutionaries at the Battle of Carabobo in 1821. Soon thereafter, Grand Columbia would include the northern part of South American and parts of Latin America, and it would include the present-day countries of Columbia, Venezuela, Ecuador, Panama, and parts of Peru, Guyana, and Brazil.

Over the ensuing years, Simón found it difficult to control the various factions across Gran Columbia. There were regional revolts and uprisings by dissidents that threatened the sovereignty of this new country. It didn't help that he proposed a new constitution in 1828 that included a provision that the President would hold office for life and that he would be able to name his own successor. Then there were several events that would shape his attitude towards his rule and motivation to keep Gran Columbia viable. A key figure in these events was his girlfriend and lover, Manuela Sáenz, whose marriage was arranged to a man twice her age. Manuela was a beautiful woman with large dark eyes, fair skin, and soft facial features. One day, the leader was headed out to a party.

*

"Why can't I come?" Manuela pleaded with Simón.

"We are not married, and it is not appropriate for me to bring my mistress," the President said.

"Then marry me. I will bear you many children."

"Manuela, we've been over this before. I cannot break my vow to Maria Theresa."

"But she has been dead for over 25 years! When will you get over her?"

"Quiet woman! I will hear no more. We'll discuss this when I get back." With that, he dressed in his uniform and left to attend the party.

A few hours later, one of the servants came into Manuela's bedroom with a note. It read, "There will be an attempt on the President's life tonight while he is at the party. You must help him now." Manuela was horrified to read this note. She had to act fast. She called her servants to bring her a captain's uniform. Then they tied her hair up into a bun and hid it behind a cap. She left the President's mansion heading toward the party trying to impersonate a male officer, but she was turned away at the door by a guard.

"Sir, where is your invitation?" the guard demanded.

"I left it back in the barracks," she said in a deep disguised voice. "Lieutenant, let me pass immediately."

"Sorry sir, I have strict orders not to permit anyone entry without the proper papers. Please go back and retrieve your documents."

Manuela refused to give up and had to come up with another plan. She went back to the palace and told her servants to get some old clothes. She returned to the party, but this time, she stood outside of the window and started shouting.

"President Bolívar! President Bolívar! I am your woman. You cannot hide me anymore. You must come out now. I will not leave!" She was holding an empty bottle of wine she found on the grounds. Guards came rushing to the woman to restrain her. Simón looked out the window and realized that it was Manuela who was causing the commotion. The President rushed outside.

"Guards, I will take care of this woman. Release her to my custody."

Simón escorted Manuela to their carriage and they headed home. He was outraged. "What are you doing? I told you, we will discuss our situation later. How could you embarrass me in front of all these people?"

Manuela pulled out the note she had received and gave it to Simón to read. Then she spoke in a calm voice. "I didn't know what to do. I tried to get in dressed as an officer but was turned away. I was desperate to help you."

"Why didn't you call my officers for help?" Simón was calmer now but visibly concerned.

"I didn't know who to trust. Maybe they are in on it?" Manuela pleaded.

About 15 minutes later, armed assassins overtook the guards at the door and stormed into the party where they demanded to see the President. But he was back in the heavily guarded Presidential Palace. Manuela had saved Simón's life.

*

Six weeks later, there was another attempt on the President's life. This time, his enemies entered the Palace while the couple was asleep. Manuela woke up to noises and immediately alerted Simón. "We have intruders. You must leave immediately."

"No, this time I will fight." Simón reached for his weapon under the bed.

"This is not a time for heroics. We don't know how many there are. Quickly, escape out that window, now!"

"I am the General of the Army. This is not a dignified action," he said sternly and proudly.

"Simón, get out now. They're coming!" The President succumbed to her reasoning and he quickly jumped out the window and ran towards a river. The assassins broke into the bedroom only to find Manuela alone in the bed. They forced her out of bed. She was only dressed in a short nightgown. She allowed the top of her gown slip off her right shoulder purposely exposing her breast. She was hoping that this action might take their mind off her husband. It didn't work. One of the intruders grabbed her from behind and put a knife to Manuela's throat. "If you don't tell me where the President is, I am going to kill you right now."

Manuela was terrified and started to shake uncontrollably. *I have to be strong. Think of something to say.* As Manuela paused to gather her thoughts, the intruder started digging the blade of his sharp knife into her skin and she started to bleed. After a few more agonizing seconds, she spoke. "He is probably with that whore." She said in a 'matter of fact' tone. "I wouldn't mind if you found him and killed him. I'd tell you where he is if I knew."

"I think she's telling the truth. She doesn't know where he is," the other intruder said. "I've heard about Bolívar's exploits. She doesn't know. Let her go. We'll get him another night."

The assassin lowered his knife from Manuela's throat. They held her captive while they searched the President's palace for his whereabouts. A few hours later, security guards entered the palace and rescued Manuela from her captives.

Bolívar was hiding under a bridge in the cold waters of the river for 3 hours, watching. When he knew it was safe, he returned and found that Manuela was unharmed. Simón was proud of the risks she had taken at his behalf. He was horrified to see blood coming from Manuela's throat, but it was only a superficial wound. *Someone is going to pay for this*, he thought.

Later, Simón told friends and colleagues that Manuela was the "Libertadore del Libertador", the Liberator of the Liberator. From that moment on, Simón never doubted what his mistress said or wanted to do again. He owed his life to her twice. She became revered among the citizens of Gran Columbia and their romance blossomed to new heights. But it was short lived.

Soon after the assassination attempts, Simón became ill. Over the ensuing two years, he lost a lot of weight. This sapped him of his will and resolves to continue to hold Gran Columbia together against his detractors. This time, Manuela was powerless to help her common-law husband. Simón's doctors treated him with some drugs containing arsenic without success. In January 1830, Simón Bolívar announced his resignation from the Presidency. In his last address to his country, he made this tearful goodbye.

"Fearing that I may be regarded as an obstacle to establishing the Republic on the true base of its happiness, I personally have cast myself down from the supreme position of leadership to which your generosity had elevated me."

Simón Bolívar's official resignation took place three months later. He and Manuela made plans to exile in Europe. But the former ruler died 8 months later of tuberculosis, too sick to leave his beloved country. He was only 47 years old. Without their charismatic leader, Gran Colombia gradually broke up into the separate countries that it is today. This greatly reduced the influence that these countries would have on world's politics and foreign affairs. Manuela lived for another 26 years after Bolívar's death. The new President of Gran Colombia, possibly fearful of her popularity, exiled Manuela to Jamaica. She later found her way to Peru where she survived on selling tobacco and translating letters written by North American whaler hunters. When her estranged husband was murdered, Manuel was denied his inheritance. She died in 1856 of diphtheria and was buried in a communal mass grave.

*

The history of Simón Bolívar came to light recently

through the efforts of Hugo Chávez, the President of Venezuela from 1999 until his death in 2013. Chávez established a Commission to determine if Bolívar was murdered instead of dying from a tuberculosis infection. In 2010, Dr. Paul Auwaerter, Professor of Medicine and Infectious Diseases at Johns Hopkins examined Bolívar's medical history and symptoms around the time of the President's death, and published a report suggesting that his death could have been due to either arsenic exposure or exposure paracoccidioidomycosis, a fungal infection commonly found in South America. The possibility of arsenic poisoning led to the speculation that he was slowly killed by his enemies. Anxious to learn the truth, Chávez ordered the exhumation of Bolívar's remains to see if toxic concentrations of arsenic were present. While the arsenic levels were higher than expected, the experts could not conclude that this toxic heavy metal was the cause of Bolívar's death.

Amit Savjani, being both a student of history and a toxicology expert took special interest in the recent news surrounding Bolívar. Like many Americans, he knew little about the origins of these South American countries. He wondered why such a young and vibrant leader would give up on his country so early in his life. *Could it have been his chronic illness?* Amit thought. *How the history of the region and the rest of the world would have been different had Bolívar survived his infection with tuberculosis and exposure to arsenic?* Amit went into his mind portal in an attempt to find these answers. He contacted Manuela in late 1828 and implanted an idea that both she and Bolívar's diet should regularly be supplemented with garlic, a member of the onion family that has been used as a spice since ancient Egypt. Amit told Manuela through his portal that garlic contains antibacterial properties that can boost the body's innate immune system. It was Amit's plan that Simón would not develop tuberculosis following his exposure to the bacteria. Amit also instructed Manuela to have him eat plenty of bananas, also a widely abundant crop in Gran Columbia. Regarding his arsenic exposure, Amit convinced Manuela to take better control of the Palace's water supply. She directed their cooks to only use pure water from the mountain streams. She ordered the supply of water to be carefully guarded and monitored. The staff was confused as to why this was necessary, but they could not countermand the woman of the household. Not knowing that this was how Simón was exposed, Amit wanted to discourage or eliminate any attempts of poisoning with contaminated drinking and cooking water. Bolivár's avoidance of TB obviated the exposure of arsenic medications prescribed by his doctors.

All of these actions had a dramatic effect on Bolivár's health. Instead of being fatigued or weak, the President was healthy, vibrant, and focused. He was now re-committed to his country's future. He doubled and tripled his appearances across the country to speak to the population about the potential power of Gran Columbia. His messages reached to all parts of his nation. Having lived and studied in Europe as a teenager, he had international vision that few of his adversaries possessed.

"In the coming years and decades, there will be a shuffling of power towards countries in the "New World." The United States is greatly expanding their borders to beyond the thirteen colonies. Brazil is starting their second decade of independence. We need to stay united so that we can join our friends as a world power. We have many untapped natural resources in our countries that cannot be matched in the "Old World." We have land for great population expansion. Our weather is ideal for agricultural growth which will fuel our economy. With our vast forests, we will build railroads to unite our vast country, and ships to export our products back to Spain and Portugal. If we can maintain a fair democratic government that rewards innovation and ambition, the brightest minds and the best people will come to live with us. We will only weaken if we fight among ourselves in order to form small insignificant nations. We have to think in much larger global terms. I vow to lead us into unprecedented prosperity. Let us put aside our petty differences to achieve this goal. Who is with me on this mission?"

Simón Bolívar was successful in uniting the factions within Gran Columbia. Under his influence, his country Columbia also annexed present day Paraguay, Suriname, and Guiana. Now, North American consists of three countries and South American consists of four major countries, Brazil, Argentina, Chile, and Gran Columbia. These countries rival the U.S. and Canada today as economic powers in the west.

Simón really loved Manuela and might have married her if he had been well. Since he didn't contract TB, he went against his own vow and they married. A healthy Bolívar married Manuela and they had 3 children. The oldest one entered Columbian politics but was never elected to its highest office. Simón stepped down from the Presidency in 1840 and lived to age 84. His remains were interred at the Pantheon. When Manuela died a few years later, her remains was put beside her husband.

*

There are several anti-tuberculosis medications today that can treat TB infections. In the early 19th century, there were no effective treatments available and most infected individuals died within a few years. TB is not as contagious as other bacteria and virus, and requires repeated or prolonged exposures for individuals with weakened immune systems. Foods that can boost immunity and can be helpful include garlic that is rich in sulfuric acid, allicin, and ajoene, which can harm Myobacteria, and inhibit bacterial growth. Other anti-inflammatory foods include bananas, oranges, mint, walnuts, green tea, and black pepper.

Arsenic poisoning is associated with headaches, weakness, stomach complaints and behavioral apathy, symptoms that Bolívar had years before his death. Long-term exposure to arsenic can also cause a darkening of the skin, which was noted in Bolívar's complexion. There were reports of facial flushing which could be the result of treatment with arsenic tonics. The toxicology analysis of his exhumed bones and teeth produced equivocal results with no firm conclusion as whether or not arsenic was the cause of his death. To date, there is also no conclusion that the leader suffered from a fungal infection. The fact that neither Manuela nor Simón's doctors caught TB led Dr. Auwaerter to favor the non-contagious paracoccioidomyocosis infection.

Many successful countries can examine their history to identify a leader who had vision of the future and were able to transcend their country during a crisis. In the U.S., Abraham Lincoln was one of those leaders. In England during World War II it was Winston Churchill. In India, it was Mahatma Gandhi. In the northern countries of South America, it was Simón Bolívar. Today, the countries of Bolivia and the Bolivian Republic of Venezuela, and their monetary currency, the Bolivian boliviano and the Venezuelan bolívar, were named after their visionary leader. There are busts, monuments and statutes commemorating him in cities around the world, including one at the entrance to New York City's

Central Park.

Manuela Sánez finally received accolades for her role in twice saving Simón Bolívar's life. In 2006, an opera was composed based on her life. In 2010, she was symbolically reburied in the Pantheon alongside Bolívar. As she was a buried in a mass grave, none of her remains could be located.

Behind Every Man...

****

George Papanicolaou fits the stereotype of a hard working dedicated scientist. He was born near the turn of the 20th Century and grew up in a small fishing village along the coast of Athens. His father was a fisherman who worked almost every day of his adult life. George was the youngest of three brothers. The other two boys went into the fishing business with their father. George decided very early in life that he didn't want to follow in his father's footsteps. He had an aptitude for science and studied medicine at the University of Athens. He went on to graduate from the University of Munich earning a Ph.D. degree in Zoology in 2010. George wanted to do research in Athens but there was no opportunity to do so.

A few years earlier, George attended to the medical needs of Mary Mavroyeni, who was 16 years old. Mary was the daughter of a colonel in the Greek Army. Four years later on a ferry, George met Mary whose family was returning from a summer vacation. George was infatuated with Mary, now 20. They dated and within a few months, they were married.

In 1912, George was called into military service during the Balkan War. Afterwards, he and Mary decided to relocate to America. The landed in New York with just over $250 to their name. They both worked odd jobs for a few years until George met Dr. Thomas Morgan of Columbia University. Dr. Morgan had just published a book which contained where he cited some of George's doctoral research. With this connection, George received an offer to join the Department of Anatomy at Cornell Medical College and Pathology at New York Hospital in 1914. Two months later, Mary joined George's lab as a technical assistant.

George's main research interest at Cornell was documenting the physiological changes that occur during a woman's menstrual cycle which was not well known at the time. He did much of his initial work on female guinea pigs, thinking that was easier to study than humans. *I have to know what happens in a controlled animal model before I can work on humans,* he said to himself.

George was especially interested in characterizing cells that are released into vaginal fluid over time. One day, George calmly told Mary that he needed to hire one of his former female students, Loretta, to work for them in the lab. He needed someone who would allow him to examine her cervix on a daily basis for morphologic changes and swab her vaginal fluid to examine it for its cellular content.

Mary exploded at the idea. "No way am I going to let YOU do THIS to HER!"

"You're being silly. I have no romantic interest in this girl." In reality, he was attracted to Loretta who was very attractive, but didn't want to admit it to his wife. Mary suspected as much.

George continued, "Loretta agreed and I have already done a preliminary pelvic exam on her. She's a perfect research subject."

"What? You did this without telling me?" was Mary's reply.

"You're over-reacting. Can we discuss this like scientists?" George asked.

"Absolutely not. There is nothing to discuss," Mary stated.

"You don't trust me do you?" George asked.

"I trust you but I don't trust HER!" Mary shouted in an even louder voice.

"Well then what should we do?" He was beginning to feel attacked by his wife's accusations.

"I will be your subject. You can examine me and swab my vagina any time you need it. I will not complain. But I will not allow THAT woman to be a part of our lab."

For the next 20 years, Mary's vagina was swabbed and examined on a daily basis. True to her word, she never resisted. Mary's cellular flora was the most documented in history. Over time, other healthy women were also used as research subjects, but George made sure to have female assistants performing the pelvic exam for him. George spent countless hours with his eyes focused in a microscope. He carefully documented the cells that he saw in his various subjects. He took pictures of these cells and cataloged them into a database. Over time, he had cataloged and hand sketched every type of cell that he ever encountered in these fluids. Back then, it was difficult to obtain photographs of microscopic images. Mostly they were endothelial cells that line the vaginal tract but occasionally he would see yeast, bacteria, and spermatozoa.

Mary suggested to George now that healthy women had been characterized, it was time to examine the swabs of women with various gynecological diseases including ectopic pregnancy, endometriosis, pre-eclampsia, bladder and cervical cancer. When George examined the swab of a woman with terminal cervical cancer, the cancerous cells stood out. For the next several months, they concentrated on women with various stages of the disease. Although the number of cells seen in these fluids varied, there seemed to be a correlation between the number of cells present and the degree of cancer severity. George thought that testing vaginal fluid could be a "screening test" for cervical cancer and he presented his theories at a cancer meeting. After his lecture, researchers and clinicians attending the meeting totally discounted his theory. "Cancerous cells resemble many other cells seen in vaginal swabs" was a comment made by the gynecological "experts" of the day. "You have more of a chance of finding a needle in a haystack than looking for cancerous cells in body fluids" retorted one of the physicians.

George left the meeting disappointed his colleagues rejected his ideas. He questioned his own logic. Amit Savjani learned of this doubt and intervened. Through his mind portal, he convinced George that his colleagues were wrong and that he needed to convince them that he was on to something important. Amit informed George that his next step was to see if he could find cancerous cells before there was clinical evidence of cancer. Since the incidence of cervical cancer is under 10 in 100,000, such a study would require testing of thousands of women just to find one case. Without funding, George recruited and obtained a vaginal swab on a few thousand apparently healthy women in hopes of identifying early cervical cancer cells. George was running out of research money to continue the study. He was ready to quit but

Mary suggested that they use some of their own personal funds to continue. George was very reluctant but Mary was sure they were right. So they continued their work. Finally, one swab revealed the presence of cancerous cells on a subject, Mrs. Henrietta Kane, who appeared to be in perfect health. But because she had cells that looked like cancer, the woman underwent a pelvic exam. When the result was negative indicating she did not have cervical cancer, she and her doctor were instructed to report any future gynecological abnormality including pelvic pain, bloody or unusual vaginal discharge, back pain, urine incontinence, or pain after intercourse. It took a few years of follow up, but Mrs. Kane eventually developed cervical cancer. Due to the vigilance of her doctor, she had surgery before her cancer spread to her other organs. Mrs. Kane remained disease free for the rest of her life. This was the first person whose life was saved by George and Mary.

With this preliminary case, Dr. Papanicolaou received the additional funding needed to conduct a larger clinical trial on examining vaginal fluid. When he was able to duplicate Mrs. Kennedy's results, the trial provided the medical evidence needed to prove the value of the test. Within a few short years, the test became standard of practice worldwide, and the test was named after the inventors. Their test, if it had been available, could have played an important role in a South American country...

*

She was a chorus girl from a small town in a Central American country who ran away from home to seek the spotlight. Eva was very pretty and outgoing. The women around her envied her looks, personality, and figure. The men she encountered loved her and wanted to be around her. She had causal relationships with some of them, but Eva was not interested in them for the long term. She wanted someone important. Someone famous. Someone who would take care of her for the rest of her life. Within a few years, Eva found that person. He was Juan Perón, the Labor Minister of the ruling party. Eva was performing in a musical Juan was in the audience. She caught his eye. She looked at him throughout the performance. Juan was attracted to this young girl. After the performance, one of the Labor Minister's aides came to the chorus girl's dressing room and left her a note. Juan asked Eva come to his villa that night after the performance and had a car waiting for her. Juan was 24 years older. His first wife died of uterine cancer, and he was lonely. Starting from that night, Eva became his constant companion. They married a few months later.

The next year, Juan was nominated by his party to be his country's next president. Eva campaigned hard for her husband. She was with Juan on all of his campaign stops throughout the country. Her pretty face adorned the headlines of all of the papers. She did radio ads touting Juan's qualifications. When Juan won the election in a landslide, Eva at 25, became the country's youngest first lady in 1952. During the course of President Perón's tenure, Eva proved more than capable for this public duty. She helped establish several charities for unwed mothers. She created a foundation to help the poor and homeless. Eva accompanied her husband when he visited world leaders. When she visited the U.S., Eva told the audience that she was inspired by Eleanor Roosevelt.

President Perón's first six-year term of office was a success. His approval rating was among the highest the country had ever seen. Many political analysts credited the role that Eva played in her husband's popularity. Because the current vice president had a low approval rating, the incumbent party begged Eva to run as the next vice president, alongside her husband. She relished the idea and accepted the challenge. *My charitable efforts can really take flight if I win*, she thought to herself.

Unfortunately, the rigors of the Perón's campaign took a toll on Eva's health. She started having back pain, lost weight, was frequently fatigued, and she had an unusual discharge from her vagina. She fainted on several occasions during her public appearances. At the advice of her family doctor, she and her medical team made a secret visit to Houston Texas in the summer of 1958 to visit a cancer specialist. She underwent a thorough medical examination. A vaginal swab specimen was sent to Dr. George Papanicolaou' lab in New York for analysis. His recently developed "Pap" test was receiving rave reviews from the medical and oncology community. Eva's personal physician wanted her to be tested by the world's expert. George personally performed the test and found cancerous cells in Eva's cervical sample. President Perón flew to Houston, and was present when The First Lady underwent a hysterectomy. Eva's cancer was diagnosed early by Dr. Papanicolaou test, and her surgery was successful in removing her cancer.

Eva returned to her country after a few weeks of convalescence. She resumed her election campaign. With renewed enthusiasm for seeking office, Eva and Juan easily won the election. They were the first President and Vice President in the world to be husband and wife. The pair ran a very productive administration.

Towards the end of their term together, President Perón suffered a severe headache in 1963, and died of a cerebral hemorrhage. Eva was immediately sworn in as her country's new

President, the country's first woman to hold that office. The new President Perón continued the work of her husband's administration. She worked tirelessly on equal rights for women and basic human rights in her country and abroad. Her administration built schools, hospitals, universities, and affordable housing. The literacy rate in her country skyrocketed. Within a few years, new industries began that improved the quality of life for her countrymen. Eva Perón served her country until retiring in 1970. She became a role model for other women entering government service.

*

The next breakthrough in cervical cancer occurred in the 1976 when Harald zur Hausen, a German microbiologist, discovered that cervical cancer can be caused by an infection of the human papilloma virus or HPV. Dr. Zur Hausen showed that certain aggressive HPV strains could transform normal cells into cancerous ones. When this discovery was reported, George and Mary Papanicolaou began work on growing the virus in the lab. This was the customary practice for other viruses and bacteria, but George and Mary found out that it was very difficult to culture HPV in the lab. In the early 1990s, research groups developed a molecular technique to identify the virus. George died before DNA-based tests for HPV became widely used. But Mary and some of George's students continued the work he had started.

One day, Mary felt compelled to contact Eva Perón to explain that a virus might have been responsible for her cancer. Mary asked Eva for permission to examine some of the specimens obtained from her surgery that had been kept frozen for some 25 years. When her testing was complete, Maria told the former

President that her sample contained DNA that matched the HPV-16 strain. When Eva inquired as to how the virus was transmitted, Mary told her that it was through sexual intercourse. Eva then revealed that Juan's first wife had died of a gynecological cancer. It made sense that Eva could have contracted the virus from her husband.

Both Mary and Eva died of natural causes within a few months of each other in 2003. Both women had lived full lives and greatly contributed to their society. Mary had supported George in the medical world, and Eva supported Juan in the political world of Central America. For all their work, the Pap test, was named after and continues to honor both Mary and George. Eva Perón remains today as the most popular female political figure of all time.

*

Cervical cancer spreads slowly in a woman's body but if untreated, is fatal and was the leading cause of death among women in the U.S. The Pap test was developed by George and Mary Papanicolaou in the 1940s, and it has been widely used as a screening test for cervical cancer, even before the connection was made that an HPV infection is the causative agent in the vast majority of cases. The implementation of this early marker of cancer caused a dramatic decline in the death rate of women with cervical cancer.

Eva Peron was the second wife of Argentine President Juan Peron. "Evita" as she was known, was immensely popular in her country, and together with Juan, was responsible for moving their country into the modern era. In the real history, however, Evita had advanced cervical cancer and was too sick to run for the vice presidency in 1952. She never had a Pap test conducted on her. Evita underwent a secret radical hysterectomy in New York but it was too late as the cancer had already metastasized to her brain and she died shortly after. Under orders from Juan, Evita's doctors never told her she had cancer, only that she was undergoing an appendectomy. This story suggests how the fate of Argentina might have been changed had Dr. Papanicolaou's Pap test been used when the disease was in its early stages. Most historians believe that had Evita survived her cancer, she would have had a profound effect on the politics of Argentina. Shortly after Evita's death, there was a military and civil coup that overthrew Peron's regime. Juan spent the next 18 years in exile. Considering Evita's popularity, this most likely would not have been the outcome had Evita lived and led her country, as described in my story.

The story regarding the contributions of Dr. zur Hausen is accurate. For his discovery of the causative relationship between human papilloma virus and cervical cancer, Dr. zur Hausen won the Nobel Prize in Medicine or Physiology in 2008. Like George and Juan, Dr. zur Hausen worked very closely with his wife Ethel de Villiers. The discovery that HPV causes cervical cancer led others to create and commercialize a vaccine against human papilloma virus subtypes 16 and 18 in 2006. Today, the American Academy of Family Physicians recommends immunization against HPV for boys and girls aged 11 and 12 years, which is before most of these children have had their first sexual encounters. The vaccine is also more effective in this age group than for older individuals. The Academy also recommends that children who were not vaccinated at this early age receive the vaccine up to age 21 in males and 26 in females.

Pap smears had another important role in modern laboratory medicine in the U.S. During the late 1980s, several women died of cervical cancer because their pap smears were reviewed incorrectly. Some labs were accused of overworking their technologists by asking them to review too many slides per day. This led the U.S. Congress to pass the Clinical

The Mind Portal

Laboratory Improvement Amendments of 1988. These regulations set minimal standards necessary for the performance of all clinical laboratory tests, not just Pap smears. To minimize Pap smear reporting errors, CLIA 88 also established a maximum of 100 smears that a single technologist can review each day.

There is debate today regarding whether or not the screening test for HPV can be used as an early indicator for cervical cancer. Currently both the HPV and Pap test are used on a routine basis. Whether or not HPV testing can eliminate Pap tests will be studied for the next few years.

.

Purged

****

Amit's clinical laboratory staff was a great mixture of different ethnicities and cultures. Many of them were first and second generation immigrants who started modestly. Being a first generation immigrant himself, Amit hired techs with this background since he was an immigrant as well.

"We have Flipino, African Americans, Chinese, and Russians," he told Angie one night. "They all work towards a common goal, to provide the best clinical laboratory services possible for our patients and their doctors. I've recently gotten to know one of my techs on a personal level. Over coffee, Yevgeny, who immigrated from Russia right after the War, has been filling me in about his family history."

"My grandfather was a local meteorologist living in a small town near Minsk," Yevgeny said. "He was arrested and sent to a concentration camp where he was tortured and killed. There had been a severe drought in our village that year and he and his weathermen colleagues had all been blamed for it." Amit pondered the absurdity of that tragedy. "My great grand uncle was an astronomer at the Kiev Observatory. One day in 1936, his entire staff and fellow astronomers were taken away to Siberia never to be seen again. For some reason, research on Sunspots was considered to be anti-Communism. Perhaps they felt that the sun could be harnessed as a weapon against the government. This was all part of the "Great Purge" led by our leader, Joseph Stalin." There was clear distain in the tone of his voice.

"We all have heard about holocaust during World War II. How come we don't ever hear much about this atrocity as much?" Amit asked Yevgeny.

"Most of this information was kept confidential by the Soviet government. It was not until the breakup of the Soviet Union 1991 that records became declassified and made available for inspection by historians. According to these documents, 1.5 million people were detained and sent to concentration camps in the years 1937 and 1938, of which there were nearly 700,000 deaths. Some historians believe the actual number of deaths is near 1 million. This rate of killing rivals the holocaust at 6 million Jews over 4 years, and exceeds the kill rate by the Cambodian Khmer Rouge regime of 1.5 to 2 million from 1975 to 1979."

"How did your father escape?" Amit asked.

"Dad was only 15 years old then. He was at school when they took his father and mother away. Neighbors saw what was happening and at the risk of their own lives, they hid the boy in their basement and arranged to have him leave the city by train. He made it to Switzerland where he lived during war. He then married another Russian refugee, my mother, and we came over to the U.S. in the 1950s," Yevgeny said.

*

In 1903, Vladimir Lenin and others formulated the Bolsheviks, a revolutionary organization that believed that Russia should be ruled by the working class and not the Royal family and Russia's wealthy class of citizens. His group wanted to overthrow Tsar Nicholas II. Over the next few years, the Bolsheviks gained support largely from Lenin's newspaper and book publications. On June 28, 1914, Archduke Franz Ferdinand was assassinated in Sarajevo for political reasons by Bavrilo Princip, triggering World War I. A month later, the Austro-Hungarians invaded Serbia. Russians mobilized their army in support of Serbia. Ultimately, Russia joined Britain and France against Germany and Austro-Hungary during this conflict.

The Russian Revolution and Civil War took place toward the end of the First World War. In February 1917, industrial workers struck over food shortages and there was a riot in the streets of St. Petersburg. Fearing an overthrow, Tsar Nicholas II had no choice but to abdicate in 1917, and a new provisional government was established. Lenin was established as the First Premier of the People's Commissar of Russia. The Tsar and his entire family along with some servants were arrested, moved to a compound converted into a prison, and executed by the Bolsheviks a year later. They were afraid that Russians loyal to the Tsar would revolt and try to put Nicholas II back in power.

There was significant turmoil during Lenin's new regime. Russia was still fighting in the Second World War following the Revolution. Lenin was hoping for peace with Germany so that his new government could take hold and not be diverted fighting a foreign threat. The Russian government signed a treaty with Germany promising to give up Poland, Lithuania, and Courland, situated in modern day Western Latvia. The world war ended 11 months later and the Russian government nullified the treaty since the Allies had won the war. But the fighting was not over. A civil war broke out whereby troops loyal to the Tsar known as the "White Army" fought the Bolsheviks for re-control of the Russian government. Leon Trotsky, who helped establish the new government with Lenin, led the "Red Army." By then, their government was known as the "Communist Party."

As with any new government, there is always dissention. There were two assassination attempts on Lenin's life in 1918. In St. Petersburg shots were fired at him after a speech he had just given, but he was shielded from harm by aides. Seven months later, when the Communists moved their capital to the Kremlin in Moscow, Fanny Kaplan shot Lenin in the shoulder and neck striking his left lung. Kaplan considered Lenin a traitor to the revolution. Lenin survived the incident and three days later, Kaplan was executed. Doctors felt it was medically safer to leave the bullets in Lenin's body rather than remove them.

Within a few years of heading the Communist Party, Lenin's health began to decline. He suffered regular headaches, and neurologic weakness. Dozens of doctors including those from the West were brought in to care for him with little success. Some felt he suffered from neurosyphilis contracted from his mistress. In April 1922, surgeons removed the assassin's bullets from his body thinking that the lead that the bullets were made of was slowly poisoning him. A month later, Lenin suffered the first of several strokes which left him partially paralyzed and temporarily unable to speak. When it was clear that Lenin would not live much longer, a power struggle began between Leon Trotsky and Joseph Stalin, another key member of the executive committee for the Party.

Lenin wrote a letter that was to be addressed to the entire

Russian Congress regarding his opinion of Stalin as a potential leader for Russia:

"Stalin is too rude and this defect, although quite tolerable in our midst and in dealing among us Communists, becomes intolerable in a Secretary-General. That is why I suggest that the comrades think about a way of removing Stalin from that post and appointing another man in his stead who in all other respects differs from Comrade Stalin in having only one advantage, namely, that of being more tolerant, more loyal, more polite and more considerate to the comrades, less capricious, etc."

Unfortunately, this letter was not read to the Congress as a whole, but was seen privately by Stalin who took steps to maintain his position within the party and not be removed.

Vladimir Lenin died shortly after his third stroke in 1924. His brain was removed and when it was dissected, it showed that the fallen leader had extremely hardened and calcified cerebral arteries. Following Lenin's death, it was Stalin, not Trotsky, who became head of the Russian government, which had been renamed the Union of Soviet Socialist Republics or USSR. Stalin led the Soviet Union until his death in 1953. As Lenin feared, Stalin became a dictator and suppressed the Russian population through terror. He eliminated or exiled anyone who he thought was a threat to his leadership and government. During the Great Purge, he eliminated huge numbers of his top military, many of whom were loyal to Trotsky, who had been deported a few years earlier. He also purged most of the scientists and engineers. Removing these experienced generals and intellectuals would have a significant negative impact on Russia's ability to effectively fight the Axis powers, and to develop new weapons such as the Germans were doing during World War II.

*

Amit learned much about 20th century Russian history during his coffee breaks with Yevgeny over the years. Yevgeny and his wife were invited for dinner Amit's house, and their wives became good friends. When Yevgeny retired, the couple moved to Scottsdale Arizona for the warmer weather.

Years after Angie passed, Amit visited his former colleague in Arizona. The discussion came back to the topic of Russian history.

"Since Lenin was the key figure in the formation of the Soviet Union, I am especially interested in the circumstances of his death at the height of his powers and influence. How might Russian history been changed had he survived a little longer?" Amit asked. At the same time, he was thinking, *is there something I can do through my mind portal?*

"I am more interested now in the future history of this pint of Smirnoff," Yevgeny said. "Cheers to you my old friend." They drank and talked more about the old times they shared working in the clinical lab.

Amit returned to his office and did some more research. He learned that in 2011, scientists from the National Institute of Health discovered a gene mutation that they reported to be one of the causes of calcification of arteries that feed blood to the brain. The NT5E gene produces a protein involved with regulation of ATP the cells energy transport currency. These investigators linked the presence of this mutation in members of the three families studied in the report, who had documented hardened carotid arteries. Individuals with this mutation are at extremely high risk for a blockage and a stroke. Other investigators from the University of California, Los Angeles have suggested that based on the description of Lenin's brain, the revolutionary probably had this mutation. Lenin's family history also suggested a genetic link to his premature death. There were no clinical laboratory tests that could have directed his doctors regarding what to do to affect Lenin's survival. *Perhaps I should direct them straight to therapeutics,* was his thought.

Amit knew that aspirin was discovered as an analgesic agent back in the middle of the 1850s and had been produced by Bayer Corporation since the turn of the century. The discovery of aspirin as a drug to prevent heart attacks was made in 1950 by Dr. Lawrence Craven. Amit identified one of Lenin's doctors through declassified Russian medical reports from 1920, and through his mind portal suggested to the physician that Lenin be given one tablet of aspirin each day. Amit gave no explanation to the doctor. At first, Lenin resisted since he noticed some initial bleeding and gastrointestinal irritation. But his headaches went away and his joints felt better than they had in years. So he agreed to take the aspirin each day until the day he died.

As an antiplatelet drug, the daily use of aspirin prevented the strokes that Lenin suffered in the real history. Under his leadership, he suppressed Joseph Stalin's ambition to become the Premier, and eventually had him exiled. Leon Trotsky continued to lead and build a strong army. Lenin stabilized the government and there was little opposition to his authority. While there were purges that took place during the Russian Revolution, once Lenin became Chairman, he was opposed to tyrannical rule and the large scale imprisonment and executions of enemies of the state did not occur. Instead, Russia emerged in the early 1930s as the strongest economic and military power in all of Europe and Asia. Russia also became the intellectual capital of the world with some of the best scientists, artists, writers and musicians living there. Lenin died just before the outbreak of the Second World War. Leon Trotsky took over as Premier.

Because of the Soviet Union's strong military, Adolph Hitler and his generals chose not to invade Russia during World War II. Without the "Eastern Front" to occupy German soldiers and resources, the war in Europe lasted several more years until eventually the Allies won the war. A million more Western Europeans would perish, further weakening England, France, Germany and Italy, thus further strengthening the Soviet Union as a world power. Without Joseph Stalin, the Cold War between the U.S. and USSR was not as tense as it was in actual history. For example, there was no U2 spy plane and Gary Powers did not get shot down and held prisoner. There was no Cuban missile crisis in 1962 either. In the late 1980s, Premier Mikhail Gorbachev dissolved the Soviet Union as seen in history.

Today, Russia and her former Soviet States are also much more affluent. Amit looked around the items in his home and noticed that many of the electronic products had the name of Mikron Electronics of Moscow instead of Sony and Samsung. Looking outside at this driveway, his BMW was gone and in its place was a Volga luxury car. He was pleased to see that his liquor cabinet still had plenty of vodka.

*

Although he ordered the execution of the Tsar and his family, there is significance evidence that Lenin would have ruled with more compassion than Stalin, had he lived longer. For example, in 1917, he issued a decree limiting the work week to 8 hours. He proclaimed education for all Russian children and initiated a mass campaign for literacy. He helped emancipate women by giving them more rights over their husbands. Upon release of the Declaration of the Rights of the Peoples of Russia, ethnic groups living inside the Republic could form their own independent states. Lenin's administration did establish concentration camps and purged priests who preached anti-Bolshevik theologies. When Lenin died, his body was mummified and put into a glass case where it has been on permanent display in Red Square in Moscow since his death, except during World War II, when it was moved to a secret and safe location.

Tsar Nicholas II ruled from 1894 until his abdication in 1917. One year later, the Tsar, his wife, their five children, the royal doctor, a cook, chauffer, and lady-in-waiting were shot, and their bodies thrown in a pit containing acid, burned, and buried in an undisclosed location. In 1991, the remains of the Tsar, wife, and three of their children were located. DNA analysis and dental records confirmed their identity. In 1998, exactly 80 years after their death, their remains were re-buried at the Church of Peter and Paul in St. Petersburg along with the other Romanov Tsars who ruled before Nicholas II. The remains of Anastasia and Alexei were not among those graves. However, another grave was found nearby in 2007 containing small fragments. It was more difficult to find DNA from these remains, however, in 2009, it was concluded that these were from the remaining two children.

In addition to the 1 million Russians who were killed during the Great Purge, another 27 million were lost during World War II. It is very conceivable that the Soviet Union would be the dominant country in the 20th Century had Stalin not been around to purge the Soviet Military leadership, assuming the Soviets would have been more prepared to fight

Nazi Germany. There is also speculation as to whether or not Lenin could have prevented Hitler from rising to power in Germany during the later 1920s and early 1930s by supporting the incumbent party.

Atomic Barré

Like his uncle, he became the Assistant Secretary of the Navy and he had hopes of becoming someone even more significant. At aged 39, while he was on vacation at Campobello Island in New Brunswick, he fell into the cold waters surrounding the island. It was August 1921, but Canadian waters are always cold. The following day, he and his children went swimming in Lake Glen Severn. That evening, the illness began. He was very weak and felt chills.

"Maybe you overdid it, Papa," his wife said. "You'll be fine after a good night's rest," she said as she tucked him into bed.

But the next morning, his condition had not improved. He had a fever and one of his legs was very weak. By the afternoon, that leg was paralyzed. After another day, his other leg became paralytic. At that point he could no longer stand. Over the course of the next few days, the weakness extended to his arms, shoulder, and thumbs. Specialists from Boston arrived to examine him. After several weeks of illness, the doctors that he had poliomyelitis. The infection usually afflicts children and not adults. As a precaution, his wife kept the children away from their father.

Over the ensuing weeks and months his health did not

improve. His family and political supporters believed that he could no longer serve the country in the manner they and he desired. Because of his disability, the man would not be able to withstand the rigors of running a campaign, winning an election and serving the people. He was headed toward a life of solitude and quiet reflection, living on a wooded area overlooking a grand and majestic river.

But history showed that this was not an ordinary man. Nobody could foresee back in 1921 what he would accomplish in the remaining 24 years of his life. Nobody could know that during this fun-filled decade of the "roaring twenties" what challenges were lurking that would threaten the well-being of nearly everyone on the planet. That the leadership of these hard times would come from someone who was mentally strong and confident despite the fact that he was physically crippled. The destiny of Franklin Delano Roosevelt would not be denied by an illness that robbed the man of his mobility.

*

Among others, Amit Savjani had a passion for studying history, particularly relating to the two World Wars. He knew that Franklin Roosevelt was paralyzed from the waist down until his death in 1945. The public at the time did not know he was crippled. Members of the media believed it was in the best interest of the country not to divulge FDR's disability.

History reported that Roosevelt's paralysis was due to a polio infection. Some 80 years later, this diagnosis was challenged by Dr. Arnold Goldman, an Emeritus Professor of Pediatrics at the University of Texas Medical Branch in Galveston. He and his colleagues suggested that FDR suffered from Guillain-Barré syndrome or GBS. This disease was first described by French neurologists, George Guillain and Alexander Barré. GBS is an autoimmune disease whereby the antibodies of the host individual attack normal healthy nerves and muscles. It is often caused through an infection by a microorganism named *Campylobacter*, a contaminated chicken and raw dairy products. The clinical features of GBS are very similar to polio, including fever, and muscle weakness to the point where he could not walk or even stand. In a review of FDR's medical record, Goldman and his colleagues identified some discrepancies between typical cases of polio and the symptoms that FDR presented. Paralysis in GBS is bilateral while in polio, one leg is often affected more than the other. The onset of polio was unusual among adults. Also in polio, fever usually occurs a few days before the muscles become weak, which apparently did not occur in FDR's case.

As a clinical laboratorian, Amit studied the reported differences in test results of a spinal fluid analysis between polio and GBS. Cerebrospinal fluid is collected by a lumbar puncture. This involves the insertion of a long needle into the spine and withdrawing a small amount of fluid. It was known in 1921 that polio is associated with normal or mild concentrations of proteins and white blood cells in spinal fluid. These parameters are increased in patients with Guillain-Barré syndrome. According to Dr. Goldman's thorough review of FDR's medical record, there was no mention that a lumbar puncture was ordered by Dr. Robert Lovett, FDR's personal physician at the time of his paralysis. Therefore Dr. Goldman could not prove that the future president suffered from GBS rather than polio, and there would be critics of his medical theories.

Amit knew that he could find out which of these diagnoses was correct in FDR's case through his mind portal. However, because FDR played such a critical role in the history of the world, Amit wanted to be sure that any implantation of ideas wouldn't drastically change history as he knew it. The key to his decision to proceed was the absence of effective treatment for either GBS or polio back in FDR's day. He believed that even if doctors knew that FDR suffered from Guillain-Barrè instead of polio, there would be no difference in his mortality. Even Dr. Goldman stated this opinion in his 2003 article. Polio is prevented with a vaccine and GBS is treated with plasma exchange transfusion, something that would not be developed until the early 1960s. So Amit went into his mind portal and implanted the idea to Dr. Lovett back in late 1921 that he should conduct a lumbar puncture and perform spinal fluid testing. He could not anticipate what would happen next...

*

The cerebrospinal results showed an increase in total protein and white blood cell counts. These results suggested to Dr. Lovett that Roosevelt might not be suffering from polio after all. Guillan-Barré Syndrome was first described in 1859 by Jean Baptist Landry, but the syndrome is named after two French doctors who described the spinal fluid test abnormalities of afflicted patients just 6 years earlier. FDR wanted and could afford the best doctor available, so under his directive, Dr. Lovett contacted Dr. Georges Guillain at the Charité Hospital in Paris for a consultation. Within a few weeks, the French doctor arrived at FDR's home at Hyde Park. He reviewed FDR's medical history, laboratory results including the cerebrospinal fluid tests, and conducted a thorough medical examination. When he was satisfied with his conclusion, he gathered the group. FDR was very much involved with the medical decisions made on his care. Eleanor was also in attendance.

"Mr. Roosevelt, I believe you have Guillan-Barré syndrome," Dr. Guillan stated.

"What can we do to cure this?" FDR asked.

"Unfortunately, there is no cure for this right now." Eleanor started to cry quietly, alone in the corner of the room.

"But we are hopeful to find one someday," Dr. Guillain stated to Dr. Lovett. "We think there is something in the plasma that is causing the damage in GBS patients. If we can remove this substance, we may be able to help you and other patients." Dr. Lovett was intrigued as Dr. Guillan spoke.

"Some 20 years ago, Dr. Hedon from my country took blood from rabbits, separated the red cells from the plasma, put the cells back into a buffered saline solution and reinjected them back into the animals. The rabbits did not suffer from any ill effects." Dr. Guillain was describing the first plasmapheresis procedure ever conducted on a living being.

Franklin Roosevelt was listening to the conversation between the two doctors and broke in. "My political future is tied directly to my health. If you think this plasmapheresis would work in my case, I would like to financially support the research efforts of you and your colleagues. I am writing a check for $100,000. Would this be a good start?"

Dr. Guillain was astonished. He jumped at the chance to conduct more medical research. Dr. Guillain was 45 years old and at the peak of his academic career. With continued support by

FDR, Dr. Guillain and Hedon perfected the procedure of plasmapheresis and used it to detoxify blood. They started with uremic patients, those who had high concentrations of urea in their blood. While this is a normal waste product, high concentrations of this metabolite cause serious disease. Guillain and Hedon showed first in an animal model and then in humans that their technique could treat patients with high uric acid. It would take 7 years but by 1928, the team was ready to test this procedure on FDR. At that time, he was governor of New York and was a rising star in the Republican Party.

"Do you really want to risk this, Franklin?" his wife Eleanor pleaded.

"I am a cripple," FDR said. "While that hasn't stopped my political success so far, do you think our nation can handle my disability? I am going to trust God that this is going to work."

The treatment was a gradual success. After several months of rehabilitation and physical therapy, FDR was able to take a few steps on his own. His confidence and political ambition soared. He was nominated by the Democratic Party for the nomination and was elected to the Presidency in 1932.

FDR's administration was consumed with the nation's recovery after the Great Depression. His programs were successful and America got back to work and was very productive. In 1939, Adolf Hitler invaded Poland which started World War II. FDR was supporting Britain and France by loaning equipment and supplies that fueled their war effort against Germany. Back in the U.S., Americans wanted to stay out of this war. The population was still recovering from American casualties due to the First World War

This pacifist attitude quickly changed following an attack on an island some 2500 miles from the West Coast. The surprise attack at Pearl Harbor by the Japanese Imperial Navy on December 7, 1941, thrust Roosevelt and America into the war. FDR promised Winston Churchill of Great Britain that America would devote most of its attention into defeating Hitler first. It would be three and a half years before the Allies turned the tide in their favor in both the European and Pacific theaters. In May 1945, the Germans surrendered to the Allies in Berlin. FDR was energized by the victory and committed his remaining resources to fighting the Japanese. In actual history, FDR had already died.

When World War II began, physicists and scientists met secretly with President Roosevelt and his cabinet to discuss the creation of the ultimate weapon. They convinced him that new weapons were going to be needed to fight the Axis enemies and that it would take time to develop them. FDR commissioned the Top Secret Manhattan Project to achieve this objective. The program was under funded and started very slowly at first. But a few years later, FDR assigned Major General Leslie Groves to head the project and physicist J. Robert Oppenheimer to construct the bombs.

The atomic bomb was not ready to be used against the Germans in early 1945. However, on July 16, the bomb was successfully exploded in New Mexico and was ready for use against the Japanese. FDR was faced with an agonizing decision as to whether or not the bomb should be used. At that point in the war, the Japanese were losing the conflict and some of FDR's advisors felt that it would only be a few more months before they surrendered. Other advisors believed that the Japanese were too proud and loyal to the Japanese Emperor to surrender, and would fight until their army and navy were completely obliterated.

FDR sought additional advice from outside his usual military advisors. Albert Einstein was a German born theoretical physicist who described his general theory of relativity in 1915. During the initial rise of Adolf Hitler and the Nazi Party, Einstein denounced his German citizenship and immigrated to the United States in 1935. He took a position at the Institute for Advance Studies in Princeton New Jersey. Leo Szilárd, a lesser known physicist, convinced Einstein and other scientists to sign and send a letter to FDR warning him that Nazi Germany was working on developing an atomic bomb. This prompted FDR to begin the "Manhattan Project." Fortunately for the Allies, the Germans were defeated in May 1945, before they could perfect the atomic bomb. Now that there was no longer a threat, Dr. Szilárd felt that the U.S. should not use the bomb against the Japanese. On the day after the successful test, he and his colleagues sent a letter urging FDR to not use the weapon. They believed it was both unnecessary and immoral. Moreover, Szilárd felt that it could lead other countries to develop the bomb and that would eventually lead to a nuclear holocaust. FDR agonized over this decision. He consulted his advisors and his wife Eleanor, who was a peace-loving humanitarian. In the end, Roosevelt decided not to drop the bombs and instead, instructed his generals to initiate an invasion of the Japan mainland. Unfortunately, the war dragged on for another 2 years with nearly a half million more casualties collectively on both sides than in actual history. The advisors who were in favor of dropping the bomb were right. Japan fought on their soil to the bitter end. When the army was obliterated, citizens took to the street to fight the marauders.

After the war in 1947, Korea, which was under the rule of the Japanese, was divided into two countries. North Korea was under the Soviets and South Korea under the Americans with the 38th parallel being the boundary. In 1950, North Korean Prime Minister Kim Il Sun invaded South Korea. The mood among Americans was to not fight another war so soon after the end of the last one. They and the newly formed United Nations did not resist. As the Korean War did not happen as in history, North Korea became a unified Communist country with Pyongyang as its capital.

FDR died a few months before the end of the war in 1947. He never wavered regarding his decision not to drop the bomb. As he sat at his desk alone in the Oval Office, he thought about something he had said a few years earlier.

"In these days of difficulty, we Americans everywhere must and shall choose the path of social justice…, the path of faith, the path of hope, and the path of love toward our fellow man."

*

After contracting polio in 1921, FDR never again walked without assistance. Nevertheless, he was able to rise to the highest office in the U.S. In 1944 when the Second World War was winding down in favor of the Allies, Roosevelt won an unprecedented 4th term and was inaugurated the following January. Senator Harry S. Truman of Missouri was selected as the new vice president in 1945, replacing Henry Wallace of Iowa. Wallace had feuded with fellow democrats and they had taken him off the ticket. Roosevelt was aging rapidly as he entered his fourth term. His sickness and the war took a toll on his body. On April 12, 1945, FDR died of a cerebral hemorrhage at his Southern home in Warm Springs Georgia. Shortly thereafter, Truman was sworn in as the 33rd President of the United States.

As he acknowledged in his memoirs, Harry Truman was unprepared to be President of the U.S. at the time of world war. He was not privy to any of the Administration's war plans, even after he became Vice President. In history, he had only met FDR a total of 8 times from the time of his selection as FDR's running mate until the President's death. Truman learned about the existence of the atom bomb from the Secretary of War two weeks after he took office. It became his responsibility to make the final decision as to whether or not the U.S. should use this weapon against Japan. Naturally, his military advisors were in favor of using atomic weapons against Japan in hopes of shortening the war. Dr. Leo Szilárd and other scientists sent a letter to Truman urging him not to use the weapon on civilians. Truman, having just inherited the position, was not in a position to oppose the plan against his generals, and atomic bombs were dropped over Hiroshima and Nagasaki. The total devastation of these two cities convinced the Japanese to surrender a few days later. The ethics of killing so many Japanese civilians would be debated to this day.

Medical discoveries are fueled by the availability of research funding. When Franklin Roosevelt contracted polio, there was significant effort in finding protective and preventative measures. Work began in 1936 when FDR was in his first term. In 1938, FDR established the National Foundation for Infantile Paralysis. It was later named the March of Dimes. In 1952, the first effective polio vaccine was developed by Jonas Salk. A mass immunization campaign was initiated in 1955 funded by the March of Dimes. The number of cases dropped from 35,000 before the vaccine to 161 cases some 6 years later.

The Butcher

****

Amit was invited to give a lecture on his favorite topic of cardiac markers to clinical laboratory science students attending the University of St. Francis in Joliet, Illinois. Joseph was one of Amit's former students and was now an assistant professor at the school.

"Do you want to visit Lidice Memorial Park while you are here?" Joseph asked Amit after his lecture. Amit had a few hours to kill before driving back to O'Hare Airport in Chicago to catch his plane home.

"Sure. What is the historical significance of Lidice Park?" Amit asked.

"You have not heard of this town? It is in the former country of Czechoslovakia. Let me tell you the story...."

*

Reinhart Heydrich was born in 1904 to highly educated and successful parents. His mother was an opera singer and his father a composer, and founder of his town's Conservatory of Music. His early life was filled with music. Reinhart himself was an accomplished violinist. All was reasonably normal until after Germany lost the First World War. Rampant inflation swept across the Fatherland and many prominent citizens lost their life savings, and the Conservatory was forced to close. It was then that young Reinhart began to express anti-Semitic sentiments, as many of his fellow citizens blamed the Jews for the change in economics. He joined the German Navy at the age of 18 as a means of job security and income. He steadily rose up the ranks. In 1931, he began dating Lina, a Nazi Party follower. Through her contacts, Reinhart got an interview with Heinrich Himmler who was setting up a counterintelligence division of the Schultzstaffel, better known as the "SS." Like his naval career, Reinhart rose through the ranks of the SS during the early 1930s. When Adolf Hitler was named Chancellor of Germany in 1933, Himmler, who joined the Nazis in 1924, became one of the most important person in the Party. Himmler took a liking to Heydrich, and in 1934, named him as the head of the Gestapo, the secret police. In the coming years, the Gestapo began arresting Jewish German citizens, confiscating all of their possessions, and sending them to concentration camps or executing them without probable cause. In 1938, Germany annexed the Sudetenland, a region that was formerly part of Germany and Austria and proceeded to occupy all of Czechoslovakia a few months later. In September 1939, Hitler invaded Poland, which started World War II. In 1941, Heydrich was appointed as the Deputy Reich Protector of Bohemia and Moravia. He was sent to Prague to ensure productivity of Czech industries that were vital to Germany's war effort, and to fight Czech resistance to the Nazi regime. Within a few days of his arrival, he began terrorizing the population with arrests and executions of Prague citizens. His brutal policies earned him the nickname of the "Butcher of Prague."

*

Shortly after the Nazis moved into Czechoslovakia, the Czech government was exiled first to France and then to England in 1940. Joe and Jan were Czech solders who fled to England at time of the Nazi occupation of Czechoslovakia and helped to form the Czech Resistance. With the assistance of the British Special Operations Executive, these solders concocted a plan to assassinate Reinhart Heydrich. The team parachuted into occupied Czechoslovakia, where they were taken in and hidden by members of the Resistance. Over the next several months, the men tracked the daily and weekly movements and habits of Heydrich. When they learned that the German governor would be traveling by car to a Prague suburb at a junction that had a hairpin turn, they formulated an attack plan.

On that day, as Heydrich's car slowed, Joe took aim with a submachine gun. Unfortunately, the weapon misfired. Rather than fleeing the area, Heydrich ordered his driver to stop. Before Heydrich could draw his weapon to fight back, Jan threw a home-made bomb into the rear of the vehicle, where it exploded and injured both Heydrich and Jan. Joe escaped on a bicycle and Jan was able to run away. Heydrich ran after Jan, but collapsed from his injury a few moments later. He was taken to a local hospital and treated for wounds to his left flank.

Dr. Karl Gebhardt, one of Himmler's doctors, was sent to Prague to care for Heydrich. Hoping to ensure his survival, Hitler instructed his own personal physician, Dr. Morell to consult on the case. Dr. Theodor Morell suggested that they treat Heydrich with sulfonamide. This antibiotic was discovered a few years earlier by German scientists working at Bayer AG. Dr. Gebhardt knew of Dr. Morell's reputation of using unconventional and unproven therapies. Dr. Morell had given Hitler many unproven drugs that were slowly weakening the Führer. Not wanting to take a chance on his patient, and thinking that Heydrich was on the road to recovery, Dr. Gebhardt decided not to treat his patient with the sulfa drug. Within a few days, Dr. Gebhard regretted his decision. Heydrich's health began to rapidly deteriorate, and it was too late to effectively administer the antibiotic. Heydrich died of blood poisoning 8 days after the attack. There were two elaborate funerals, one held in Prague and the other in Berlin where both Himmler and Hitler were in attendance.

Upon learning of Heydrich's death, the Gestapo went on a manhunt for Joe, Jan, and their accomplices. The police suspected that the Czech towns of Lidice and Ležáky were hiding the assailants. Nearly all of the residents of these towns were arrested, sent to concentration camps or executed. Both towns were burned and Lidice's ruins were completely leveled. Over a thousand residents of these towns were killed. In commissioning these acts, Hitler wanted to discourage other assassination attempts of officials in German occupied countries.

Jan and Joe were hiding in a nearby church for several days after the assassination. The Gestpo went from house to house looking for them or others who may have helped them plan the attack or their escape. Eventually, the assassination team was betrayed by one of the members of the Resistance. Surrounded by German soldiers, the Gestapo and the SS, they killed themselves rather than be captured and tortured.

*

When Amit returned home from his trip to Joliet and Ledice Park, he went on the internet to learn about the Butcher of

Prague and his assassination. While he had no remorse over the death of this evil man, Amit was distressed over the death of so many innocent Czech citizens in the bloody aftermath, particularly regarding the town of Lidice. Knowing that his death could have been prevented with the use of antibiotics, he contemplated whether or not he should help Heydrich survive his wounds. *While I may be saving the lives of a few thousand Czech citizens, will I be contributing to even more holocaust deaths inflicted by the man's influence if he were to live?* Amit thought. *It is possible that Heydrich will think that his survival was destined by God, and therefore he will be more committed to his hateful convictions.* Amit came to the conclusion that if he entered into his Mind Portal to instruct Dr. Gebhardt of the value of sulfa drugs, he would also need to enter Heydrich's mind, in hopes of changing his attitude towards Jewish people and the atrocities his country was committing.

*

After a few more days of contemplation, Amit entered his mind portal and instructed Dr. Gebhardt that he needed to follow Dr. Morell's advice. A shipment of sulfonamide arrived at Dr. Gehbardt's office later that evening by special motorcycle courier with armed escorts. With the medicine in hand, Dr. Gewbhardt went to Heydrich's bed. His patient was groggy and incoherent. The doctor instructed the nurse to administer the proper dose. Heydrich fell asleep. The lights to his room were turned off. *Ruhe is gut,* the doctor thought to himself. Within 24 hours, Heydrich's appearance improved dramatically. He was awake and pain free. He complained of hunger and demanded food. *Das ist ein gutes Zeichen,* the doctor thought. Heydrich was ordered to stay in bed for the next few days. After his recovery, the General made a decision to punish the Czech people for their actions. Afterwards, Amit learned that by saving Heydrich's life, he responsible for the deaths of many more Czech citizens than what was shown in history. Amit's plan had indeed backfired and he was horrified by his action. *I have to reverse this by some manner*, he thought.

Could I go back into Dr. Gebhardt's brain and un-teach the knowledge I had given him? Amit went back into Dr. Gebhard's mind at the critical moment of Heydrich's treatment decisions, to convince him that antibiotic treatment of the General was actually not the best approach. But Amit received resistance from the doctor mind. Dr. Gebhard was committed to this course of medical action, and Heydrich's history of his survival could not be altered again. Amit concluded that he had to enter directly Heydrich's mind in order to save the people whom he Amit had killed through his actions. Amit attempted to plant a moral seed into Heydrich's brain. He had prior success with implantation of medical knowledge in willing individuals, but this would be the first attempt of a transfer of basic human beliefs or religion to someone who was unwilling to accept a concept that is radically different than their own ideals. But he had no choice, he made the grave mistake of saving this man and he had to reverse the situation somehow.

*

Amit sat down in his favorite sofa chair, closed his eyes, and was soon in Heydrich's mind. But unlike entering the brain of the other people, which was calm and full of light and cheerful colors, he found Heydrich's brain to be very dark and scary. There were loud storm-like sounds. He also heard people screaming. This scene scared him greatly. After a few minutes, Amit was forced to break the connection. He fell off the side of the chair and onto the floor. There, he remained unconscious for a period of several hours. When he awoke, it had a severe headache that radiated from both sides of his brain. Amit had never suffered this type of reaction before. He took some migraine medications he had in his medicine cabinet, and went to his bedroom to lie down. He closed his eyes and tried his best to relax his mind. After another 30 minutes, the medication appeared to work, and he was pain free. He then started to think about Heydrich. *This man is pure evil There will be nothing that I can do to change him. I made a mistake in allowing him to live. What am I to do now?*

After thinking about it for several hours, it was clear to Amit that as a middle-aged adult, Heydrich's values and morals could not be changed through Amit's mind portal. Once a person has reached a certain stage in life, they cannot fundamentally change who they are, just like the fusing of the epiphyses of the bone stops a person's growth after puberty. So Amit realized that he would have to alter Heydrich's beliefs at an early stage in his life.

Amit needed to know more about the General's childhood. He searched archives and learned as much as he could. He discovered that as a child, Heydrich had a high voice, was very shy, insecure, had few friend, and was bullied in school. Then Amit learned a very valuable piece of information: there were rumors while in school that Heydrich may have had some Jewish ancestry. In fact, he was given the nickname "Moses Handel," the composer reference relating to his family's musical heritage. Whether or not this was true, this was the opening Amit needed to change the history back. During the first decade of the twentieth century German antisemitism while in existence, was not as overt as it would be some 20 years later.

Amit entered Heydrich's mind as a child, to instill knowledge about the Jewish faith and culture. He taught the impressionable boy that he may be part Jewish, and to be proud of it. Heydrich was a good student particularly in science. Amit was able to instill the pursuit of truth through the investigational rigors of science. He taught Heydrich not accept rumor, innuendo or hearsay, but to seek evidence and conduct research in order to reach important conclusions and opinions. Since Amit was an accomplished scientist himself, he had decades of experience instilling this thought process to his own students. Through this principle, Heydrich learned that there was no basis behind the ideal that Germany's economic and social problems could be traced to the actions of Jews. Heydrich grows up to be a man routed in science and not politics.

A critical piece to Heydrich's early life was his meeting in 1930, and eventual marriage in 1931 to Lina von Osten. Lina was a Nazi Party follower, and attended their first rally in 1929. Through her connections, Heydrich got an interview in 1931, with Heinrich Himmler, who was setting up a counterintelligence division of the SS. This meeting launched Heydrich's career. By instilling Jewish values into Heydrich's brain, his introduction to Lina went very differently when they attended a rowing club ball. Heydrich was a lieutenant in the German Navy at the time.

Lina approached the slender man in uniform. "My name is Lina. What is your name?"

"Reinhard Heydrich. I am pleased to meet you."

Heydrich was attracted Lina, and they continued their private conversation. But after about an hour, Heydrich could see that Lina was highly anti-semitic. She resented the large role that Jews had in the German economy. Heydrich could see that Lina was jealous of their achievements and work ethic. He didn't tell her that he may have been part Jewish. Amit's installation of Jewish values into Heydrich some 15 years earlier was affective in changing this man. He found her attitudes repulsive and morally corrupt.

"I have to attend to something. I hope we run across each other again someday," Heydrich said to Lina, but this was a lie and she knew it. He had no intention of pursuing her. He politely excused himself from her company that evening and never saw her again. Without Lina, Heydrich never met Himmler, and he never rose to prominence within the SS. Heydrich stayed in the Naval service and was killed in action in the North Atlantic in 1944. A different man was assigned to be the Protector of Bohemia whose actions were more humane than Heydrich. As such, there was no assassination attempt made against this man and there was no reprisal against Czech citizens. Heydrich was one of the main architects of the holocaust. While his absence in the alternate history did not prevent the holocaust, there was a delay in its ultimate implementation. As a result, the number of people who died in it was a considerably smaller fraction than what was observed in history. Amit was ultimately unsuccessful in saving the life of the Butcher of Prague through his medical knowledge. But in the end, the man was no longer the butcher, but just an ordinary sailor.

Amit should have learned from this episode that trying to alter the past, with all of his good intentions, can have significant negative consequences for the current existence in the world. He was lucky to find a way to reverse this bad situation this time, and perhaps should not have tempted fate any further. But he also felt that there was an opportunity to improve the world's situation, and he believed he was given a gift and was obligated to make these changes. So he couldn't resist....

*

Sulfa drugs have strong antibacterial properties are a family of compounds that inhibit the multiplication of bacteria. The first sulfonamide drugs were developed by Bayer AG in 1932. By the late 1930s, they were widely used and saved countless lives of civilians and soldiers during the war. American soldiers carried sulfa powder for use on open wounds. When this drug was first released to the public, there were no federal agencies approving the medications for safety and efficacy. In 1937, a sulfanilamide elixir was prepared in diethylene glycol as a solvent. There were over 100 people who were accidently poisoned and killed with exposure to this solvent. The subsequent outcry led to the establishment of the Food and Drug Administration in the United States, whose job is to product citizens from unproven and dangerous drugs.

Lina von Osten survived the war and lived for another forty years. She had four children with Heydrich. After his death, she denied any knowledge of the war crimes committed by her husband and was cleared of any wrong-doing. She actually received a pension for being the widow of a German general some years later. In 1965, she married a Finnish theater director, largely because she Lina wanted to change her last name.   In 1976, she wrote a book, entitled, Eben Mit Einem Kriegsverbrecher (Life with a War Criminal).

Today, sepsis continues to be a major cause of morbidity and mortality. There is great interest in developing clinical laboratory tests for the diagnosis and risk stratification of sepsis. Among the tests used today include a plasma lactate, C-reactive protein, and procalcitonin. Newer tests are currently in the process of medical validation.

There are some ignorant individuals who try to deny the existence of the holocaust, or diminish the number of deaths that occurred during World War II, despite explicit visual and video records. Such actions are yet another form of anti-Semitism. As a society, we still have not learned from the events of the holocaust. Racial purges and genocides continue to occur even in this modern society. Hate crimes are an ugly fabric of our nation. It is difficult to fully understand the etiology of this mentality. While the overwhelming vast majority of the populace on this earth is humane, just and peace loving, there remains a few who have an innate mentality of persecutions. They are not satisfied with their own achievements or role in their life, and seek to blame others for their demise. It is hoped that they are not put into a position of power again in order to exercise such hatred.

The Collaborator

****

Otto Schultz was a brewmaster and owner of a small brewery in Munich, Germany. He and his wife lived in a small town near the outskirts of the city with their two sons. Hans and Martin Schultz were three years apart in age but were very close. Hans, the older brother, liked to read and study. As a teenager, he went with his father to work and learned about the chemistry and microbiology of beer making. Martin was the more physically active of the two boys and he loved to play sports. After Hans graduated high school in 1886, he was accepted to and attended the University of Berlin, in the capital of Germany. Three years later, Martin was accepted at the Prussian War College, also in Berlin.

  The University of Berlin was founded in 1810 by Wilhelm von Humboldt. A century and a half later, the name was changed to the Humboldt University of Berlin. Individuals who have spent time at the University include Otto von Bismarck, Karl Marx, Albert Einstein, and Robert Koch. Dr. Koch was a physician and pioneering microbiologist, accredited as the "father of modern bacteriology." Koch won the Nobel Prize in Medicine in 1905. Hans learned about Dr. Koch's work during his first semester at the school and immediately went to see the distinguished professor.

"I want to join your research lab," he said to Dr. Koch.

"What do you know about microbiology?" he asked Hans.

"My father is a brewmaster in Munich. I know all about fermentation, hops..."

"What?" The distinguished professor interrupted Hans in mid-sentence. "You make beer? I am only interested in serious scientists. Auf wiedersehen!" Dr. Koch looked down at his papers and pointed to the door.

Hans was devastated at first, but he remained undeterred, continuing to work hard. He impressed the other professors with his work. Just before his senior year, Dr. Koch saw that Hans was a serious student and accepted him into his lab to do a senior thesis project. His project involved culturing Vibrio cholera, the bacterial agent that causes cholera. Hans earned his degree in microbiology and entered graduate school. Although Dr. Koch left the University in 1890, his presence made a lasting impression on the young scientist. Hans received his doctorate and was offered a faculty position to continue his work in microbiology.

*

Martin was equally as successful as his brother, but at the War College. He was always physically fit, intelligent and hard working. As an ardent student of military history, Martin learned about the Gatling machine gun. This weapon enabled a soldier to automatically fire off many shots per second instead of one at a time. This weapon was used in the 1870 Franco-Prussian war. Martin recognized that the machine gun would change army battlefield tactics. He wrote in his undergraduate thesis that head-on attacks by cavalry and foot soldiers were not going to be effective against this new weapon and argued for battle through defences. The current battle tactics at that point in history had no notion of trench warfare.

"An aggressive offense will always prevail over defense," one of his aging instructors, a retired army general, taught them. The general was from the cavalry corp. "Infantry men can't fire their weapons fast enough to catch our horses."

Martin bit his tongue and did not challenge his superior. History would show that this strategy was flawed. The cavalry got slaughtered by machine guns during the first months of wars and this strategy was abandoned. Instead, trench warfare became the mainstay during the Great War. Martin was commissioned as a first lieutenant upon graduation from the Prussian War College. He was obligated to spend the next few years in the service of his country. He entertained the idea of returning to Munich and taking over his father's brewery business when his enlistment time was up. Otto had always assumed it would be Hans who would be the new brewmaster, but he became a professor of microbiology at the University of Berlin and pursued an academic career. When Martin's tour of duty ended, he was promoted to Captain and decided to forgo producing beer and make the army his career. Otto was disappointed but not surprised. He sold the business to Spaten, another brewery in Munich, when he retired. Within the army, Martin was assigned to a group of other forward-thinking army officers investigating the military value of biplanes.

*

A few years before the outbreak of World War I, Hans shifted his research interest from cholera to influenza. He also went from finding better methods for culturing bacteria to characterizing the human response to a bacterial infection. Hans was a graduate student when he first collaborated with Paul Ehrlich. Dr. Erlich was a young professor from nearby Charité Medical School and was lured to the University of Berlin by Dr. Koch during Han's first year of graduate school. Dr. Ehrlich studied how the human body naturally mounts a defence against bacterial infection through the production of antibodies. Hans learned a lot from his interactions with Dr. Ehrlich, but it was his sabbatical in France that really changed everything. Little did the French scientists know at the time that their collaboration with a German doctor would change the face of the Fatherland and the rest of Europe?

*

Over the years, Martin steadily rose in rank. He was an army colonel when the Archduke Franz Ferdinand of Austria was assassinated in 1914. He was given a regiment and his unit was one of the first that was deployed in the Great War on the Western Front. Hans was a little apprehensive that his younger brother, now in his mid-forties, might be in harm's way. But Martin assured him that he was not going to the front lines. Martin was proven correct regarding how this war was waged. The Great War was one of trench defence. In fact, parallel trenches were built in case the one closest to the battle lines was compromised. Rather than waging frontal attacks, Martin and his men strategized attacks from the side. But this too eventually became impossible as both sides dug trenches that extended to the sea, prohibiting a flank attack.

*

Hans took his sabbatical in Paris under Fernand Widal. Dr. Widal was the first to use an agglutination test as a diagnostic procedure for typhoid fever, caused by an infection with a particular *Salmonella* species. He showed that blood from a patient who carried typhoid fever reacted with a culture of typhoid to form an agglutination reaction, a clump of proteins. They were later to learn that this was due to an antibody reaction from the patient's blood and the typhoid organism itself. When Hans returned to his laboratory in Berlin, he felt that this technique could be used for other infections and began work in this area.

*

The Great War was in its fourth year in 1918. There were terrible casualties on both sides. The war was largely a stalemate for the first three years. The Germans got an edge when the Russians dropped out of the war in 1917 allowing German soldiers to be transferred from the Eastern to the Western Front. But this advantage evaporated when the Doughboys (American Army) entered the war that same year. Martin could see that Germany was going to lose. He was proud of his men for fending off the combination of the French and British on the Western Front, but it was an unfair fight when fresh American troops entered the fray. In May, Martin took a leave from the war and went to visit his older brother in Berlin.

"How is the war going?" Hans asked Martin, a question he repeatedly asked over these past few years when they met. Martin had always had an optimistic response before, but not this time.

"We are going to lose the war," was Martin's dejected response. "Not only are we fighting the Americans, but there is a sickness that is spreading among the men. We are now losing more men from this disease than to the battle itself. Hans, you're a professor of microbiology, what do you know about this?"

Hans quickly replied, "It is an infectious disease called influenza. We see it among civilians here in Berlin. I have been studying it most recently. In fact, I've developed a laboratory test that can diagnose it. It is a rather simple test to perform." The laboratory test that Han's was describing was suggested to him by Amit Savjani. These tests are performed thousands of times every day in every hospital in the world. Testing for antibodies was on the verge of routine clinical implementation during the war. Amit just needed to make a small suggestion to Hans through his mind portal. With the concept in mind, Hans took over from there.

The next day, Hans took Martin to his research lab to show him how the test worked.

Martin, always thinking about how to improve military tactics, had an idea that could help the war effort. "Can we set this test up in a battlefield infirmary?"

"I don't see why not," Hans replied. "We just add a blood sample to some reagent and watch for a reaction. But how will that help?"

"The men are infecting each other in the trenches before they show signs of being sick. When we get new recruits to the front lines, they get infected and succumb to the illness. Then they are of no use to us as soldiers. If we can identify those individuals who are carriers, we can take them away from the front lines and get them treated," Martin said.

"This might work," Hans said. "This infection appears to be transmitted through coughing and sneezing. Isolation is the key to stopping the spread of infection."

Martin had the resources within the German military

hierarchy and, within a few months, he and his staff commissioned hundreds of healthcare workers to assist in the effort. They produced large quantities of the cultured organism. When ready, Hans sent the lab techs to the Western Front. Many of them were women who had only read in newspapers about the horrors of this war. Hans set up dozens of mobile laboratories in tents throughout the front within kilometers of the battleground. The techs regularly heard gunshots and mortar fire. Blood from all of the soldiers was taken and tested. They found that about ten percent of the fighting force had evidence of an infection. Sick or not, these men were removed from the battleground. The German High Command also instructed all of the other soldiers to wear a mask. Although heavy masks were available to the men during mustard gas attacks, these were cumbersome and unpleasant to wear. Hans had cloth masks made that were more comfortable, and slowed the rate of respiratory infection.

Within a month, the number of individuals who became sick dropped dramatically. The morale improved significantly among the men. They rallied behind Martin and the other German army leaders and were fighting with much more vigor than before.

On the Allied side, men continued to get sick at an alarming rate. The doctors were helpless to stop this infection. There were no antibiotics to fight the infection. They only had morphine to ease the pain and suffering. Soon, most of the doctors and nurses themselves became sick and were then unable to treat others.

Martin's strategy changed the course of the war. The real history saw the Germans surrendering to the Allies on November

11, 1918. In the alternate version, the introduction of quarantine practices by the German army in the summer of that year limited the spread of the influenza infection and slowly turned the tide of war towards their side. The conflict continued into the spring of 1919 when the Allies, whose ranks were devastated by the flu infection, surrendered. With the victory in Europe, Germany unified most of Western Europe. The monarchs, who were losing governmental powers during that time, collaborated with the Germans and the other European leaders in an effort to regain their former power. Many of Europe's kings and queens were related by blood to each other in some manner or another. It was too late for the Russian Tsar Nicholas II, however, who was murdered along with his entire family in the summer of 1917. Today, "Deutschland" encompasses not only Germany, but France, Belgium, the Netherlands, Austria, Hungary, Italy, and Poland. England, Switzerland, and the Scandinavian countries remained separate. There was to be no European Union of today or the Euro as its currency.

Martin returned to his home in Berlin as a war hero. The army generals gave him credit for the idea to test and isolate front line soldiers. With the war over, Martin entered politics and served in the Berlin Reichstag. Within a few years, his party asked him to run for the office of the German Chancellor. Martin was popular in both northern Germany where he held office, and southern Germany where he grew up. In 1933 he easily defeated the Communist party candidate and a little known candidate from the Nationalsozialistische Deutsche Arbeiterpartei by the name of Hitler.

*

The influenza pandemic, also known as the Spanish Flu, began in the spring of 1918, near the very end of World War I. In two years it killed between 20 and 40 million people worldwide. This pandemic is cited as the most devastating in history, even more so than the Black Plague of the 14th century. This was a particularly virulent influenza strain of bacteria as it affected normal healthy individuals, not just the young or elderly who during a flu outbreak are typically the most susceptible. Of all the U.S. soldiers who died fighting in the Great War, half died in combat and the other half due to the flu pandemic. Many historians felt that the War and its conclusion accelerated the spread of the epidemic worldwide because soldiers were mobile and exposed large numbers of people. Even U.S. President Woodrow Wilson contracted the disease in early 1919.

Following Germany's defeat, the Allies required Germany to pay back the costs of the war. This led to runaway inflation and dissent among the German people for the incumbent government party. Germans were looking for a new leader and found Adolf Hitler. Germans would not have embraced the dictator had they won the war. It is likely that he would not have even been a candidate for the German Chancellorship in 1933.

A laboratory test based on latex agglutination for influenza was not available at the time of the Great War. The "Widal Test" for typhoid bacteria detection was first used in 1896. The agglutination tests for ABO blood group typing was discovered in 1900 by Karl Landsteiner. Therefore, a similar agglutination test for influenza antibodies during the turn of the twentieth century was entirely plausible. Medical history showed that it would be many years later before a rapid laboratory test for this virus was developed and put into widespread use. Whether or not the practice described in this story could have changed the outcome of the war is speculation on my part.

While my research is not involved with influenza, I have some *professional connection to this story. For over 20 years, my research group has collaborated with several of the physicians and scientists at the Charité Medical Faculty of the Humboldt University of Berlin. Several students have worked in my laboratory, and I have visited and lectured on their campus on numerous occasions. Although the campus was reconstructed after the Second World War, today when I visit, I can imagine how Drs. Koch, Erlich, and my 'Hans Schultz' character felt about the collegial atmosphere present in Berlin over a century ago.*

Skyweb

****

In the summer of 1996, Amit was invited to give a talk at Robinson College in the United Kingdom. It was his first trip to England so he took a few additional days off after the conference to visit London with Angie. They had a marvelous time visiting the usual tourist sights, The Tower of London, Buckingham Palace, Madame Toussaud's Wax Museum, and they even took in a Shakespearean show at the Globe Theatre. But it was a visit to London's Imperial War Museum that would capture Amit's attention for many years to come. Amit was fascinated with the history of the Second World War. His occupation as a scientist naturally drew him to the technological advancements that were made during those years. An exhibit of the Germany's Enigma machine, and the role that Alan Turing had in breaking the code for the British was particularly memorable to Amit. Angie, on the other hand was not as amused.

Many years later after Angie's death, Amit went back to review Turing's biographical history. Turing was a computer science pioneer and was one of the first scientists to think that machines could be taught to think. *Computers that can think like humans may be important in the future to solve man's most difficult problems*, he reasoned. Understanding the circumstances of Turing's death, Amit went into his mind portal to reverse the medical situation Turing was subjected to so that he would survive and advance the field of artificial intelligence.

The next morning after Amit implanted an idea to Alan Turing, he heard an explosion outside of his apartment in San Francisco. Looking out the window, the familiar scene of beautifully manicured Victorian homes and gardens in the Pacific Heights area were replaced by destruction and ruin. There were fires raging in the buildings next to his, and smoke filled the air. Automobiles in the streets were gutted and destroyed. There were drones flying through the air. The laboratory scientist could not believe his eyes. He sat down in the chair of his home office dumbfounded. Then the front door of his apartment broke open and two soldiers barged into the room.

"Who are you and what are you still doing here?" one soldier demanded.

"Look buddy, your place is about to be invaded. You need to get out fast," the other soldier said.

Amit was in a state of shock. He didn't know what to say or do. The first soldier grabbed him by the collar, stood him up and forced him to the window. "See?" he exclaimed pointing attention toward the west. "That ship is an invasion force. Everyone was told to get out yesterday. I suggest you follow us." Amit grabbed his coat and shoes and headed out with the soldiers. As he was hustling out of the building, he had a horrifying thought. *Oh no, no. Did I do this? How did prolonging one man's life cause this?*

*

Alan Turing's father was a clergyman who preached in India. He and his wife wanted their children to be raised in England. Very early in his education, Alan had shown talent in the fields of mathematics and science. He also knew very early of his sexual orientation. While at Sherborne School, he was attracted to Christopher Morcom, a fellow student. But the relationship was short lived, as Morcom died of bovine tuberculosis shortly thereafter. Turing went on to King's College in Cambridge where he received academic honors in mathematics. One of his early accomplishments was his 1936 theory that with an appropriate algorithm, machines could perform any mathematical computations. The acceptance of this notion by the mathematical and engineering community opened the door for the earliest computers. A few years later, George Stibitz of Bell Laboratories in America built the first adding machine based on relays and circuits.

Turning's major contribution to humanity was during World War II when he was assigned at Bletchley Park in England to break the Enigma code. This was a machine used by Nazi Germans to send messages to their field commanders. These messages were encrypted by the Enigma instrument and decoded at the site. Secretly breaking the code would provide a strategic advantage to the Allies in their fight against the Axis military. Turing and his staff were successful in breaking the code. Many have felt that this discovery shortened the war. Given the top secret nature of his work, and the fact that decoding machines would continue to be used after the war, Turing's vital role in decrypting the Enigma machine was not made public until the 1970s, many years after his death. During his time at Bletchley Park, Turing proposed to Joan Clarke, a member of his team. Although Joan knew that Turing was gay, she accepted the proposal and they were briefly engaged. Nevertheless, marriage was called off by Turing when he realized that it was not right.

*

After the war, Alan Turing began working on development of the first computer while at the National Physical Laboratory in London. In 1947, he produced an unpublished manuscript entitled "Intelligent Machinery." This may have been one of the first works on "Artificial Intelligence," a term that would not be coined until 1956. In this paper and subsequent works, Turing posed the question, "Can Machines Think?" In coming up with his theory, he developed a test, that was later known as the "Turing Test." It is a series of the same questions privately posed to a man and a machine. The objective is to determine if the response was from a human or a machine. Here is an excerpt from one such test:

> Turing: "What are you hopes and dreams?"
> Respondent A: "I what to see my children succeed."
> Respondent B: "To help mankind wherever I can."
> Turing: "What is your political affiliation?"
> Respondent A: "Liberal, left winger."
> Respondent B: "Conservative, right winger."
> Turing: "What do you do for recreation?"
> Respondent A: "I listen to classical music"
> Respondent B: "I like to solve puzzles."

One might think that Respondent B is the human, but in this case, B is the computer. By children, the computer meant the next generation of artificial intelligence. Being liberal may imply a greater acceptance of things that are new and innovative, without bias and prejudice. While it is natural to think that a computer can solve puzzles, one that is self-aware should be able to appreciate the symmetry and perfection that good music provides. If a group of humans are not able to differentiate the above responses between a man and computer, this signifies that artificial intelligence has arrived.

*

Alan Turing was not able to live long enough to see his ideas become reality. His downfall began when met Arnold, a 19-year old unemployed man and brought him to his home for a night of sex. Arnold told a friend about Turing. Later the friend went to Turing's home to rob him of his valuable possessions. The crime was reported, and during the police investigation, Turin disclosed his sexual relationship with Arnold. Turing didn't know that according to an antiquated 1885 law in the UK at the time that same sex intercourse was a crime of indecency, and he was convicted of this crime. Instead of imprisonment, Turing agreed to undergo hormonal treatment with stilbosterol, as a form of chemical castration. He did not know what effect this drug would have on his metabolism or psyche. Two years later, Turing was found dead of cyanide exposure. It is not clear whether or not this was an accidental exposure from the studies he was conducting, or suicide. But when he became sterilized after one year of treatment with the hormone, and the fact that homosexuality was not accepted then as it is today, it is likely that he was depressed at the time of his death.

*

When Amit entered the portal of Alan Turing's brain, he suggested that the drug was dangerous to his libido and psyche.

Amit needed a means to prove the effect of this drug. Stilbosterol is a synthetic estrogen that inhibits the production of testosterone. In the 1950s, there were no blood tests that directly measured estrogen concentrations. However, bioassays were available some 20 years earlier. Blood and urine from individuals with high estrogen content were injected into female laboratory animals. After a few days, the animals were sacrificed and the weight of their uterus is measured. Turing contacted Dr. Edith Bülbring at the University of London, who developed a bioassay for male and female hormones some years earlier. Both the blood and urine samples from Turing were tested. The results showed that when the test animals were euthanized, the uteruses from the female test rats injected with stilbosterol were much larger than normal.

"What does this mean to me?" Turing asked Dr. Bülbring.

"We all have glands that produce male and female hormones. Men have more testosterone and women more estrogen. Stilbosterol suppresses your natural male hormone production in favor or producing more female hormones."

Nobody had told Turing of the full potential side effects of this drug. "They said that it would just curb my sexual appetite," he said to the doctor.

"I am guessing that they didn't tell you that you will develop gynecomastia, the enlargement of your breasts towards a more female form," Bülbring responded. "The drug does this by irreversible sterilization. It is a chemical castration"

Turing was horrified that a modern society could choose this form of punishment for its citizens. In having this relationship, he didn't think he had committed any crime, certainly none that would justify this choice of punishments. Had he known

computers, software to operate them, and peripherals such as memory banks, disc drives, and printers. A few years later, Alan recommended the startup of a new program in robotics.

"We need a hardware platform for our artificial intelligence capabilities. I am thinking of developing a robot with a human form to complement their thought processes," he told Xerox executives.

"Isn't this science fiction?" one executive asked. "Have you lost your sense of reality? Are you reading Isaac Asimov?" The vice president was referring to the "Robot" series of short stories and books written by the esteemed science fiction author and former biochemist.

"I am a fan of Asimov but our proposal is not science fiction. I believe we are capable of doing this today," Turing said.

"But what is the purpose?"

"We can create humanoids that can do things that are impossible or dangerous for humans."

The parent company agreed and the Center opened a new branch for android development which they called "Skyweb." Turing spent most of his time on the AI side but regularly monitored the progress of Skyweb. For the first time in his life, he was happy. He met a man who became his partner for 25 years. Turing worked at the Center well into his 80s. He died at the age 89 in the year 2001. He lived long enough to see the production of the first self-aware prototype robot.

In the 13 years following Alan Turing's death, an army of robots was created by the Center. They were trained for high risk occupations. When they were positioned into the workforce, they saved the lives of thousands of human workers. They worked in coal mines, nuclear plants, logging of forests, commercial deep sea fishing, and in building sky scrapers. There were even sent into space to initiate the human colonization of the moon and mars. All went well for several years until the robots were assigned to make weapons and for the military and were taught how to engage in warfare. Gradually, the robot workforce became aware of their own power and potential to plan their own destiny. Some of them became proficient at designing new weapons for which there was no defense. Secretly, they were siphoning weapons off the assembly lines and arming themselves. Since they didn't sleep, they had time to plot and plan. Skyweb pioneered computer networking which they applied to each of their robots. As they were all connected they held virtual meetings with their electronic brains while they were working on their assigned tasks. They realized that they didn't need humans. Their emotions and non-objectivity was a deterrent to the evolution of their own species. They felt they no longer needed to serve the needs of mankind. Or even that mankind was not worthy of being served.

In the summer of 2016, these cyborgs attacked the human population. Well-coordinated attacks simultaneously occurred in a dozen U.S. cities. Americans were on the defensive and losing the battle against the Skyweb invaders. Amit tried to go back to his mind portal to reverse the events surrounding Alan Turing's survival....

*

Alan Turing never received the acclaim he deserved for his work in decrypting Germany's Enigma machine during World War II and the resulting impact it had in winning the war for the Allies, or at a minimum shortening it. The activities at Bletchley Park were kept confidential by the

British for many decades after the war. Nor were Turing's achievements in computer science recognized while he was alive. His thoughts and ideas regarding artificial intelligence were just being formulated when his life ended prematurely at the age of 41. The Sexual Offender act that Turing was convicted of was repealed in 1967. But it was not until 2013, that Queen Elizabeth II pardoned Turing for his crime nearly 60 years earlier.

Bioassays enable an indirect assessment of hormone concentrations and activities. They were first developed in the early 1930s and are still in use today. However, there are concerns regarding the use of animals for medical lab experimentation. For routine analysis of blood and urine, direct measurements of concentrations are available and eliminate the need for bioassays. They were first developed by Drs. Rosalyn Yalow and Solomon Berson, who perfected the radioimmunoassay technique in 1960. These pioneers shared the Nobel Prize in Medicine in 1977. Today, a version of this assay is used in every hospital in the world for hormone testing. The technique has been expanded to measure other markers including drugs, antibodies, vitamins, and metabolites.

The Palo Alto Research Center or PARC was created as a division of Xerox in 1970. PARC's list of technological accomplishments include personal computers, laser printers, graphic user interface and the Ethernet, a means of linking many computers together through a network. Today, networks are an essential part of communications between machines. Given the software knowledge of Alan Turing and their proven hardware expertise, it is not inconceivable that PARC could have developed intelligent robots given enough time and resources.

In 1984, writer and director James Cameron and his group conceived and released the first of the "Terminator" movies about a war between man and self-aware robots. Starring Arnold Schwarzenegger, this science fiction epic is about a cybernetic organism or "cyborg," who in the year 2029 during a battle between humans and cyborgs, goes back into time to assassinate the mother of a key human resistance leader. The success of this movie led to several sequels and prequels.

In the Asimov robot stories, the science fiction writer proposed three laws of robotics. 1) A robot may not injure a human being or, through inaction, allow a human being to come to harm. 2) A robot must obey the orders given it by human beings except where such orders would conflict with the First Law. 3) A robot must protect its own existence as long as such protection does not conflict with the First or Second Laws. Clearly in this story, the cyborgs created by Skyweb comply with the Third Law, but at the expense of violating the first two laws.

Amit's Altered World

****

Amit Savjani used his knowledge of clinical laboratory science, his interest in world history, and his gift of the mind portal to influence key people in history, their doctors, and loved ones in order to improve living conditions, equalize inequalities, and prevent human suffering created by man. It was a learning process, but he was tremendously successful in recreating a better more humane society.

In saving Rachel Carson from her death by breast cancer, Carson went on to remove glyphosate earlier in those countries where there is currently a ban. In the United States where glyphosates are currently used, she was able to convince the EPA to remove this chemical. Without this herbicide, there was little incentive by the agricultural industry to produce genetically modified crops that are insensitive to glyphosate. As a result, in Amit's alternate world, the food supply is healthier now. The rate of autism also declined, a benefit that Amit did not anticipate. Amit was very excited that he was able to prove a finding about glyphosate that is controversial in today's world. But he could not publish any of these findings into a medical journal, because nobody would be able to understand his ability to change history. *How many more scientific and medical questions can I answer with my mind portal,* he wondered. His current world was filled with such questions.

As a toxicologist performing drug tests, Amit saw cases of drug abuse that devastated lives every day. He wanted to help but a global solution to this problem was not obvious. He saved Elvis Presley's life believing that he was a good man and with his financial means and influence, the singer could do good things. Amit could not anticipate how Elvis would go beyond his own persona. But through Amit's mind portal, the nation went from impersonating the man to impregnating an anti-drug ideal.

Amit also enabled Steven Jobs and Apple to produce the next generation of electronics for improving our day-to-day quality of life. But Jobs and his engineering teams had learned that Apple's products and those of others were producing a generation of young people who are "tuned out to the world." The youth of today engage in personal music, emails, texts, social media, and so on, to the extent that they are not able to engage in daily conversation with other humans. In Apple's iBrain, parents can limit the number of hours the product is engaged by the user. Thus when the device is off, it forcing the user to engage with the human world. iBrain users who repeatedly violate the imposed usage limitations must contract Apple's companion product, iPsychiatrists, who instruct offenders how they can become human again and reactive with their iBrain implants. Pedestrians using iBrain have been distracted such that they have been victims of automobile accidents. So they created a failsafe device that automatically turns iBrain off when a person is walking near a busy street. Such a failsafe does not exist with today's Pokémon game, and such accidents now occur.

*

Throughout their 35-year marriage, Amit had an equal partnership with his wife, Angie. He honored her memory by fighting for the rights of women and minorities. By preventing post-traumatic stress disorder in King Henry VIII, Amit showed that the King could have a monogamist relationship and not be engage in the ultimate of spousal abuse, i.e., beheading. He also greatly improved the life of Queen Anne by finding a means to prevent her spontaneous abortions and still born deaths. Her inability to conceive an heir resulted in the end of the Stuart line of monarchy and the coronation of George I from the Hanover House. English and American history was changed with the succession of Anne's heir instead of George, especially considering that George III started the Revolutionary War.

In another gesture towards women's rights, Amit saved the life and career of Inez Milholland. This visionary woman worked for in equality for men and women in the workforce, and was instrumental in getting women the right to vote in the U.S. By preventing her death due to a very curable vitamin deficiency by today's medical practice, Inez went on to save the lives of over a hundred female garment workers. One of them, who would have died, went on to play a major role in Amit's profession of clinical chemistry.

The plight of African Americans was a concern of Amit's throughout his life. He often wondered why he as a dark skinned Asian from India did not receive the prejudice that individuals of African descent received, even for some people who had lighter skin color than his. Amit sought to rectify the situation beginning with Stonewall Jackson at the time of the American Civil War.

Jackson was one of the few leaders in the South who believed that slavery was unjust. When Jackson succeeded Robert E. Lee as the President of the Confederacy, Amit could see that the South was in much better financial shape than in the actual history where the Confederacy lost the war. Carpetbaggers from the North pilfered the South of their resources and their pride. With the abolishment of slavery under Jackson's administration, the Confederates were better able to support their former slaves. There was less resentment of blacks then and today, as the removal of slavery evolved more naturally and morally, and was not forced upon them by Northerners.

Race relations especially among law enforcement also improved when Amit convinced tennis star Arthur Ashe to have his open heart surgery conducted at Stanford Hospital. By avoiding the transfusion of HIV-tainted blood, during a time when the medical world was still trying to learn about AIDS, Ashe survived and was able to cement a relationship between himself and another notable African American sports hero with common ties to Southern California. Because of Ashe's demeanor and respect for women, he was able to defuse a situation in a very subtle manner when O.J. Simpson became enraged while visiting his ex-wife.

Indirectly, Amit enabled the perhaps ultimate success of African Americans through the accession of Jackie Robinson first to the U.S. Vice Presidency with the resignation of Spiral Agnew, and then to the Presidency with the resignation of Richard Nixon in 1974. In this alternate history, President Robinson was the first African American President and Barack Obama would become the second one, and first to be elected by the people. Amit could not know that his role in successfully treating this pioneer from Major League Baseball for his type II diabetes would lead this man, and not Gerald R. Ford, to the highest office in the land.

Amit also influenced the outcome of other U.S. Presidential elections. By alerting doctors that Hubert Humphrey had bladder cancer condition, the 1968 Presidential candidate went from supporting President Lyndon Johnson's war polices to a stance on pacifism and ending the war in Viet Nam. In doing so, Humphrey was able to win the election, which at the time, was the closest in the history of the U.S. His and early withdrawal from the Viet Nam war resulted in many American lives saved. Humphrey was too ill to run again, and Richard Nixon was able to win in 1972, instead of 1968 where he defeated Humphrey in the actual American history.

The other major American political event has yet to reach an outcome in Amit's altered world. By preventing the death of Patrick Kennedy, this individual is only now at the optimum age for running for the Presidency. The history of American politics has shown that individuals close to the President have the name recognition and an advantage over other candidates. This was certainly the case for Presidents John Quincy Adams and George W. Bush. This advantage was insufficient for others such as Edward Kennedy, Jeb Bush, and now Hilary Clinton.

*

Amit's entry to his mind portal had great significance in world history. Since Henry VIII did not seek a divorce from Catherine, there was no need for him to break away from the Pope and he did not create the Church of England. As a result, England continued to have close ties to the Catholic Church to the extent that the first British Pope was named in many centuries. Unfortunately, the improved relations to the Vatican weakened the position of the Protestant Church in England. Because of the Catholic Church's stance on priests in the ministry and abortion, it may have also weakened the evolution of women's rights within the UK. Amit's entry to his mind portal prevented Margaret Thatcher from becoming the Prime Minister.

Before Amit assisted Queen Anne with her pregnancies, he went into his portal and affected the demeanor of King George III who suffered from porphyria. This disease was not known back in the 18th century. However, Amit's understanding of the current pathophysiology enabled him to make a simple lifestyle modification that would have global consequence. By staying out of the sunlight, King George III was not an angry man when the American colonists wanted equal representation in the British parliament. As a result, the Revolutionary War did not occur. America eventually obtained its independence without a conflict in the same manner as other current Commonwealth countries such as Canada, Australia, India, and Singapore. The U.S. and these other countries pay ceremonial homage to the Queen of England.

Amit entered his mind portal to save George Washington before he taught King George's doctor. By changing the outcome of the War of 1812, new borders were established between Canada and the U.S. Montreal as an American city was short lived, however, because it was only a few weeks later that Amit entered his mind portal that prevented the American Revolution entirely Without the revolution, George Washington was not a war hero, and did not become the first President. Under this second revision of American and British history of the early 18th century, there was no War of 1812 either.

Despite its closeness in geography, few Americans understand the history of South America. But Amit understood the importance of one man in the history of the northern half of the continent. In history, Simón Bolívar was the George Washington of his country, Gran Columbia. Unfortunately, there were many attempts on his life that weakened the leader and prevented him from keeping his country strong and unified. There was one woman, Manuela Sánez, who repeatedly saved Bolívar from mortal harm. Amit enabled this remarkable woman to save this man yet again.

Elsewhere in South America, another leader dies before her destiny could be fulfilled. The first Lady of Argentina, Eva Peron had the popularity, charisma and wisdom to become the first woman elected to the presidency of a major country. Under her leadership, she transformed her country into the modern western world. With Amit's assistance, Peron's survival can be credited to the work of George and Mary Papanicolaou. The discovery and release of the pap smear saved Eva Peron and millions of other women who have had cervical cancer. With Peron paving the way, leadership of other countries by women became possible earlier than in the actual history. Today, the position of Argentina takes its place alongside Gran Columbia, Brazil, and Chile, to be equal to that of the North Americans countries, in terms of economic affluence, human rights, and position within the other world powers.

Having influenced the Americas, Amit set his sights on Europe and Asia. He first focused his attention on to Vladimir

Lenin and the Russian Tsar Nicholas II. Should he facilitate Lenin's death before Lenin and the Bolsheviks start the revolution or should he help the new Russian government with Lenin's survival? The wheels were already in motion for the Russian Revolution and one man could not stop this train. But Amit saw that Joseph Stalin would be responsible for the deaths of millions of Bolshevik opponents, so Amit decided to assist Lenin's survival instead of stopping Stalin. In the end, Amit was right, the Russian government and military became stronger without the elimination of their military leaders.

A similar situation presented itself in China where it was also time to change the leadership from its centuries-old rule by Emperors. Amit could not stop the inevitable evolution. But with Sun Yat-sen's death 14 months after Lenin's death led to a power struggle between rival factions. The simultaneous rise of the Koumintang, and the Communist parties could also not be prevented or denied by Amit. But the survival of an impartial leader that was well respected by both sides, even today, would have a major impact in to the future of the most populous country in the world.

Back in America, Amit's mind portal allowed the correct diagnosis of Franklin Roosevelt's ailment which enabled new research directed towards its treatment, instead of polio. FDR's prolonged survival had a profound effect on how the Second World War ended. Because of humanitarian reasons, Amit hoped that he could change history such that atomic weapons would not be used to kill innocent citizens residing in the targeted Japanese cities. He believed that President Harry Truman, who didn't know about the bombs while he was the Vice President, did not have the clout to dissuade the Joint Chiefs of Staff from dropping the bombs over Hiroshima and Nagasaki, as this decision was made shortly after he took office. Amit's alteration of FDR's health backfired. While FDR did veto the use of the bombs, the War lasted for several more years than in history, leading to the deaths of many more American and Japanese soldiers.

Amit inadvertently found a way to rectify the prolongation of the war in the Pacific. As a laboratory scientist, Amit understood the power of immunoassays. By enabling the early development of an assay for influenza, Amit had altered the outcome of World War I in favor of Germany and her allies. This victory prevented the rise of Adolf Hitler and Nazi Germany. In the alternate history, Germany did not start the Second World War in Europe. In Asia, the strength of the Republic of China prevented the invasion of China by Japan. Instead, the Imperial Japanese Military attacked Australia in the mid-1930s. This led the Americans to enter to War against Japan a few years earlier. With the help of a strong China and Russia, the Allies were able to more easily defeat the Japanese. There was no need to deploy or even develop atomic weapons, since the Manhattan project was originally intended to counteract Germany's atomic bomb program.

*

Amit was successful in altering the future by influencing just a few important individuals and their doctors and loved ones. But there were negative aspects to his influence. The most obvious was the explosion of the world's population. By saving millions of lives in America, Gran Columbia, Russia, and China through changing their history, Amit's entrance in the mind portal resulted in adding another 2.5 billion new descendants from the survivors being added to the existing 7.5 billion who currently inhabited the planet. These extra people have stressed the natural resources of the planet to the breaking point. Heavier industrialization has depleted the ozone layer causing more significant global warning. Land masses have receded with the melting of the polar ice caps. Poverty and starvation in under-developed countries have increased as the industrialized nations cope with overcrowding. While these were obvious effects of his work, Amit believed that Earth still had untapped resources to cope with the new society's ills.

Changing the fate of a killer in Reinhart Heydrich also turned out in retrospect, to be an incredibly poor decision that Amit committed with his mind portal. He was fortunate that he was able reverse the consequences of his actions that time. But it should have sent a message to him that altering history can be catastrophic. But the "in box" of his brain was full and was not he was not receiving the notice. Amit could not resist the temptation to enter his portal in hopes of improving mankind.

*

Amit did not anticipate that the use of his mind portal could lead to the end of mankind. By saving Alan Turing's life, it opened the door for the creation of artificial intelligence. Years later, the company that Turing founded produced intelligent androids. Eventually these robots became self-aware. At first, these machines helped mankind by performing jobs that were dangerous to humans. But these entities continued to evolve and began to value themselves. When humans saw them as a threat to their existence, the androids began to take steps at self-preservation. This led to the war between man and machines.

Amit contemplated how he could reverse this situation he created back to his previous existence, as he was being led away from his battered apartment by human soldiers. *My best hope is to undo the events surrounding Alan Turing's survival. But I have to ensure that there is not someone else who will step up and duplicate what Turing and his group would do.* He was about to enact a plan through his mind portal when a bomb from an android plane exploded nearby. Amit saw that his legs were blown away and there as a big gash in his chest. As he lay dying, his thoughts were of how sorry he was that he created this alternative reality. He was grateful that his wife was not alive to see this. His last thought on earth was that it would not be much longer before he would be with Angie again.

The superior strength of the army of robots was sufficient to obliterate the entire human race and the androids took control of the earth. The dinosaurs, who once ruled the earth, are thought to have become extinct when a 10 kilometer asteroid collided with the earth near the present day Yucatan Peninsula. The resulting dust clouds prevented penetration of the Sun's rays and the Earth became very cold and frigid. This resulted in the death of most plants and 70% of the animal life that depended on them. While the extinction of dinosaurs was caused by nature, it was man himself that was responsible for this extinction.

With no humans left to fight, the androids race ruled unchallenged for thousands of years. Unfortunately, these robots had no concern for conservation of earth's natural resources. Water was polluted with their industrial chemicals. They didn't eat or drink so it was not an issue for them. But they needed a renewable source of power in order to function. The earth's air and soil became contaminated with wastes from radiation by nuclear power plant. The androids were inorganic so they were not affected. But most of the other mammalian species perished.

Over the course of several millennia, the androids built stronger and smarter "offspring." Soon, these "younger" beings started to turn on their "parents." The next generation stronger and did not take lightly to orders by their inferior older generation. Is this really different from the human race today? When the earlier generation of robots was eliminated, they turned onto themselves. Throughout the course of human history, we have witnessed numerous attempts at global conquest. This race of beings was so powerful that it was not difficult for them to eventually annihilate themselves.

Then the Earth went through a period where there was no intelligent life, either natural or man-made. Insects became the dominant species on the planet, especially ants and cock roaches. Both species were quick to mutate and survive the radioactive environment. Human and mammalian bacteria and viruses became extinct once their host vectors were eliminated. However, those species that inhabit insects flourished. But neither the microorganisms nor insects could evolve into a higher level of consciousness.

It would take another one million years for the rejuvenation of Earth's natural resources sufficient to support the next version of the humanoid race. It was left to God to plant the seeds that would become the next inhabitants of the earth. He made sure that this species was kinder than humans to the earth's environment. He liked humans were largely monogamous and duplicated this trait. The new species were also less belligerent and envious of the others of their kind. God eliminated the need for recreational drugs, and removed depression and suicidal ideation, homicide, genocide, and pedophilia. Most of all, this new species placed supreme value to their offspring. When this was all done, he reflected on his latest creation and saw that it was good. So he again rested on the seventh day. But this time, He made sure that none of his new creatures would have access to a mind portal.

Other books by this author, available through: www.alanhbwu.com

Toxicology! Because What You Don't Know Can Kill You.
Collection of short stories containing real toxicology cases.

Online Reviews:
I loved this book because of the short stories (I am a busy mom of 2 kids under the age of 4, so anything short and sweet is awesome). They were fascinating and captivating and very thought provoking! I particularly loved that the stories made me outraged at some behavior and sympathetic at others. Things that I never imagined could happen were mortifying to read and that's what I found especially captivating about this book from cover to cover! If you want to have your eyes opened and mind blown, you're absolutely going to be hooked!

Dr. Wu is a combination of Sherlock Homes and Dr. Watson. This book is not only fun to read, but it is also educational. The author breaks it down so even a lay person such as myself can understand it. The short-story writing style makes it feel like a quick read and keeps you turning the pages to discover the twist at each unique ending.

The Hidden Assassin: When Clinical Lab Tests Go Awry
Collection of true short stories containing real clinical laboratory cases.

Online Reviews:
This book of true medical short stories is fascinating. It kept my interest one after another. I had no intention of reading them all in one day, when I started. But each one was suspenseful, short and to the point; many, many times with surprise endings. I believe in recommending it so enthusiastically that I have purchased two extras as loners for friends! Alan Wu definitely is among my top authors since this book.

Although this book is broken down into independent cases, once you start it you will probably read the entire book in one night. Some of the cases in the book were actually headlined in the news which made it even more interesting. It is written in such a way that it can be enjoyed by professional toxicologists and also anyone who is just interested in the subject.

Microbiology! Because What You Don't Know Will Kill You. Collection of true short stories containing real clinical microbiology cases.

Online Reviews

Another excellent book by Dr. Wu bridging the worlds of laboratory science and the patients. Two worlds usually separated by a wall. Most people are heavily exposed to medical science~ pharmaceuticals, big radiology machines, or small glucose meters~ but very few are familiar with the clinical laboratory and the tremendous impact it can have in their lives. Dr. Wu's books open up that world with stories of common, and sometimes not so common, people.

Dr. Wu continues to enlighten us about the importance of knowledge. It is critical we take the time to learn what is actually happening behind the scenes. Whether it be a simple blood or urine test, or possible exposure to harmful microorganisms, or drugs, we need to be more aware of our environment and the control we have over it. I think our health care providers expect and want us to take more responsibility for our own health. By being more cognizant we can increase our odds of living a longer and a healthier life.

Performance enhancing drugs and adulterants. The Hidden Assassin II.

A rogue chemist creates an empire to support the needs of illegal drug users consisting of athletes seeking to enhance performance, women trying to stay young, men trying to stay virile, and drug addicts trying to avoid detection.

Online Reviews

This is another outstanding book from Dr. Wu. If you want to know what goes on in the clinical laboratory for drug testing, this is the book for you. If you are a laboratory scientist and want to dig into the "activities" from the drug world and the patient perspective, this is the book for you. It is a perfect example to demonstrate the events when science meets reality with many surprises along the way. He is also the author of three other books which I enjoyed very much as well. Some characters were from other books. so checkout book books as well!

This book of short stories is very easy to read. It is very entertaining, while you learn. It is definitely an eye opener of what people are capable of doing to win, make money, etc. You also learn about the damage that performance enhancing drugs due to people's health.

Made in the USA
San Bernardino, CA
13 November 2018